Choose Me

CHAPEL COVE ROMANCES

WHEN LIFE BEGINS AT FORTY...

A Chapel Cove Romance
~ Book 4 ~

By

USA Today Bestselling Author

MARION UECKERMANN

Contact Information: marion.ueckermann@gmail.com

Scripture taken from Holy Bible, New International Version®, NIV® Copyright ©1973, 1978, 1984, 2011 by Biblica, Inc.® Used by permission. All rights reserved worldwide.

Holy Bible, New Living Translation, copyright © 1996, 2004, 2015 by Tyndale House Foundation. Used by permission of Tyndale House Publishers, Inc., Carol Stream, Illinois 60188. All rights reserved.

Cover Art by Marion Ueckermann: www.marionueckermann.net

Edited by Ailsa Williams.

Cover Image ID 156650268 purchased from Depositphotos © ArturVerkhovetskiy
Logo Image Chapel ID 164957864 purchased from Depositphotos © verity.cz

ISBN: 9781088501795

PRAISE FOR *Choose Me*

I am always delighted with the way Marion weaves the love of God into her romances. She reminds us that we are chosen by Him for a very special purpose. How Hudson and Julia find their purposes takes us into a discovery of the power of forgiveness. And never once did I feel preached at. The story spirited me away into a deeper understanding of things I thought I already knew. That's genius and the call of God in action.

~ Judith Robl, JR's Red Quill Editing

Choose Me by Marion Ueckermann is the most delightful Christian romance that will warm your heart. It is the fourth book in the Chapel Cove series but can be read as a stand-alone. I, however, enjoyed my return visit to the cove.

Marion Ueckermann writes novels that wrap around the reader like a cozy dressing gown. *Choose Me* has some wonderful wholesome characters with huge hearts bursting with love.

Choose Me is a most charming read. I could not put it down and read it in just one session. I adore all Marion Ueckermann's novels. I think they would all make wonderful Hallmark movies... any producers out there please take note.

~ Julia Wilson, Book Reviewer at Christian Bookaholic

Choose Me describes two of the most traumatic experiences for any woman. What a joy to walk with Julia from a place of despair to one of forgiveness, healing and finally to a deep satisfying joy. The significance of the book's title is skillfully woven through the story and offers hope to both the characters and the readers. Be warned! This is an emotional rollercoaster well worth the read.

~ Ailsa Williams, Editor

Marion Ueckermann always manages to pull out all "the feels" when it comes to her writing! *Choose Me* was rather a surprise for me—the story took me on an emotional roller coaster in quite a good way!

Julia and Hudson are two of the most engaging main characters I have read in a while. My heart wept and leapt with these two all the way through the novel, and I truly cried happy tears in the end. It is so refreshing to read about two very God centered people that have their own personal relationship with the Lord!

I am so grateful that this is part of series so that I can continue to follow along with their journey! Thank you, Marion, for another great story that will stay with me for a while!

~ Paula Marie, Blogger and Book Reviewer at Fiction Full of Faith

Heartwarming is definitely a word I always associate with books by this author, and *Choose Me* is no exception! The reader can almost hear the title "Choose Me" ... "Pick Me" ... reverberate throughout the book. So much more than just a clean romance, this book has a great depth and is filled with treasures of wisdom about life. Some of the topics included are: heartbreak, rejection, shame, unforgiveness, trust, cancer, adoption, healing, our identity in Christ, the quiet confidence that God really is in control and will work all things for our good because He loves us so greatly, and so much more. This book is one that will capture the heart, mesmerize the reader, and not only entertain, but also cause one to be enriched by having read it. My only regret is that the story ended!

This author is immensely gifted, expertly telling a story and creating characters who will remain in the reader's heart, and appear to be almost real. My favorite quote is: "Hey, everyone has a story. The thing we need to remember is that it's all about allowing God to use our stories to bring glory to His name."

Well done, Marion! The title is whispering, "Choose Me!"

~ Becky Smith

The characters in this book are all truly inspirational and wonderful people. You will feel God working throughout this wonderful book.

~ Debbie Jamieson

We all have dreams of what our life will be like and what our future will be. However, sometimes life takes a different turn than what we had hoped for. Sometimes those things are in our control and other times they aren't. It's how we handle those unexpected changes that make our life rich or sorrowful.

As I read this book I was overcome with buckets of emotions. WOW! In this wonderful story, we find hope in place of despair, and how God can work all things for His good. *Choose Me* is packed with many rich Bible references and lessons of God's love for us. This is one of the reasons I choose to read anything Marion Ueckermann writes. She doesn't just add a little verse at the beginning and call it good; she weaves these lessons throughout her character's lives. These are lessons we can all benefit from.

If you like romance, this book has lots of it, and if you're like me, you'll tell your husband about some of the ways Hudson tries to romance Julia, just to give him some suggestions.

This story has so many sweet moments yet also some fun humorous parts. It is a delight to read.

The author, Marion Ueckermann, is a truly gifted writer. She brings such life to each of her characters. From the crazy ladies of the bookstore, the kind, confident receptionist of the clinic, to the grumpy Mr. Patterson. I loved all the banter with each and every one of these characters. Some of the characters I really got a kick reading about.

I highly recommend you pick it up. Also look for the next books in this series. Hopefully, there will be more!

~ Marylin Furumasu, MF Literary Works

Marion delights us once again as we journey back to Chapel Cove, Oregon and its delightful characters with so much charm.

Julia and Hudson's story is one to treasure. Knowing that you can face your fears while letting God lead the way, true happiness can be found. And that's exactly what these two did. Sharing their deepest fears with us shows us God's unconditional love for us. A story not to miss as Marion weaves God's love into Julia and Hudson's hearts.

~ Sharon Dean

Marion Ueckermann has written another compelling story of hope and Gods mercies.

We often have big dreams but life has a way of making us think those dreams are impossible, but with God nothing is impossible.

Choose Me by Marion Ueckermann is a story that shows though the dreams God gave Julia and Hudson seem to be thwarted at every turn, God has bigger plans than they can even imagine.

Julia has secrets she wishes to remain that way. The pain is too much to bear.

Hudson has been living the life of a renowned Doctor but is disillusioned and unfulfilled. He returns to the small town where he grew up to find his dream of a family.

Nothing seems possible for Julia and Hudson when they meet but God has new unexpected dreams for them both. What does the future hold? How will it come to be?

Read this story and see how marvelously God works in our lives.

~ Renette Steele

God has exciting things planned, not only for Dr. Hudson Brock and Julia Delpont, but the growing community of Chapel Cove, Oregon. Throughout this inspiring story Marion Ueckermann weaves the theme: Miracles still happen, especially when people feel vulnerable and need to feel loved and be loved by God and others. A page turner, gut wrenching at times, story with a believable resolution. Chapel Cove with its unique residents is my kind of growing town.

~ Renate Pennington, Retired English, Journalism, Creative Writing
High School Teacher

I always love reading Marion Ueckermann's books. This was no exception. It was a beautiful romance and dealt with some serious issues in such a loving way. Her words kept me entranced until the end. I loved the characters and their interaction with the hero and heroine. This book is highly recommended for those who love Christian romance. I look forward to her next book.

~ Linda Rainey

Whenever I open a book of Marion Ueckermann's, I know that I'm in for the long haul! I take my time to read and digest, savor every detail, and feel thankful for an author that moves me! *Choose Me* is one of these books!

~ Mattie Henderson

I LOVED this book!! I knew going into the story that Julia was struggling. What I didn't know too far in advance, was that her struggles were a subject near to me as I have friends who've struggled with the very same issue.

I love the way Marion showed that Hudson could look beyond Julia's problems, and that he knew God had brought Julia into his life. I also love that Marion used Hudson to bring Julia into a different view of God through the way he loved her. It made her walk with God stronger, and showed He is faithful, and does work things to the good for those who love Him. It won't be the same for everyone, but this story shows that, no matter what, we can give God our difficulties, insecurities, feelings, and He can still use them to bring good things to us and bring glory to Himself.

~ Trudy Cordle

Dear Reader

Sometimes it's hard to forgive…
Even harder to forget.
Especially when situations don't make sense,
when they seem unfair,
when it feels like the world is against you
and God doesn't seem to care about your pain.

But He does see.
He does care.
And He's on your side.

Don't allow unforgiveness to rob you of your peace.
There's freedom in forgiveness.
Try it—you'll see.

Live Romans 12:14-21 every day.
Bless those who persecute you; bless and do not curse.
Live in harmony with one another.
Do not repay anyone evil for evil.
If it is possible, as far as it depends on you, live at peace with everyone.
Do not take revenge…but leave room for God's wrath.
"If your enemy is hungry, feed him;
if he is thirsty, give him something to drink.
In doing this, you will heap burning coals on his head."
Do not be overcome by evil, but overcome evil with good.

Be blessed,

Marion

To Marylin Furumasu ~
my Oregon girl.

Thank you for reading my stories
(and for being in this one).

"For I know the plans I have for you," declares the Lord, "plans to prosper you and not to harm you, plans to give you hope and a future."

~ Jeremiah 29:11 (NIV)

CHAPTER ONE

Thursday, April 19

TODAY OF all days, Julia Delpont needed to forget about the world. Searching for the latest crime novel to devour might just help. In little over an hour, she'd be meeting a new client, and she could not afford to be distracted by thoughts of her past.

She paused in front of the moss-green, two-story Victorian house. Ivy's on Spruce. Since moving south to Chapel Cove nearly eighteen months ago, she'd come to love the quirky bookshop. It would be good to see the gray-haired owner, Ivy Macnamara, again. It had been two weeks since Julia's last visit to the bookstore. She only hoped she could avoid seeing Ivy's meddlesome shop assistant—always trying to push some castles-in-the-air romance novel into her hands.

1

Romance? She didn't need it. Didn't want it.

The doorbell jangled as Julia entered Ivy's. She headed straight for her favorite section, noticing two things on her way there: the store looked different—cleaner, more organized—and never before had she seen the tall woman with long, dark hair who'd straightened up from behind the counter. Who was she?

And *where* was Ivy?

The woman adjusted her wide-rimmed glasses which had slipped down her nose and offered a smile.

Julia barely acknowledged the greeting as she flicked her hair over her shoulder. She wasn't here to make friends; she was here to buy a book. The more distracting, the better.

But even the blood-splattered knife that loomed large on the cover of the paperback she soon held in her hands couldn't tear her thoughts from the distressing memories. If anything, it made her think about what she'd still like to do to James Miller.

Forgive me, Lord. I know Your Word says "You shall not murder." And truthfully, I don't really want to kill him. I know that You require us to forgive if we want to be forgiven, but it's still so hard to do that after what James put me though. Raising my hopes for a happy ever after, just to smash them into a million little pieces.

It was difficult to comprehend that in just four days, two years would've passed since her most humiliating and most painful moment.

Even more painful than the doctor's diagnosis.

And time had not yet healed the wounds caused by her ex-fiancé.

Would it ever?

She released a heavy sigh. Somehow, the days leading up to the anniversary were harder to get through than the actual anniversary itself. At least, it had been that way last year, and this year looked to be heading in the same direction.

"I... I do." James's deep voice slithered into her memory as everything blurred, the books around her morphing into the quaint, white chapel on Echo Bay with its large windows at the altar that overlooked the Pugent Sound waters of Hale Passage. Eight miles north of Echo Bay had been home for thirty-two years. Gig Harbor—how she'd loved that small town. Never wanted to leave. But she did. She had to.

At James's hesitation, she should've realized something was wrong. And yet, when the minister asked, "And do you, Julia Rose Delpont, take James Alexander Miller as your lawful wedded husband, to have and to hold, from this day forward, for better or for worse, for richer or for poorer, in sickness and in health, to love and cherish until death do you part?", she had hurtled ahead with her own "I do."

How could James have made that very same pledge, only to take it back moments later? She'd kept no secrets from him. He knew full well what he was getting himself into when he'd asked her to marry him. And despite her numerous pleas to ensure he was certain, he reassured her that being with her for the rest of his life was the only thing that mattered. Still, when he'd taken that gold band with trembling hands from his best man, ready to slide it onto her finger and recite his own vows, *then,* and only then, did James suddenly find the courage to whisper, *"I–I'm so sorry, Julia. I can't do this. I thought I could, but I can't."*

After she'd been honest with the other men she'd dated, they had called a halt to the relationship before marriage was even a possibility. At least they hadn't embarrassed her in front of her family and friends.

Julia hadn't waited to listen to any more. She'd hitched her long, white bridal gown and run down the aisle as fast as her heels could carry her, eyes focused on the red runner beneath her shoes.

She hadn't stopped until she came to the end of a nearby jetty where she crumpled into a heap, like melted vanilla ice cream. That was the moment she allowed herself the luxury of tears. Out there alone, just her and the cold water surrounding her.

Her parents afforded her the time to grieve her loss and humiliation before seeking her out and driving her home.

She had stayed on in Gig Harbor for six long months, but the town was too small, too many people talked and stared. So when the owner of the Real Estate Agency she worked for offered her a position with his branch in Chapel Cove, she grabbed the opportunity to start again.

And not once had she looked back.

Here, people didn't know her history. Here, they didn't know her story, and she planned to keep it that way. Never again would she allow a man to break her heart. She was done with them.

"Miss Julia, what about this one? It's a new romantic suspense with very good reviews."

Violet's brittle voice drew Julia from her bitter walk down memory lane. Not that she wasn't grateful for being yanked from that prickly path. But it was the reason Violet was at her side that irked Julia.

Her brows drew together in a frown as her head snapped toward the elderly woman with her purple hair. Julia waved Violet away. "No! I've told you so many times, Violet. Just plain suspense books, not romantic suspense. No romance. None. Zip. Zilch. Please!"

When would this woman get it into her thick skull what her reading preferences were? Better still, when would Violet understand that she was quite capable of selecting her own reading material?

Without having had a chance to glance through the book she'd held in her hands for the last few minutes, Julia shoved the thick paperback back on the shelf in the open slot.

Whirling around, she stomped out of the bookshop with nothing to read. At least her annoyance with Violet would consume her thoughts for a while, not James.

She glanced at her wristwatch as she slid into her silver sedan, parked just outside on Spruce Street. Still forty-five minutes before her two o'clock appointment.

Julia jammed the key into the ignition and turned it. The engine roared to life. Might as well head on down to the prearranged meeting place at the boardwalk. At least she had time to grab a cup of coffee at The Pancake Shoppe before she walked to Wharf Road with her Patterson Properties folder in full view so Mr. Brock could identify her. Good thing she'd lost her appetite or she might've been tempted to order one of Melanie's delicious pancakes. She definitely didn't need to meet a prospective client with sugar granules or cream clinging to the sides of her mouth or chin.

She hoped and prayed that Hudson Brock wasn't a difficult customer, because he certainly seemed to have very specific requirements for what he wanted in a house. Or should she rather say, in his words, a home. She was in no mood for any man's nitpicking today.

Not even a new client's.

CHAPTER TWO

DR. HUDSON BROCK hurried to sign the anti-inflammatory pain medication script he'd just written, checking his watch as he did so. He had ten minutes to get down to the boardwalk. He'd hate to be late for his appointment with the new real estate agent. The woman came highly recommended by a patient he'd seen on Tuesday, so he'd decided not to continue using his current agent. After several showings, she still didn't comprehend what kind of house he sought, not to mention totally ignoring the listings he'd wanted to see. Hudson had little doubt that Samantha Lawson saw dollar signs and a big commission for herself attached to his title of doctor.

He tore the script from his pad and handed it to Dorothy Winters, sitting in one of the chairs on the other side of his desk. That chore over, he rose hoping to discourage the elderly lady from lunging into yet another conversation. She'd already taken up way more time than he'd envisaged, and he wasn't talking about the time it took to take and examine the x-rays, apply a cold compress to reduce her pain and swelling, and finally immobilize her swollen wrist with a compression wrap.

He glanced at the graying gent seated beside her. George Winters, who must be near retirement age himself, if not already retired, had barely uttered a word in all the time Hudson had been treating his mother.

"Thankfully it's only a sprain, Mrs. Winters, albeit quite a nasty one." This was the second time he'd seen Dorothy for a fall in the short time he'd been back in the small coastal town. The last time, though, a friend had brought her to the clinic. She really should consider moving to an assisted living center or step-down facility—her next fall could be far worse. But he needed to first chat with Dr. Johnson about what to recommend before discussing the matter with her son.

Taking Dorothy by the arm that didn't rest in a sling, Hudson helped her out of the chair. "Now you go straight home, take two of those pills, and rest. Do you have someone who can help you?"

She nodded. "Yes. I live with my son, George." The wrinkles on her brow deepened. "I didn't tell you?"

Hudson shook his head. She'd told him a lot of things, but who she lived with hadn't been one of them.

Her mouth turned down as she shrugged. "Hmm. Old age. Gray matter." She tugged at the wispy, silvery hair covering her head. "When George's wife passed away a few years ago, I sold my house and moved in with him."

"Mom…" George reprimanded. "I'm not the patient here. Dr. Brock doesn't need to know my personal details."

Hudson cleared his throat. "George, please take note of the side effects of the medication and keep an eye on her." If only he had time to discuss his concerns for Dorothy's care, and the possible need of more full-time care, but if he didn't leave now, he'd be late. Besides, he could just be overreacting.

He had a weak spot for the elderly—maybe because his father had died alone. Hudson had been in Seattle completing his second last year of medical studies. Heath, his older brother, had just moved to Portland to attend Bible college. And their eldest brother, Hunter…well, who knew where he was getting up to mischief at that time? After his first stint in jail, Hunter had managed to dodge the long arm of the law for twelve years. But finally, his crimes had caught up with him, and he had been serving his eighth year of a ten-year sentence.

Thankfully, when their father's brother, Uncle Trafford, took ill and died, Heath had been there for him in his time of need.

Hudson hoped and prayed that he'd have children who would look out for him one day when he no longer could do so himself. Life was tough for old people. Even with a support system, many families were just not equipped to handle those twilight months, lingering sometimes for years.

"Don't worry, doctor. George will take good care of me." Mrs. Winters's skin wrinkled into furrows with her smile.

"That's good to know." Returning her smile, Hudson opened the door of his office and let his patient and her son out.

Holding onto George's arm, Dorothy tottered across the clinic reception floors. She turned and waved. "Until next time, Dr. Brock."

Hudson tipped his head in acknowledgement. Hopefully there wouldn't be a next time. But if there was, he would definitely ensure he found some private time with George Winters to discuss his mother's ongoing care.

After grabbing his doctor's bag from beside his desk—one never knew when one would need it, so he never went anywhere without his bag, or a first aid kit in his car—Hudson shut his office door and headed toward the exit, thrilled about the prospect of meeting Julia Delpont. He had a feeling this real estate agent had some great options—even one of the houses he'd been trying to get Samantha Lawson to show him.

Perhaps *this* property person would live up to her reputation because for him, Samantha certainly hadn't.

As he passed Marylin's desk, he paused. "I'll be out for the afternoon looking at houses. Say a little prayer that I find a suitable one this time. And please remind Doctor Johnson that I'm not here the rest of the day. He does know I have the afternoon off."

Marylin smiled. "Will do, Dr. Brock. Happy hunting." She gave a quick wave then returned to her work.

At exactly 2 p.m., Hudson pulled his electric blue SUV into an open parking space and hopped out of the vehicle. Up ahead, he noticed a tall, neatly-dressed woman with long, dark hair. Could it be Julia Delpont? He'd seen the slightly bigger than thumbnail image of her on Patterson Properties' website, but hadn't taken too much notice. He'd been more interested in examining the houses than the person selling them.

She tugged the edge of her black, tailored jacket then smoothed a hand over the matching skirt that complemented her hour-glass figure.

Hudson strode toward her, his mouth curving upward as he recognized the logo on the folder she held in her hand. It *was* her.

Nearing, he extended his hand toward the attractive woman. "Julia Delpont?"

Her lips, shaded with a faint pink gloss, parted in a wide smile that stretched across her face as she shook his hand. "Mr. Brock. Glad you could make it."

"The feeling is mutual, Miss Delpont." Or was it Mrs.? His gaze flicked to her left hand, her pale skin a stark contrast to the dark folder her hand clutched, before settling back on her face. Was that a flicker of relief he'd felt at seeing no ring?

And those eyes? Surely the darkest brown he'd ever seen. The color reminded him of the intense, bittersweet chocolate slabs— 85% cocoa—he loved to indulge in every so often.

Speaking of indulgence, he wouldn't mind staring into the depths of those dark spheres for an interminable amount of time.

Seriously, Hudson?

Focus.

And he did. He focused on the fact that she hadn't corrected him on her title. Then again, he hadn't corrected her on his either. And for good reason. He didn't want to risk his being a doctor influencing Miss Delpont in her work, as had clearly been the case with Samantha Lawson. Strangely, Hudson found himself hoping Julia Delpont was single. But could that purely be because one of the main reasons he'd come home to Chapel Cove in the first place was to find a wife and raise a family? Was he destined to measure up every female he met in Chapel Cove, prematurely deciding whether or not they were marriage material?

He couldn't...no, shouldn't find himself attracted to the first beautiful woman to cross his path. Not that Julia Delpont was the first to do so. Several attractive women, single and married, had come to the clinic requesting an appointment with *him*. Not Dr. Johnson. According to Marylin, they specifically asked to see Dr. Brock. And on examining them, Hudson was left with serious doubts regarding the authenticity of the symptoms several of the women described, finding absolutely nothing medically wrong with them.

Then there was Samantha Lawson. Despite being pleasing to the eye, there'd been no spark between them—at least not from Hudson's side. Not like right now with this beautiful, dark-eyed brunette with her open smile.

10

"Please, call me Julia. We can use my car. No point in driving to the various locations in two vehicles."

Julia's voice drew him from the sweet land of chocolate and dark, dreamy eyes that he'd returned to with ease.

Hudson cleared his throat. "Um, yes. Sounds like a good idea. And you'll need to call me Hudson." He glanced around. "Where did you park?"

"Just over there." She pointed to the silver sedan close by, the car beside it just pulling out.

Julia strode ahead, and Hudson found himself admiring the shapely stockinged calves beneath her knee-high, pencil skirt, the fabric a few shades darker than her eyes.

There he was, back to thinking about those eyes that seemed to draw him in like a siren's call.

As she stepped off the curb, Hudson heard a soft crack, and the next minute, Julia face-planted the asphalt beside the driver's door of her car. The folder she'd held skidded toward the back tire, while her handbag landed in the empty parking space.

She groaned before letting out a low, "Ow, ow, owwwuch!"

Rushing to Julia's side, Hudson knelt down next to her. "Are you all right?"

"Do I look all right?" she retorted as she rolled over. Remaining seated on the ground, she scrunched her face in obvious pain, pulling her injured leg up into a V to examine the broken skin beneath the ripped stocking. Blood oozed from her knee, as well as from her chin. She dabbed the back of her hand against the tip of her jaw, then moaned when she saw the red streak across her skin.

"You're hurt. Wait right there." Hudson ran to his car and grabbed his first aid kit—it had more of what he'd require in this instance than his doctor's bag. He rushed back to Julia.

As he knelt again, he reached for the strap of Julia's handbag and tugged it closer. Wouldn't do for someone to park there and drive over the bag.

The handbag safe, he set the first aid kit down and unzipped it before examining her knee. "I'll clean this up. It'll probably burn, but better that than risk an infection, right?"

Julia nodded, tears brimming in her eyes. Did it hurt *that* much, or were those tears and her abruptness the result of something else?

"But first, we need to stop the bleeding." Hudson reached for a pack of sterile gauze swabs.

Leaning forward, Julia lifted the offending shoe, the heel broken clean off from the sole. No wonder she'd fallen. Up ahead, a small hole in the asphalt—about the size of a quarter—indicated the reason for her sprawl.

"Ugh, and these were my favorite shoes." Julia dropped the shoe back onto the dark gray surface then swiped her cheeks. She dabbed her chin with a finger.

"Don't touch that," Hudson cautioned. "You don't want to contaminate the wound."

He rubbed his hands with sanitizer then snapped on a pair of blue, nitrile gloves.

Dark, doe eyes stared up at him. "Are you an EMT?"

Unable to lie, he shook his head. His cover was blown now. Up until that moment, he'd just been Mr. Brock, and he'd intended to stay that way until the purchase papers had been signed. He could've been the local plumber for all she knew. He glanced at his smart trousers and leather shoes. Well, maybe not the plumber.

But now he was about to become Dr. Brock to this woman.

He offered up a quick prayer that it wouldn't impair her ability to do her job as had been his recent experience, and then answered, "I'm a doctor."

"*You're* the new doctor in town." Her jaw dropped and surprise coated her words. "You never said—"

"It's a long story. Maybe I'll let you in on it someday." Once the right house was signed, sealed, and delivered. Well, not quite delivered, but at least having the keys in his possession.

Hudson removed a few swabs from the now unsealed pack and placed them on her patella. Wrapping his fingers around her knee, he pressed down firmly.

With his free hand, he applied the same treatment to her chin.

Minutes passed by in deathly quiet, but when Hudson checked the wounds, the bleeding had subsided on both. He rinsed her knee and chin with a sterile saline solution then checked to ensure that no dirt was embedded in either. Her chin was free of grit so he applied a topical antibiotic ointment over the road rash then covered the injury with a small adhesive wound dressing. The transparent waterproof film would keep the site dry for days. But there was surface debris in her knee. Using clean tweezers, he set about slowly removing the tiny bits of gravel.

Julia winced.

"I'm sorry. Did I hurt you?"

She shook her head. "Not really. I'm just a little skittish. I–I haven't had skinned knees since I was a kid kicking up dirt in Gig Harbor. Didn't like them then; don't like them now."

So, she was a small town girl. He liked that fact.

"That's okay. I never liked them either, and I got a lot of them playing football in school and college." Hudson smiled. "Gig Harbor? Such a beautiful place. I visited there once when I was studying in Seattle. How long did you live there?" This woman intrigued him, and perhaps through small talk, he could not only distract her from her injuries—and without a doubt her humiliation at taking such a dramatic fall in front of a new client—but also find out a little more about her. He definitely didn't want to slide back into the silence that had existed while he'd concentrated on stopping the bleeding.

Julia drew in a long, deep breath. "My whole life. Except for the past eighteen months when I...when I decided it was time for a change. An opportunity to transfer to Chapel Cove came along, so I grabbed it."

"With Patterson Properties?"

She leaned closer to examine Hudson's handiwork on her knee. "Yes. Bill Patterson has been very good to me, even though he's quite a tough boss."

Bill Patterson? Could that be the same William Patterson, Chapel Cove property mogul that his family had feared, thanks to big brother Hunter? Did they still even live in this small town, although it had grown somewhat over the years with the luxurious developments to the south on the other side of the river near the Cape Cod-style home Heath owned, thanks to their Uncle Trafford? But Heath deserved it. Most of those were holiday homes for rich Portlanders, but there had also been development over the years toward the lavender farm. That was where his first choice of house was situated. If it was the same man, the growth of the town was thanks, no doubt, in part to him.

"Does he have a daughter? Olivia?" Hudson asked.

Julia's eyes brightened. "Yes. She works for the company, but she's upstairs in a different division—new developments. You know her?"

So Olivia was still in Chapel Cove. What would Hunter do with that information when he got out of prison? Would that be motivation enough for his wayward brother to come back home to the Cove? And behave?

Assuming, of course, Olivia was unmarried. Although, would that even matter to Hunter?

"I do." Hudson shrugged. "At least, I did."

Tiny lines crinkled Julia's brow as she narrowed her eyes. "Did? Haven't you just moved to Chapel Cove?"

"Yes, but I grew up here...well, mostly. From twelve to my late teens when I left to study medicine." He'd been the fortunate one of the three brothers who'd scored a football scholarship.

"S–so how do you know Olivia?"

Could Hudson even hope that was the tiniest touch of jealousy he heard in her voice?

Don't be stupid. You've only just met.

"Olivia and my brother, Hunter…they were a hot item around town for two years." Before Hunter had blown things and gotten himself arrested. William Patterson had probably been overcome with relief to have Hunter out of Olivia's life. He'd never thought Hunter, or any of the Brock boys for that matter, were good enough for his princess.

"Wow, small world. When did they break up? Olivia and your brother?"

Hudson chewed on his bottom lip as he did the math. "Must be twenty-two years ago, at least."

The grit out of Julia's knee, Hudson placed the tweezers back in his first aid kit then cleaned the wound again before applying the antibiotic ointment to the cut and covering it with the same transparent film as her chin, only a bigger size. "Keep that, and your chin, closed and dry. I'd like to see you in five days' time, unless you notice any signs of infection before then like redness, swelling or heat, fever, or weeping green or yellow fluid. Then you call me immediately, doesn't matter what time of day or night. You have my number."

Julia nodded then grinned. "Yes, doctor."

"When was the last time you had a tetanus shot?"

Lips pursing, Julia raised her shoulders. "No idea. Probably when I was ten or twelve."

"So not in the last ten years?" Hudson checked. A smile tugged his mouth. "Not since kicking up dirt in Gig Harbor?"

Julia's laugh floated on the cool, early afternoon air. "I *was* a bit

15

of a tomboy in my day. But, yes, definitely not since about then. I am way older than twenty-two."

"I would never have guessed." The flattery slipped out of his mouth before he could stop himself. Although beautiful, she did look older than twenty-two, and for that he was grateful. Wouldn't do for a forty-year-old man to be dating someone that much younger than himself. *If* he and Julia ever got to the stage of dating. Who knew? Besides, he couldn't see himself being with someone where there was more than a decade's age difference. Then again, he probably couldn't date anyone his age if he wanted a few children to fill his house.

Hmm, would Heath and Reese try for children now that they were back together again, even at their ages? He wouldn't be surprised if wedding bells rang in Chapel Cove before the summer ended. Not that he would blame them. His brother and the love of his life had already wasted too many years apart. If Hudson found the right girl, he'd sweep her off her feet and marry her in a heartbeat.

Realizing he was staring into Julia's big brown eyes, he quickly looked away and zipped the first aid kit closed. "As a precaution, we should probably get you down to the clinic and give you a tetanus shot." Rising, Hudson slung the bag over his shoulder and extended a hand to help Julia to her feet.

"Right now?" Stretching to her full height, she kicked off her other shoe to stand balanced, merely two or three inches shy of his height. "Can it wait until *after* I've shown you the houses? I think some of them might receive offers pretty quickly so we need to move fast."

Hudson raised his brows. "You still want to go?"

Her jaw dropped again, and she shot him an incredulous look. "Of course. You've taken time out of your busy schedule to do this, haven't you? Besides, I'm not crippled. I can still walk, albeit it barefoot." She lowered her gaze to her stockinged feet. "Well, as good as barefoot."

Hudson raised a finger. "I have a solution for that. But let me drive us in my car so that you can rest your knee." He stooped to pick up the broken shoe and heel, as well as the whole one, then offered his elbow to Julia. "Feel free to use me as a crutch for the afternoon, if you like."

Julia's eyes flicked to the extended limb, apprehension washing over her face. Without taking him up on his offer, she took a step. Faltering and nearly taking another nose-dive, she reached for his elbow. "I–I think I might need to. But just for a while, hopefully. Thank you." Leaning on him for support, she limped the short distance to his SUV. Hudson considered scooping her up in his arms and carrying her, but didn't think the gesture would go down well, no matter how well-meaning.

Maybe she needed something to dull the pain, so he asked, "Do you need a painkiller?"

She shook her head. "I'll definitely ask for something if this throbbing gets any worse."

With a nod, Hudson unlocked the vehicle and opened the passenger door for Julia to slide in. Soon as she'd buckled up, he hurried around to the back and popped the hatch. After setting her shoes and the first aid kit down, he rummaged inside another bag and pulled out two matching items. Only once he was behind the steering wheel, did Hudson hand the two blue shoe protector booties to Julia.

Holding up the thin pieces of fabric, she stared at them, the slightest wrinkles forming at the tip of her nose.

A pretty cute nose he must add.

"Part of a fun farewell gift from the surgical staff at the hospital I worked for in Dallas," Hudson explained as he started the engine. His coworkers had given him a bag full of protective hospital wear and told him that any time he missed the OR in his little coastal clinic, he could play dress up. What they couldn't grasp was that he didn't intend for Chapel Cove clinic to remain just a clinic. His vision was to expand it into a small hospital with at least one OR. With the right funding from the government and community, he could accomplish that long before he retired. Maybe not before Dr. Johnson did though.

He smiled at Julia "Those might at least keep your feet from getting dirty. And your stockings."

"Ha, my stockings are ruined already. Soon as I get home, they're going into the trash. But thanks anyway." Leaning forward, Julia slipped the booties over her feet. She relaxed back in her seat and turned to him. "So you were a *surgeon* in a large city and you've moved back to *this* small town that doesn't even have a hospital?" She shook her head as if Hudson had made the biggest mistake of his life.

Had he? Was he going to be satisfied with no surgeries, treating sick people—the odd broken bone or sprain here and there—and writing scripts?

The feeling deep in his gut told him that no matter how mundane his job might initially seem compared to what he'd come from, he hadn't. He'd followed God's leading—yes, admittedly his own heart too—so how could he have made a mistake? God had exciting things planned for him, of that Hudson was sure.

Three times, in the space of one day, he'd stumbled across the verses in Matthew, Mark, and Luke where Jesus told the paralyzed man to get up, take his mat, and go home. Once in his daily reading. Another time at the bottom of an email from a Christian colleague. By the time the third one came in the form of a meme on Instagram, he knew God was trying to get his attention. It was that very same night he saw Dr. Johnson's tiny ad in a medical magazine looking for an interested partner in the clinic.

When he and Dr. Johnson got to talking, Hudson's adrenaline had surged at the prospect of what he could do in and for Chapel Cove. That was the moment he realized he was the paralyzed man, stuck in a life he seemed to be living for himself alone.

After a three year stint as an army surgeon in Afghanistan—seeing the worst atrocities, patching and stitching what realistically shouldn't have been fixable—he'd settled into a cushy surgeon's job at a large Dallas hospital where, for several years, he'd avoided the ER, performing only scheduled surgeries. After all that time, he was still no closer to finding the life he really wanted for himself.

He was certain he was about to find it in Chapel Cove.

Slowly his head moved up and down, agreeing with Julia. "Yes, there's no hospital for now. But this town is growing." It had changed much in size since his father had moved him, his siblings, and their mother there almost three decades ago. "And it's getting to the point of needing a real hospital, even if it's small. I want to be part of that groundbreaking process."

He shifted the vehicle into reverse, the thought of that groundbreaking process once again getting his adrenaline pumping. He could achieve so much for this small town. And that's why he didn't want a house like Samantha Lawson was trying to sell him. If he'd still been in Dallas, yes. But he wasn't. He was in Chapel Cove, and part of the profit he'd made from the sale of his previous, luxurious apartment had gone to buying into the clinic. Another portion he'd set aside for a down payment on a modest home where he could raise a family. The balance, along with his healthy savings account, he planned to invest into upgrading the clinic to a hospital. Better still, building something from scratch.

But the townsfolk and government would need to come to the party in that mammoth task. He couldn't do it on his own, that was for sure. He'd set money aside, but not *that* much.

But he had faith. God *had* called him home to Chapel Cove, and a family was only part of the reason for such a drastic move.

CHAPTER THREE

AS THE SUV pulled away from the boardwalk, Julia rattled off the first address and directions on how to get there, doubt suddenly flooding her. Had she understood his housing needs correctly? He was a doctor for crying out loud—a surgeon. The places she'd shortlisted to show him might be a little too homely for someone of his standing.

Julia reminded herself that Hudson Brock had been very specific about what he was looking for when he'd emailed her. So specific, in fact, that she'd been certain she was meeting a middle-class man with a wife and half a dozen kids in tow. Okay, maybe not half a dozen, but at least two or three. Of course, just because they weren't here on this excursion, didn't mean they didn't exist.

Well, it was nothing to her if they did or not. She was here to sell him a house. That's all.

Then why had she noticed how good-looking he was, or how bursts of green and brown, or was it gold, seemed to radiate outward from the pupils of his hazel eyes? Why had she noticed that he wasn't wearing a wedding ring? And why did it feel as if, deep down inside, she wished for something more than just a brief business transaction? She didn't like the thought of never seeing him again once she handed over the keys to the house he purchased.

Ridiculous! She was merely more vulnerable this week, that's all—the need to feel loved, to *be* loved, heightened by the vivid memories of her almost wedding day. Love, happiness, and forever after…they just weren't on the cards for her. Hadn't been for many years. She had to accept her lot in life and the inevitable fact that she'd most likely end up like Ivy Macnamara, the only exception being that she'd be selling houses until she was old and gray, not books.

As for all those animals… No, *that* she could not imagine. No old cat lady, dog lady, or bird lady like Ivy was.

A smile twitched at the thought of her gray self being surrounded by and talking to cats.

Julia shoved the ridiculous image away and shuddered.

Yanking the visor down, she examined her taped up chin. At least it seemed the good doctor had cleaned up any blood stains on her neck. She could have sworn she'd felt the warm, red liquid trickling over her skin, but she couldn't remember Hudson mopping it up, though he must have. Either that or she'd imagined the extent of the bleeding on her chin. Which was entirely possible. Stranger things had happened to her today. Hadn't the bookshop morphed into the small, white chapel on Echo Bay earlier?

Her gaze drifted to her ruined stockings—runs heading both up and down her legs like a game of snakes and ladders—and then to the blue booties on her feet. Her palms burned and she turned her hands over. Even they hadn't escaped unscathed.

She looked such a mess.

She was a mess.

But today, of all days, could God not have kept that mess on the inside where it usually hid?

"You hurt your hands too…"

Her head snapped up at the sound of his voice beside her. For a brief moment, she held his gaze until Hudson focused his attention back on the road ahead.

So did Julia. "I–It's nothing. Just a few tiny scrapes. I'll wash my hands when we get to the first house."

"I'll give you some disinfectant. It'll help avoid any infection."

"It's not necessary," she snapped, finding his concern a little unsettling. She'd vowed never to allow herself to be attracted to a man again. That way she could avoid having her heart broken once more. Now she had a one date policy. As a result, she'd only been out for dinner three times since moving to Chapel Cove—there just weren't that many eligible bachelors in this town.

But here she was feeling things she hadn't allowed herself to feel in a long, long time.

Butterflies.

Attraction.

Hope.

Definitely no 'one date' policy for Dr. Brock. A 'NO DATE' policy was best where this handsome, kind doctor was concerned.

Relief flooded Julia as Hudson drove away from the second house she'd shown him. She *had* understood his requirements and shown him exactly the kind of houses he was looking for. Not only had he said so—more than once—but the expression on his face also declared that she'd been right in these choices.

However, she'd kept the best for last...the one property Hudson had specifically requested to view. And she didn't blame him. If she were buying a house, this was the one place she'd choose out of all the homes in Chapel Cove. She had always loved this house. In fact, she'd been sorely tempted to buy it for herself when it came on the market last week. But her long-term plans were still too uncertain. She had no idea whether she wanted to settle in Chapel Cove for the rest of her life. She'd only been here for eighteen months, and although she loved living in this little sleepy hollow of a town, Mr. Patterson had talked about establishing an office in sunny California, seemingly in the not too distant future. *And*, he'd hinted at her running it.

So for now, putting down firm roots wasn't in her plans. She had to be sure that both the job *and* the town were what and where she wanted to grow old, because that was all she had to look forward to in her future.

No husband.

No children.

No grandchildren.

Just herself and her career.

Hudson glanced in his rearview mirror. "I really liked that place. More than the first house—although that was a good choice too." He flashed Julia a smile.

Her stomach did a somersault and she swallowed hard.

Not quite trusting herself to speak yet, Julia filled her lungs then exhaled slowly. "Well then, you're going to love the last place I have to show you today." She pointed ahead. "Turn left at the next crossroad, then drive toward the lavender farm. You know where that is?"

His smile returned, spreading into a grin. "Of course I know where that is. Are we going where I think we're going?"

She nodded. "You *did* request to see that place, but I wanted to save it for the last showing today." There was no doubt in her mind that once he'd seen the house overlooking the lavender farm, the others would pale in comparison, and her client deserved to have some good places with which to compare so that he could make an informed choice.

As the afternoon had worn on, Julia had come to realize that Hudson was a really nice guy. Warm. Caring. And oh so easy to talk to. Slowly, she'd relaxed and was able to just be herself, someone she hadn't been for far too long.

"Your wife and kids will love this place."

Groan. What on earth had made her say that?

Probably because the longer she'd been in his presence, the more the desire to know his marital and family status had grown. She would've made a colossal fool of herself if he were still single. Her pulse thrummed at the thought. Come to think of it, he hadn't mentioned a wife or kids. Not once. Surely any normal family man would say things like, "This kitchen is exactly what my wife is looking for," or "Oh, my little girl would love this bedroom," or "Man, my son will have so much fun in that treehouse."

But he hadn't made any such statements. Not one.

Perhaps he hadn't said anything because she'd been somewhat aloof with him initially as they'd viewed the first house. She'd only been trying to remain professional, trying to maintain her composure despite her ripped stockings, bandaged knee and chin, and those ridiculous blue booties covering her feet.

She lifted one foot to check underneath. That blue fabric, now a shade of brown where it covered the soles of her feet, might survive one more house before shredding.

Nearly overshooting the turn, Hudson yanked the steering wheel to the left. The SUV's tires screeched as the vehicle skidded around the corner. Thankfully the road was devoid of other cars.

25

Despite the seat belt, Julia couldn't prevent herself from careening sideways and slamming into Hudson's right bicep or her palm from landing on his thigh. Her fingers clamped around the hard muscle for a second as she attempted to steady herself.

Yanking her hand back, she righted herself almost as quickly as Hudson had straightened the vehicle's course.

He chuckled, low and deep. "I'm sorry." He shot a glance her way, concern in his eyes. "You okay?"

"I'm fine." Ugh, that sounded way too clipped again.

"Good. You caught me off guard with what you said about my wife and kids, and I lost concentration. I guess that's why I nearly missed the road you'd told me to turn onto."

She shrugged, a smile gently tugging the corners of her mouth. "It's okay."

It was a simple question though, so why had he lost concentration? Surely he didn't want to hide his wife and family from the world? Although Julia was beginning to think that if he *was* married, he did.

"I'm not married, Julia. And I don't have any children."

Hearing that, her heart skipped a beat. Relief washed over her. "Y–you're not? You don't?" She didn't understand.

He shook his head. "Why would you think I was married?"

Mouth dry, Julia blurted out, "B–because you specifically asked for a house a woman would love, one kids would enjoy growing up in." She raised a brow, eyeing him. "A family home were your exact words."

"You're totally right. It's like this…" He inhaled deeply. "I'm *not* looking to make a statement with the house I live in. That's why I stopped working with my previous agent. We both had totally different ideas about what kind of house I need."

"Who was the agent?" Julia asked.

"Samantha Lawson."

26

"Humph, that explains a lot. I take it she's your long story?"

Hudson tipped his head.

"Let me guess... Knowing you were a doctor, she saw dollar signs."

Once more, his head bobbed up and down.

Julia raised her brows. "And you thought *I'd* be like that?"

Hudson's mouth skewed as he worried his bottom lip. "Well... I... I just didn't want to take any chances I might waste more of my time, which I'm really glad to see I haven't."

Nearing an intersection, Hudson slowed the SUV to a stop. He turned and fixed his eyes on hers. "All I need is a normal house—a home—not the palatial ones Samantha kept showing me. I want to settle down and start a family...*when* I find the right woman to fall in love with, of course."

"Of course." After what felt like forever, but was probably merely seconds, Julia forced herself to look away. "Continue to go straight. It's not far down this road. One more turn—the last part's a dirt road."

Hudson pulled away slowly. "So you see why it's really important that I buy the right property, one that checks all the boxes for my hopefully not too distant future requirements."

Up ahead, neat rows of small, well-tended bushes came into view, the faintest tinge of purple skimming their tops. Julia sighed. She would never grow weary of that sight, although it was best in two or three months' time when the lavender was in full bloom. She could only imagine how peacefully people in this area must sleep at night with the fragrance of lavender wafting on the air.

As if reading her thoughts, Hudson opened the window and took a deep breath. "Ah, that smells good. Although the fragrance is way stronger in the height of summer."

Of course, he'd grown up here so he would know.

The wind whipped her hair across her face, and Julia brushed a hand over her head to smooth the wayward strands.

"Did you know that, according to research, those tiny purple flowers are nature's answer to anxiety, insomnia, depression, and restlessness?" Hudson continued.

She did know, but it was good to have a doctor confirm that fact. Maybe she should make an excuse to go home and not show him the house, put in an offer herself. Because she could certainly do with some tranquility.

She glanced at his chiseled profile out of the corner of her eye.

Especially now.

She could always sell the place again if California was on the cards for her.

Realizing where they were, Julia shouted, "You need to turn left here!"

Her instruction coming too late, they skidded around the corner again. Once more, Julia slammed into Hudson's shoulder and grabbed his leg. Talk about a groundhog day!

Hudson laughed. "Are you deliberately trying to make me take these corners sharply?" His mischievous gaze flicked to her hand on his leg.

Like the first time, Julia quickly pulled away. "Of course not!" A nervous chuckle spilled from her lips as heat rose up her neck, rushing for her cheeks.

Hudson's brow quirked as the SUV bounced down the dusty road. "Are you sure?"

Her heart thumped against her ribs. *Had* she subconsciously made him swerve the second time?

CHAPTER FOUR

THE PHOTOGRAPH on Patterson Properties' website didn't do the one-and-a-half-story Cape Cod justice. The place was more impressive, in a quaint sort of way, than Hudson had imagined, a photo unable to capture its full beauty.

And he and Julia hadn't even gone inside yet. They still stood rooted on the pathway leading up to the central front door framed by two tall, round pillars supporting the flat roof of the porch. Granted, the house didn't have the large front porch that he desired, but maybe just as well—it would be a pity to hide the pristine front of the house with its white, shiplap walls and double hung symmetrical windows, dark green shutters flanking each side. Not to mention the neatly trimmed shrubs edging the house on one side, verdant grass on the other.

He turned to Julia and grinned.

Her eyes lit up with her own smile. "So, what do you think?"

"I *really* like what I see so far, especially the enormous balconies on either side of the house. What rooms are those beneath them?"

Julia pointed to the left, and Hudson couldn't help staring at her slender, perfectly manicured fingers. A miracle she hadn't broken a nail with her fall, but then, her palms did bear the brunt for her hands—probably saved that cute chin from a nastier injury. "That's a guest bedroom. And on the right," she shifted the direction of her finger, "is the kitchen."

"The view over the lavender farm must be beautiful from up there," Hudson said, eager to take a look.

Julia offered a slight tip of her head. "It is. Well, from the main bedroom's balcony, at least. Bonus is, with the farm being on a slight incline, on a clear day you're able to see the ocean from the other balcony."

"Fantastic!" This house offered even more than he'd thought, which he might've known if he'd had the time to do more than just look at house photos. But life had been somewhat hectic since he'd arrived in Chapel Cove merely eleven days ago, and he'd wasted a lot of precious spare time looking at houses that were way too big and way too elaborate for his liking. He should have cut Samantha Lawson off at the pass with that very first unsuitable house.

He stared up at the house again. Between the two balconies, three dormer windows broke the dappled gray of steep shingles, as did stone chimneys on either side of the roof. The twin stacks, pointing toward the cloudy skies, promised warmth on cold winter nights. This place was exactly what he wanted in a home.

Julia took a step forward. "Should we go inside?"

Hudson nodded. "Please."

Judging from the outside of the four-bedroom house, Hudson should have known that the interior would be equally impressive.

But he hadn't realized it would be *that* impressive. Best of all, large doors in both the living and dining room opened onto the backyard and that expansive porch he'd so desired. Seeing the view across row upon row of lavender bushes at the neighboring farm, he could understand why the house had been built with the porch on the back.

But besides that, there was so much else he loved about the house—the wooden flooring throughout, the fireplaces in the living and dining rooms as well as two of the upstairs bedrooms, and the well-designed kitchen with all the modern conveniences one could wish for. Already he could imagine breakfasts with his wife and children around the big kitchen island or the built-in breakfast nook, windows opening the heart of the home to fragrant fields of lavender.

A vision of Julia completed that image.

Strange.

He should ask her out for dinner.

But not now.

Maybe another day.

Or later.

Standing outside on the ocean-facing balcony, Hudson narrowed his eyes as he peered into the distance. Didn't help. There'd be no catching sight of the sea on a cloudy day like today.

Julia leaned forward. As she rested her arms on the wood railing, Hudson noticed her taking the weight off her injured knee.

He turned to her. "Much as I'd love to stay here gazing into the sunset," *with you,* "you really need to get off your feet now and rest that knee." After she'd fallen, he should've insisted they reschedule, but somehow he knew he wouldn't have won that battle.

She continued to stare across the low vegetation that spread out from the edge of the yard. "Waiting for the sun to set would be stretching this visit quite a bit since it doesn't set until eight—three hours to go. Besides, I doubt there's anything out there to see today except gray clouds."

He almost said "I'm willing to wait if you are," but she was right. And the sunset line was really cheesy, especially as there was no sun shining today, and they'd barely met.

"Well, let's swing by the clinic first so that I can give you that tetanus shot. Then I'll drop you off at your car."

Or take you out for dinner.

Right…like she'd go with a sore knee, a Band-Aid on her chin, blue hospital booties on her feet, and runs in her stockings. Of course, she could go home and change. But would she?

Probably best he didn't ask.

Best? Why then did he have this overwhelming urge to throw caution to the wind and do exactly what he knew he shouldn't do?

At least, shouldn't do just yet.

"Do I really have to? I hate needles." Dark brown doe eyes pleaded with him.

"It's for the best. Don't worry, I'll be very gentle. I promise." Hudson touched her arm lightly. Just as in the car, she pulled away, even though her gaze told him something different. What was this fascinating woman's story? He really wanted to know. In fact, he wanted to know everything about her.

Back at the clinic, it didn't take long for Hudson to administer the tetanus vaccine.

As he secured a small piece of cotton ball over the puncture site with surgical tape, Julia shifted her gaze from the top of her arm to Hudson's face. She smiled. "You were right. You *were* gentle. I didn't feel a thing. Well, *almost* nothing."

"I did tell you I'd be gentle, and I'm a man of my word. If I say something, I'll do it—no matter what."

"That's good to know."

Hudson turned to dispose of the needle in the medical waste can. Done with the procedure, he pulled the blue, nitrile gloves from his hands and disposed of them too before turning back to Julia…his patient. Full on doctor mode kicked in.

"You might experience some redness and swelling at the injection site," he began. "If you do, it should fade within a couple of days. Advil or Tylenol may help. Body aches, fever, and headaches are also possible side effects, although less common. Again, over-the-counter meds may help. If you feel tired or fatigued, make sure you rest as much as possible."

Still seated on the examination table, Julia pursed her lips. "You might've told me all of that before jabbing a needle into my arm."

Her deadpan face made it difficult to tell whether she was serious or joking.

She burst out laughing, and Hudson exhaled in relief.

"Oh, Miss Delpont, I'm not done with all the side effects. Those are just the common ones."

"Stop!" Julia stared at him wide-eyed. "I'm regretting allowing you to talk me into having this shot."

"I'm sorry, but as your doctor, it's my duty to let you know." Although she was right—he should have warned her before injecting her. But she was so distracting, and he was so concerned that she needed the shot before he took her home, that he'd totally forgotten.

"The risk of contracting tetanus isn't worth it, Julia. One out of ten people die from the disease. So rather safe than sorry and suffer a little discomfort now. Right?"

She eyed him, her head slowly moving up and down.

"Any severe reaction would happen shortly after administering the drug to a few hours later. Remember I'm only a phone call away if you need me… I mean, should you have any concerns."

"I'll certainly do that." Julia eased off the table and reached for her jacket. "So back to that man-of-your-word... Does that mean that once you tell me you want to buy a certain house, I can be assured you'll stick to your choice and won't change your mind?"

"I never change my mind. Once I commit to something, Julia, I'm all in. All or nothing."

For a moment their gazes locked.

"Just make sure you're ready, Dr. Brock."

Hudson quirked a brow, allowing his mouth to drop open in mock astonishment. "Dr. Brock? Are we back to being formal again? After all we shared this afternoon? Enjoying the sunset from the balcony of my new home... You falling for me..."

"I did not fall for you! My shoe broke. I fell. Nothing more." She slid her arms into her jacket, then flicked her long, dark hair over the collar. "Besides, you just said that you were my doctor. And, FYI, there was no sunset."

Her eyes narrowed. "Wait a minute... Did you just say your new home? Does that mean—?"

"Yep. I want to put in an offer to purchase the lavender farm house." He loved everything about that property, so why look any further?

"A wise choice. You won't regret it. It wouldn't have remained on the market for long. I'll draw up the paperwork tonight and extend your offer to the seller tomorrow morning."

"I've got a better idea." Hudson shrugged into his own jacket. "Call the seller and tell them you have a serious buyer and a firm offer. Then tackle the paperwork in the morning. Have dinner with me tonight instead."

So much for waiting, but the words just tumbled out, although Hudson didn't regret saying them.

Julia shook her head. "I... T–that's not a good idea. You don't want to have dinner with me... Ever." She turned to go.

Hudson reached for her arm. "But I do. Very much."

She shied away from his touch. "Please, take me back to my car. I need to get home. I have work to do."

Chapter Five

FROM THE desk in her study, Julia gathered the papers she'd worked on last night and tucked them neatly into a folder marked *Dr. Hudson Brock.*

On the drive between the clinic and her car yesterday— thankfully a short distance—she'd managed to ignore the awkwardness between her and Hudson by asking pertinent questions regarding the sale. Anything else she'd needed to know in order to complete the offer to purchase later that evening, she'd texted Hudson. All alone in her quiet, lonely house, she hadn't trusted herself to hear his voice, because if he had been bold enough to ask her out again, she might have, in a moment of weakness, said yes.

Hudson was prepared to offer the full asking price—wanted to take no chances on losing the property he'd said. A wise move on his part, because someone would definitely have been willing to pay what the seller wanted. And that place was worth every dollar. However, having a pre-approved loan and the full deposit amount would work in Hudson's favor, not to mention speed up the process once the seller accepted his formal offer. And, being in pristine condition, Julia had no doubt the house would fly through the inspection.

She lifted the coffee mug from her desk and swigged back the last mouthful before shoving Hudson's folder into her briefcase. By the beginning of June, the good doctor should be able to move into his new home. Just in time for the start of summer and the blossoming of all those lavender bushes.

How she envied him.

And how she envied the woman who would one day share 16 Lavender Lane with him.

But not because of the house, even though she loved that place.

Ugh. She was not supposed to feel attracted to someone. After what James had put her through, she'd promised herself never again to have feelings for a man.

Not that she had feelings for the handsome doctor.

She couldn't have. They'd only met yesterday.

Then why all the butterflies in her stomach at the thought of seeing him again soon?

Butterflies? More like a convocation of eagles spreading and flapping their wings.

Breathing in and out several times, Julia tried to find some calm before she grabbed her briefcase and headed for the front door. She glanced at the clock hanging in the hall. Nine forty-five. Plenty of time to get to the clinic for the 10 a.m. opening Marylin had managed to squeeze into Hudson's busy schedule. The clinic receptionist was only too eager to assist when she heard that Julia needed to see the doctor so he could sign papers to purchase a house.

The weather cold outside, Julia wrapped a scarf around her neck. Her right arm ached as she lifted it to put on her coat. She pursed her lips and glanced at where Hudson had given her the tetanus shot. *Thanks injection.* Or had she twisted her arm when she fell? Maybe she'd ask Hudson's opinion when she saw him.

Julia gazed down at her legs as she opened the front door, grateful she was wearing long pants. But she hadn't chosen the outfit because of the cooler day. The pants covered the large patch on her knee, which she'd had to cover with plastic food wrap last night in order to take a quick shower.

She took a final peek at herself in the hall mirror before exiting her house. Pity nothing could be done about her chin. Oh well, Tuesday would be there soon enough, and all the dressings could hopefully be removed. The sooner she could rid herself of them, the easier her life would be.

And the less she'd be reminded of Dr. Hudson Brock and his gentle touch on her face and knee. If only there was something he could do to heal her heart.

At the clinic, Julia answered Marylin's questions about what happened to her chin then took a seat. One other person waited.

Barely comfortable in her seat, Hudson's door opened. Marylin had told Julia she was next. Seemed Dr. Brock was pretty punctual with his appointments.

Julia's heart thwacked against her ribs as Hudson's tall frame headed toward her. Not a good sign, but dang, he looked so handsome in his white doctor's coat, stethoscope hanging around his neck. She rose and he smiled.

Thwack.

Best she got this sale over as fast as possible.

"Julia..."

Julia's gaze flicked from Hudson to Marylin, standing behind the tall reception desk. The receptionist seemed to be writing in the appointment book, but in that instant, Julia caught the woman peering over those blue frames of hers, seemingly eager to observe the interaction between Julia and the doctor. But why? Was she just happy that someone had found her employer a house he loved? Or was it something more? Something like this middle-aged woman checking out the ladies who came into the clinic as potential romantic interests for probably the most eligible bachelor now in Chapel Cove?

"Dr. Brock." Julia held out a hand.

Ugh, that was pushing the professional envelope a little too far. This wasn't the first time they'd met.

But, she was in his territory now. It wasn't wrong to address him here by his medical title. In fact, it was probably better.

Hudson's low chuckle rumbled as he shook her hand. He leaned forward and whispered. "Formal again? Or is that just for the audience?" He tipped his head slightly toward the reception desk.

It was. But she couldn't...she wouldn't tell him that.

"Shall we get these papers signed? I'm sure your next patient will be here soon." If they weren't there already. Or were those Dr. Johnson's patients lining up?

Julia took a step toward Hudson's office. The sooner they got this deal done the better. She couldn't risk her attraction to this man growing any more than it already had.

Despite Julia's pointing to the purchase documents intoning, "Sign here, here, and here," Hudson determined to make his time with her last as long as he could.

Lifting the papers, he leaned back in his high-backed, leather chair, and painstakingly began reading the fine print. In various places, he feigned ignorance and asked Julia to please explain. Twenty minutes later, he picked up his Montblanc fountain pen and scribbled his signature or initials where Julia had once again shown him.

Disappointed that their time together had come to an end for now, he handed the papers back to Julia, resisting the urge to ask her out for dinner tonight. After all, it was Friday, the night most people ate out. But something whispered to wait until Tuesday when she came for her follow-up appointment, and then try again. After all, she'd already turned him down once.

Julia slid the papers back into her briefcase then rose.

Hudson shoved to his feet, moving to the other side of his table with lightning speed.

With her scarf and coat draped over her arm, and her fingers clenching the briefcase handle, Julia turned to go then paused. "May I ask you something?"

"Of course. Anything," Hudson replied.

"The stiffness in my arm…is that because of the tetanus shot yesterday?" She chuckled. "You rattled off so many side effects, I really can't remember if that was one of them."

"It probably is, but let me check your arm before you go. It's entirely possible you hurt it when you fell." Hudson gestured toward the examination room just off his office. Same place he'd administered the injection yesterday.

Julia waved her free hand through the air. "That's not necessary. I've already taken up more than enough of your time. Your next patient will be waiting."

Hudson smiled lazily. "That's all right. It won't hurt them to wait a few more minutes."

She clamped her bottom lip between her teeth for a moment, before gushing out, "I–I'm not here as a patient. I don't have an appointment."

Did the thought of spending time with him make her nervous? It certainly seemed that way. He'd probably made a mistake by rushing to ask her out last night. But he couldn't deny the chemistry between them, and he was certain Julia felt it just as strongly.

What if she was already involved? Perhaps that's why she feared the strong attraction.

The nauseating thought churned in his gut like sour milk. He had to find out. Hopefully, on Tuesday, he'd get a chance to do so. Now really wasn't the right time to fish for information.

Hudson's left brow slowly lifted. And just as slowly, he said, "Let me take a look, Julia. Doctor's orders."

Releasing a sigh, she set her coat, scarf, and briefcase down on the empty chair and made her way to the examination room. She removed her jacket then hopped up onto the examination table.

He gazed at the long-sleeved top hugging her arm. No way could he examine her arm with that on. Twisting away from her, he reached into the top drawer for a disposable paper gown and handed it to her. "Um…you'll need to take off your blouse and put this on. I'll give you a moment's privacy."

Hudson stepped back toward the door.

"Is this really necessary?" Julia protested.

"Better safe than sorry. And it'll only take a minute or two." He shut the door behind him then waited on the other side until he could hear Julia clambering back onto the examination table. Her voice drifted through the closed door, "I'm ready."

Hudson entered. He washed and dried his hands before turning to Julia.

Smooth, slender arms, protruded from the short sleeves of the gown, their flawless complexion resembling that of a porcelain doll.

As he touched the arm he'd injected yesterday, Julia winced.

41

"I'm sorry. Did I hurt you?" He wasn't sure how he could've. He'd been so gentle.

She shook her head. "It *only* hurts when I *lift* my arm."

Then why did she pull away?

"Feels as if a brick's holding it down," she continued.

For a moment their eyes locked. Her dark gaze failed to hide the pain, but Hudson was convinced it wasn't any kind of physical pain. Something or someone—and he'd hazard a guess it was the latter—had hurt this beautiful woman deeply. Of that, he was certain. Maybe one day she would open up to him. He only hoped that if she did, he would be able to help her work through that pain and find healing.

But that was doctoring of a different kind and certainly for another day.

Hudson examined the site. It was slightly inflamed and warm to the touch. He checked the rest of her arm then moved it to test her mobility. Besides her grazed palm, he could find no evidence to suggest that she'd hurt the limb in the fall.

"I think your discomfort is purely due to the tetanus shot, Julia. It can do that sometimes and become quite uncomfortable and sore. Those symptoms will subside in the coming days or weeks, however."

Her eyes widened.

He should have stopped at days. She didn't seem to relish the idea of her arm hurting for weeks. He hurried to add, "Apply a cold compress to your arm regularly. It'll help. Do you have a compress?"

"I should have one at home. If not, I'll stop by the drug store later." Julia slid off the table.

Pivoting, Hudson opened the cupboard beneath the counter and removed a reusable hot/cold gel pack. He handed it to Julia and smiled. "There, now you have one less thing to worry about today."

Her gaze lowered to the pack in her hands before returning to Hudson. "A–are you sure?"

"I have half a dozen of them stacked up on that shelf." He pointed toward the cupboard. "Free samples from medical reps…for patients who need them."

"Thank you." She reached for her jacket.

Hudson took that as his cue to leave the room. He shut the door behind him for Julia's privacy.

A few minutes later, she joined Hudson in his office. He hated to see her go, but he couldn't detain her any longer.

This time she put on her coat and scarf, ready to brave the cool weather outside.

"Oh, I almost forgot…" She lifted her briefcase, opened it, and dug inside. She pulled out some blue fabric and handed it to Hudson.

He immediately recognized the booties he'd given her to wear yesterday.

Her mouth turned down. "I'm sorry, the soles are almost worn through. But I did wash them thoroughly last night. Seeing as they were part of your farewell gift, I thought you might want to keep them." She started laughing and shrugged. "For sentimental reasons, perhaps?"

Hudson's chuckles joined hers as he lifted the blue fabric, raising a brow as he inspected them. But even though the protective shoe coverings were practically ruined, one day they'd be part of the story of how they'd met. He'd never throw them away. So sentimental reasons? Yes. But not the ones she was thinking of.

"Thank you." He set the booties down on his table.

Briefcase in hand, Julia made her way to the door.

Hudson followed close behind.

He reached for the door handle, pausing before opening. "So what's next?"

"Once the seller has signed your offer and the paperwork is done with the bank, it'll go to the title company to draw up the final paperwork for the transfer of ownership. As you have a pre-approved loan, you should be in your new home by June."

Hudson's mouth curved upward. "Great."

Julia glanced at the door handle that Hudson still held onto. An obvious hint for him to let her out.

He complied by cracking the door an inch.

Julia shifted forward. "I'll let you know when everything is ready for you to sign and take ownership."

That was it? Except for her follow-up appointment on Tuesday, it was possible he wouldn't see her again for several weeks. Unless he bumped into her at church on Sunday. After the way he'd raved about Chapel Cove Community Church when they'd chatted on Thursday afternoon, Julia said she would try it out. He'd had to confess to having only attended a few times over the past few years when visiting Heath, *and* that he was biased because his brother was the youth pastor, but he'd reassured her it was a wonderful church. A growing church. Now was definitely a good time for him to start attending services regularly. In his defense, he'd only been back in town for two weekends, and he'd been on call and worked both of them.

But what if she decided to ignore his sales pitch for Chapel Cove Community Church and continued attending the tiny church she said she went to every Sunday?

He had to do something more.

Pushing the door open wider, Hudson shifted into the gap. "Before you go, can you find out who owns the vacant ground on the other side of the fire station? I'm looking to expand the clinic into a hospital. As the current premises won't allow for much expansion, I'm investigating the possibility—with a lot of help from outside funding—of erecting an entirely new building. And that site is perfect."

"I can tell you right now who owns it." Apparently undaunted by the fact that he was in her way, she squeezed past him. "That's my boss, Mr. Patterson's land. In fact, probably most vacant land you'll find in Chapel Cove belongs to him. But I don't think he'll sell that particular piece of property. He has plans for riverside condos in the near future."

"Please, would you try to get me an appointment with him? Only," Hudson rubbed the back of his neck, "could you maybe not mention my name? Just tell him the doctors at the clinic would like a meeting with him."

Julia nodded knowingly. "Because of your brother? The one who dated Olivia?"

"Let's just say the Brock boys were always *persona non grata* with the great Bill Patterson."

Julia's jaw dropped. "But that was a lifetime ago—you said you were all just teens then. Surely he won't still feel the same way?"

Hudson's lips pursed, and he shook his head. "Anything's possible. I don't want to take any chances of ruining an opportunity to present my arguments for acquiring the land."

"All right. I'll see what I can do. I'll be in touch."

Julia headed toward the exit as Hudson strode across to his next patient. That little request he'd just made had accelerated his expansion plans by at least a year.

But perhaps God was the one who had prompted him to ask. Maybe the Lord wanted Chapel Cove to have its own hospital sooner rather than later. Wasn't that one of the reasons he'd felt called to move back home?

Yes, that was it. His request to Julia had nothing to do with him being captivated by her, wasn't as a result of him not thinking clearly or trying to come up with any excuse to have more contact with her.

Nope. Not at all, but then who was he kidding?

CHAPTER SIX

WHEN HE'D made Julia's follow up appointment five days ago, Hudson had deliberately scheduled it as his last appointment for the day. That way he knew he wouldn't be pressured to watch the clock. Hopefully, conversation would flow as easily between them as it had the day they'd met. Well, as easily as it had been by the time they were halfway through viewing the second house.

His pulse raced at the thought of asking her out again.

Please, Lord, let her say yes so I can get to know her.

Not a busy day, the hours had dragged by. As he strode across the floor to greet his next patient, his gaze roamed the almost empty seats of the clinic's reception. Julia hadn't arrived yet. Refusing to entertain the thought that she'd be a no-show, Hudson consoled himself with the thought that she'd probably arrive any minute now. After all, there were still fifteen minutes before her appointment.

He'd really missed her. He hadn't heard from her besides two texts—one on Friday night to say that his offer to purchase had been accepted and signed by the seller, and another yesterday to let him know that she'd managed to secure a meeting with Bill Patterson for Wednesday evening...without having to divulge Hudson's name. She suggested Hudson make the business dinner at her boss's favorite seafood restaurant on the boardwalk, reminding Hudson that the way to a man's heart was through his stomach.

He did need to soften Bill Patterson's heart if he was to have any hope of convincing the man to sell the prime property, maybe even invest in this important part of Chapel Cove's future.

At both morning and evening services on Sunday, Hudson had kept his eyes peeled for Julia. But she definitely hadn't attended any of the services. Was she just not as interested in trying out the church as she said she was? Or had she stayed away because of him? The thought did cross his mind after the evening service that perhaps she wasn't feeling well from the tetanus shot. It had taken everything in him not to text her to check whether she was ill. She had his number; she'd promised to call if she had any concerns he reminded himself over and over.

When Hudson walked his patient out of his office fifteen minutes later, his heart sank. Except for Marylin, the reception area was empty.

She looked up as he strode across to her desk.

"Has my five o'clock appointment arrived yet?" Perhaps Julia had stepped into the bathroom.

Marylin looked down at Hudson's appointment book, then up at him again. "Julia Delpont? She changed her appointment when she was here on Friday with your house papers—saw Dr. Johnson around eleven this morning."

"So she's not coming in?"

The receptionist shook her gray head. "Highly doubtful, I'd say."

"Did she say why she changed from me to Dr. Johnson?"

Marylin shook her head again, narrowing her gaze. "It was strange though, as if she'd had a sudden change of mind. She'd already walked out the door, when she paused and looked back over her shoulder. I might be wrong, but it seemed as if she was watching you walk back to your office because the moment I heard your door click shut, she spun around and came back inside. That's when she changed her appointment. At the time, I just assumed it was by mutual agreement and that she'd merely forgotten to do so until she got outside."

Hudson folded his arms. "No. No mutual agreement. It's very strange. I wonder why she did that."

Leaning forward, Marylin lowered her voice and said, "Do you want my five cents' worth on what I think the reason is, doctor?"

Did he? Would what he heard from Marylin be a valid, honest opinion, or would her take on Julia be colored by town gossip? He knew what this small town was like—he'd lived with the whispers, some louder than others, after his mother skipped town one night, never to return.

He nodded. Might as well hear what Marylin had to say— maybe it would all be based on woman's intuition, and not on gossip.

Speaking a little louder, she continued, "Violet called me over the weekend...just to chat."

"Violet?" Hudson narrowed his eyes.

"From Ivy's on Spruce...the bookstore where Violet works for Ivy Macnamara."

Ah, at least he knew one trusted name. "The woman who had the heart attack two weeks ago." Which had necessitated an earlier start date for Hudson, albeit by only a day. Still, as nobody had his on-call number—ha, which even he didn't have then—he'd had to spend that Sunday at the clinic to attend to any emergencies. And there had been one or two, although nothing serious or life-threatening. Not like the heart-attack victim Dr. Johnson had dealt with.

Although he didn't really know Ivy, Heath was very close to her. At the time their Uncle Trafford had been keen on Ivy, then fallen ill and passed away, Hudson had been trying his best to salvage and save what was left of wounded and dying soldiers.

"The very same," Marylin replied. She pushed her glasses farther up on her nose. "I happened to mention to Violet that you had bought a house through Julia, saying that I thought you two made a cute couple."

She held up a finger to him. "And don't deny it Dr. Brock, I saw those sparks flying between the two of you on Friday."

Hudson sucked in a breath, preparing to retaliate with a quick explanation of what Marylin thought she might've seen. No words came because there was no explanation. There *had* been chemistry between them when Julia came to the office with the offer to purchase.

He exhaled slowly, waiting for Marylin to continue.

She complied. "It was then that Violet confided in me about an altercation she'd had with Julia on Thursday. Seems it must've happened shortly before you met her to view houses."

"An altercation?" Hudson couldn't imagine Julia having an altercation with anyone, especially not a little old bookshop lady. Not that he knew how old Violet was, but as she was friends with Marylin, he assumed she wasn't young.

"Yes. Violet forgot that Julia only reads crime and suspense novels—you know the ones with blood-stained knives or smoking guns on the cover? Foolishly, she offered Julia a romantic suspense. According to Violet, Julia was quite rude, reiterating NO romance before storming out of the bookshop. Actually, I was rather surprised when I heard that, because Julia seems like a lovely lady."

He was surprised too. But her actions did seem to support his theory that somebody had hurt her in the past. No wonder she'd said no to his dinner invitation.

But after all that backstory on Julia and Violet, Marylin still hadn't given a reason why she thought Julia had canceled her appointment with him and seen Dr. Johnson instead.

He stared at Marylin, cocking his head to the side. "And your five cents worth is…?"

"Based on what Violet told me, *and* what I saw on Friday, I think that Julia is terrified of falling for you." Marylin's mouth curved into a smile. "And *that's* why she cancelled."

Well, he was falling for her too. Except, he wasn't afraid. The only thing that terrified him was the thought of missing a chance with her.

Placing his palms on the reception counter, Hudson eased forward.

Ha. As if he'd find what he was looking for on the other side of the desk.

He raised his gaze to Marylin. "Do you know where she lives?"

"Well, normally I'd have no idea, doctor, but thankfully she became an *official* patient earlier today, so I do have a medical file for her. And as she was supposed to be your patient…"

What? "Do you mean to tell me that in the eighteen months she's lived in Chapel Cove, she's never been to see Dr. Johnson? Not even once?"

"Nope. Maybe she just doesn't like doctors. Although, as I said before, I certainly think she likes *this* one." With a wide grin, Marylin tipped her chin at Hudson and waggled her brows. Her blue frames moved up and down with the action.

"Don't be smart now, Marylin," he reprimanded, chuckling as he did so. He stretched out his palm. "Just hand over the address."

Seated beside a window in The Pancake Shoppe, Julia stared through the glass at the ocean. The sun was shining and the temperature had risen to the upper seventies. What a perfect day! Not too hot, and nowhere near cold—not like it had been last week. A few white, wispy clouds painted the blue skies like a tie-dyed T-shirt. Summer might just arrive early this year.

Except, it wasn't a perfect day. And she could only blame herself for ruining it.

She lifted the tall, porcelain mug, disappointed to find only a mouthful of the sweet, hot liquid left. She turned to glance at the serving counter where Melanie, co-owner of this quaint establishment, was cleaning up. Of course...they'd be closing soon, and Julia would have to leave and go back to her empty house.

Her gaze roamed the almost deserted eating house before snapping back to Melanie. What the heck, she might as well.

"Melanie," she called. "Any chance I could order a final hot chocolate before you close?"

Melanie smiled. "Coming right up."

While Melanie prepared her drink, Julia finished the last of the pancake on her plate. Talk about an endorphin-filled hour. If all the chocolate she'd consumed in the last ninety minutes or so didn't transport her to a happy place, then she didn't know what would.

Instead of placing the fresh order on the table and leaving, Melanie set the hot drink down in front of Julia then lowered herself into the opposite chair. She reached for Julia's hand and touched it lightly. "So, what's on your mind, girl? I haven't seen you eat and drink this much chocolate since that first day you entered my shop nearly a year and a half ago. Three hot chocolates *and* my sinful chocolate pancake stack? What's going on?"

Oh how she remembered those first few months in Chapel Cove. They'd caused her to pick up several pounds, and she'd had to spend last summer jogging to get rid of her expanding waistline.

The thought of all the sickly sweetness she'd just consumed, not only in the drinks, but in that stack of five pancakes loaded with chocolate ganache and topped with blueberry compote, powdered sugar, and whipped cream, suddenly made Julia feel a little ill. But she would force down her drink. Perhaps that teensy bit more chocolate would tip the serotonin levels in her brain in her favor and the depressive fog that had clouded her mind all afternoon would lift.

Shrugging, Julia wrapped her fingers around her mug then took a sip before staring into Melanie's sweet face. "I... I made a stupid decision today. Actually, I made it on Friday already. I had the whole weekend and yesterday to rectify it, but I didn't."

"A business decision?" Melanie asked, concern filling her face.

Tightening her lips, Julia shook her head. Heat rushed to her cheeks at the thought of Hudson.

Melanie's eyes widened, and then slowly her mouth stretched into a smile. "This is about a man? Oh, please, please, please tell me it is."

She wished she could divulge the specifics, but she just couldn't, even though Melanie was the closest she had to a friend in Chapel Cove. For certain, Julia wasn't the only female to have her heart beating faster because of the new doctor in town. Who knew how many others had come to Melanie's pancake shop because of Dr. Hudson Brock and spilled their guts to the empathetic owner over copious amounts of chocolate in whatever form they found on the menu.

"It is. But I can't tell you anything more. Not now."

Melanie patted Julia's hand. "That's okay. Just know that I'm here when you need more than chocolate to make you feel better."

Hearing the door open, Julia looked up then quickly averted her gaze, hoping she hadn't been seen. Her heart pounded. Of all the rotten luck, *he* would be the one person to walk into this restaurant. Now.

But was it rotten luck, or a blessing?—a chance to redeem herself, to explain.

Right...

Explaining would mean admitting to feelings she preferred to ignore and keep buried until she'd suffocated the life out of them.

Finding no one home at Julia's house, Hudson drove down to the boardwalk. He needed to clear his head, and a walk on the beach would do that. Or maybe he'd skip that until later, first try out that pancake place Heath raved about. He could walk off the indulgence later.

His pulse raced as he entered the charming pancake shop, his eyes settling on long, dark tresses. He had expected to find some solace in a sweet dessert. What he hadn't expected to find was gorgeous Julia sitting there in her flowery summer dress. At least, it looked like a dress from what he could see.

Despite her looking away as he entered, Hudson didn't hesitate to head toward her. Hopefully the person sitting at the table with her wasn't a client, because he was going to interrupt. Even if it was just a friend, if there was *any* chance that Marylin was right and the reason Julia switched doctors was because she *did* like him, he wasn't going to risk losing out on a future with her—client or no client, friend or no friend, her trying to avoid him or not. Maybe she just hadn't seen him, something catching her attention at the very same moment he'd walked through the doors.

He stopped beside her table. "Julia."

She whirled her head around, a look of surprise on her face. "Oh... Hi."

"Hi," he whispered in return before turning to the pretty brunette sitting opposite Julia. He held out his hand. "Hi there. I'm Dr. Hudson Brock."

Offering him a wide smile, the woman shook his hand. "Nice to meet you. I'm Melanie Montana. You must be the new doctor in town."

"Guilty as charged." He gestured to the empty seat in front of him at the square table. "Do you mind if I join you ladies?"

Julia sucked in a breath as if she wanted to say something.

Melanie got in first. "Not at all."

As he sat, Melanie rose. "Can I get you something to drink?"

He glanced around. "Um, I'll order something as soon as I can find a waitress."

Melanie laughed. "That would be me. I'm co-owner of this place and currently the one on floor duty it seems. So, what'll it be?"

"A cappuccino would be great. Thank you." He wouldn't mind a bite to eat as well. After all, isn't that why he'd come here in the first place. Finding Julia was just the cherry on top of the...pancake stack. "Is there any chance of getting one of your famous pancakes or waffles? I've heard so much about them."

"I'm certain my mother-in-law can rustle up something in the kitchen for you. Any preferences?"

Hudson grinned. "Surprise me."

Melanie feigned thought then asked, "You like chocolate?"

Did he like chocolate? No, he *loved* it. "Absolutely. The darker the better."

He turned to Julia. "Would you like anything else?"

She shook her head.

Melanie took a step away. Then paused. "Brock? Any relation to Heath Brock, the youth pastor at Chapel Cove Community Church?"

"Y-e-p." Hudson stretched out the word. "That's my older brother. Do you attend his church?"

"I do." A moment's silence ensued before Melanie continued. "Well, I'll leave you two alone and get that cappuccino and pancake. One more sinful Chocolate Pancake Stack coming up." Her gaze flicked from Hudson to Julia, and he was certain she gave Julia a slight wink.

What was that for? Had they been talking about him before he walked in?

As Melanie strolled away, Hudson turned to Julia again. "I wasn't expecting to find you here, but I'm really glad I did."

CHAPTER SEVEN

OH BOY. Melanie come back! Don't leave me here alone with doctor hunky... I mean Hudson.

Julia flashed Hudson a smile then turned her attention to her paper napkin. Fingers trembling, she furled the corners. She should finish up her drink and leave.

Hudson's voice brought a hasty end to her fidgeting.

"I was disappointed to find that you had cancelled, or rather changed your appointment with me this afternoon to seeing Dr. Johnson earlier today. If the time was a problem, I'm certain Marylin could've squeezed you in earlier with me. I did have a few openings—surprisingly, it was a rather quiet day. For a change."

Shoot. How should she respond? She couldn't say that she'd shifted her appointment because she had a clash with a business meeting, because clearly she hadn't if he found her here at five thirty with an almost finished pancake stack and a half-empty mug in her hand.

And what if Marylin had told him she'd changed the appointment on Friday already?

"I…"

Hudson reached for her hand and gave it a light squeeze. "It's okay. In fact, it's better that you're Dr. Johnson's patient, because if you were my patient, ethically I wouldn't be able to date you."

Date me?

Was he serious, or pulling her leg, making light of the uncomfortable situation?

She glanced up into his warm gaze, sweet as the chocolate on that pancake stack she'd just enjoyed. But oh, this was so much more satisfying.

"Have dinner later with me," he whispered.

Was he for real? Clearly the man wasn't thinking straight—no way was she eating again today. Not after those pancakes. And perhaps he'd feel the same once Melanie brought his order and he'd wolfed it down.

Besides, she couldn't get involved, especially not with Hudson Brock. He had expectations for his future. High ones. Ones she couldn't meet.

Julia shook her head. "I–I already told you… You don't want to date me."

A low chuckle rumbled from his chest. "Actually, if I recall correctly, you said I didn't want to have *dinner* with you."

She waved a hand in the air. "Semantics. Dinner…date… at the end of the day, they're the same thing." Seemed he was going to be hard to persuade that she wasn't the right woman for him. "And you don't want to do either."

Crossing his arms on the table, Hudson leaned forward. "Oh, but I do. I *want* to have dinner with you—lots and lots of dinners.

Which of course will come when I'm dating you."

Julia tsked then laughed nervously. "You're impossible, but you might as well stop asking because I'm *not* going to have dinner with you, and I'm *not* going to date you."

His bottom lip pouted, his face taking on a puppy dog look as his mouth drooped. The sight was enough to make a woman's heart melt.

"Why? Are you involved with someone else?" he finally asked.

Much as she would've liked to, she couldn't lie. "I'm not involved with anyone. I just don't want—" Now *that* was a lie. She did want to. Very much. "I don't think it's a good idea, that's all. Can we leave it at that? Please?"

He shrugged, mischief twinkling in his eyes. "Okay. If you're afraid to be alone with me—"

What?

"I'm not afraid to be alone with you," Julia retorted. "We were alone the entire afternoon on Thursday."

"That we were. Well, in case you *are* afraid to be alone with me at dinner," Hudson chuckled, "why don't we start slowly? Join me tomorrow night for dinner with your boss. If not for the food or my company, do it to help save my head, which I could very well lose if Bill Patterson still has an issue with the Brock boys. It would be such a shame for Doc Johnson to be on his own again—so soon— don't you think?" He angled his head, offering her the most irresistible smile. "And, it's *seafood*. Don't you like seafood? Most people do, don't they?"

"I do. But—"

Hudson gently pressed a finger against her lips. "No buts. Just think about it for a moment. You don't have to give me an answer right now."

His fingers slid beneath her chin. Tilting her face upward, he leaned closer.

Julia yanked her head away. Was he seriously moving in for a kiss? "What are you doing?" Her voice had jumped an octave or two.

Puzzlement washed over his face. "I wanted to see how your chin was healing, that's all."

Oh.

Heat rushed up her neck to her cheeks, and with Hudson staring at the tip of her chin, there was nowhere to hide her blush.

If he noticed, he gave no indication. "It's looking good. And your knee? How has that healed?"

She wanted to snap back that if she'd wanted his medical opinion, she would've kept her five o'clock appointment with him. Instead, she shyly turned in her chair, extended her leg, and hitched her dress to just above the knee, because truth was, cancelling that appointment had been a hard decision. She was already outside the clinic, still grappling with her emotions, before deciding it was for the best and whirling around. Hudson had already closed the door to his consulting room when she'd entered the clinic again and headed toward the reception desk.

Blue bruising outlined the fresh sterile patch that Dr. Johnson had applied. "Doc Johnson is happy with the way it's healing—and my chin. Said you did a great job of fixing me up. Unfortunately, as the knee graze was deeper, I still have to keep that covered for another five days."

Spotting Melanie en route with Hudson's coffee and pancake stack, Julia twisted back in her chair.

Melanie slid the plate and cup onto the table in front of Hudson, shooting Julia a wink as she did.

Ignoring her, Julia focused her attention on the cappuccino foam and the heart pattern that Melanie had crafted in it.

"Mommy?"

Hearing the soft, child's voice, Julia glanced down to see

Melanie's four-year-old daughter hugging her mother's legs. The little girl looked sleepy, her long, gingery wisps standing in all directions

Julia smiled. "Hello, Alia. Have you just woken up, sweetheart?"

Alia retreated behind Melanie before peeking around her mom's legs again.

Hudson turned to look at Alia and smiled. "Hello there. And who are you?"

She retreated for a second time.

Grabbing his paper napkin, Hudson furiously set about folding it. Within seconds, he had a beautiful white paper swan. "Alia," he called. "I've got something for you."

Melanie twisted around and coaxed Alia to the front of her legs. "Alia, say hello to Dr. Brock."

Cat still got her tongue, Alia made speaking worse by nibbling on the tip of her thumb, twisting the finger one way then the next.

Hudson held out the swan on the palm of his hands. "Here, this is for you. Just don't put it in the bathtub or it'll break."

Hesitantly, Alia reached for the swan.

As she did, Julia noticed Hudson's brow arch for a brief moment. He glanced up at Melanie. "She's really cute. How old is she?"

"Four," Melanie said. "And not usually this quiet. In fact, she's rather a handful most days, but she just woke up from a nap. Preschool seems to tire her out somewhat."

Alia clutched the origami swan between her slender fingers, Hudson's pristine handiwork getting wrinkles where they didn't belong.

"Well, you'd better not let those pancakes get cold." Melanie turned to go. "Alia, say thank you."

Alia's soft "Tank you", not yet getting the 'th' in her words, came with a wide smile, rewarding Hudson for his gesture.

"Bye-bye, Dr. Brock and Julia," Melanie prompted.

"Bye, doctor." Alia coughed then waved as she followed her mother back to the kitchen.

Hudson's brows wrinkled again before he pulled the plate of pancakes closer. "She is really cute."

Julia's heart warmed.

And ached.

Giving Alia a final wave, Julia said, "She is. You certainly had a way with her. You should've been a pediatrician."

"Looking back, I wish I had specialized in that. With Chapel Cove growing the way it is, the town certainly could do with having at least one. And I would've saved myself seeing too much of man's inhumanity to man during my time in Afghanistan."

Julia's eyes widened. "You were an army doctor?"

"Surgeon. For three years. It was tough, but certainly prepared me to be able to handle the worst."

"And how do you plan to do that now, Dr. Brock, without an OR?"

"For now…" He took a sip of the steaming liquid then set the cup down. "That's why tomorrow night's dinner is so important. Maybe *you* could persuade Bill Patterson that my proposal for a Chapel Cove hospital is a good one."

"Okay, I'll accompany you to this business dinner. But *only* to do what I can to keep Bill from serving your head on a platter. I'll try to convince him to part with that land for a hospital. And if not that piece, then some other piece of property. But being alongside the river, that *is* prime real estate."

"Thank you." Hudson grinned. "So it's a date."

Julia shook her head. "It's not a date." But if it were, she would count it toward that non-existent one-date policy for Hudson Brock. Then she wouldn't have to see him again. At least not socially.

Cutting a chunk of chocolate-laden pancake from the round shape, Hudson speared the piece with his fork then shoved it into his mouth. Once he'd swallowed, he looked up at Julia, his expression growing serious. "Can I ask you something? And please, feel free to tell me it's none of my business."

Julia hesitated a moment before answering. "Sure."

"Melanie... Is she a good mother?"

So he had seen the bruises on Alia's arm. "She's the best. She'd give her life for that little girl." Julia wrapped her fingers around her mug. Drat, her drink had gone cold. "Look, I know where you're heading with this, but no...Melanie is not an abusive parent. Alia bruises easily, that's all. And you know kids of that age are always tripping and falling, or bumping into something or the other."

"I believe you. But Alia could be anemic, or have an iron deficiency. Maybe you could convince Melanie to bring her in one day soon for a checkup?"

"Maybe." Or maybe not. She wasn't Alia's mother. And what did she know about mothering anyway? Melanie was a good mom; she'd know whether her daughter needed to see a doctor. She might even have been to see Dr. Johnson. She might already be on medication. It wasn't her place to suggest to her friend that perhaps she wasn't being as attentive to her daughter's health as she should. Julia didn't want to rock the boat of one of the very few friendships she had in town.

Deciding to leave the rest of her drink, she rose. "I need to go. Enjoy those pancakes...they are divine." She broke off a corner of the top one and popped it into her mouth. Yum, divine. She smiled. "I'll see you tomorrow night at The Fisherman's Hook. Seven o'clock."

Hudson shot to his feet. "How about I collect you at six forty-five? It's the least I can do seeing as you're doing me this huge favor."

"Are you trying to make sure I don't duck out when the going gets rough?"

Feigning surprise at her suggestion, Hudson said, "The thought never crossed my mind. I was thinking more that I could drive you home, walk you to your front door, and kiss you goodnight."

Hudson held Julia's stare. What had come over him to be so bold? Desperation at being forty and longing for a wife and kids?

No, this went way deeper than that. He had really developed feelings for this woman. Fast. She made his heart thrum at the mere thought of her. Not to mention what it did when he saw her. He could very well be Dr. Johnson's next cardiac arrest patient.

Julia grabbed her handbag. "Ha, in your wildest dreams. I'll allow you to pick me up, and take me home, and walk me to my door, but that's all." With that, she flounced off toward the cash register, probably to settle her bill. If she'd given him a chance, he would've gladly offered to pay for whatever she'd had.

Tomorrow night, he would.

Hudson finished eating his pancakes and sipping his cappuccino. Then he paid and left.

The weather too good to waste, he took a leisurely walk to the end of the jetty where fishermen cast their lines into the sea. Some came up empty-handed then tried again, while others had already landed that big one.

He too had cast a line with Julia. Hopefully it would end up hooking her heart.

As the sun sank lower on the horizon, Hudson ambled down the boardwalk toward the beach. If only he'd invited Julia to share the sunset with him. But there would be more opportunities, he was certain. Even if Julia didn't want to admit it, he was certain she was attracted to him too. If she wasn't, she could've just said no to his plea for help with the Bill Patterson dinner.

Pausing, Hudson whipped off his shoes and socks before stepping from the wooden walkway onto the soft sand. Shoes dangling from his fingers, he strolled up the beach. Overhead, seagulls squawked, frantically searching for their last meal of the day.

It didn't take long for Hudson to realize he'd gone as far as Heath's camper. Disappointment quickly obliterated his initial excitement at the prospect of chatting with his brother. Heath's red truck wasn't there. More than likely, he was visiting Reese at Uncle Trafford's house.

Uncle Trafford's? He really should get used to calling it Heath's place. That house hadn't been Uncle Trafford's for five years.

An overwhelming urge to talk to Heath, to tell his brother he'd met someone, flooded Hudson. Should he call? It had only been a few days since Heath and Reese had gotten back together again— he didn't want to disturb them.

Sinking onto the sand, Hudson pulled his cell phone from his shirt pocket. Heath could always decline the call if he *was* interrupting.

On the fifth ring, Heath's voice boomed through the phone. "Hudson. I'm glad you called. I was actually planning to call you later to catch up. What's new?"

Not managing to touch base on Sunday at either of the services, Hudson had last spoken to Heath on Saturday morning. He'd called his brother to tell him that he'd signed an offer to purchase the house near the lavender farm. Hudson had promised to take Heath and Reese to see it as soon as he could.

"I've met someone," Hudson blurted out.

"You have? Wow, that was fast! When? Where?"

Maybe he had developed feelings for Julia fast, but Hudson certainly didn't want to follow in his brother's footsteps of waiting twenty-two years for someone. Time was not on his side.

"Actually, my new real estate agent. She's...incredible. She's beautiful. Intelligent. Fun." *Hurt.*

And Hudson wasn't thinking about her knee or chin. The sudden thought took him full circle to the earlier feeling he'd had on Friday that her heart was fragile, still healing. He must tread carefully with her, let her realize that he was someone she could trust, someone who would never toy with her heart and then break it.

"I couldn't be happier for you, Hudson. Reese and I would love to meet her. Will you bring her around for dinner sometime soon?"

"I will. As soon as I start dating her."

Heath's laughter rumbled so loud, that Hudson yanked the phone away from his ear for a second, bringing it back in time to hear Heath say, "You haven't asked her out yet?"

"I have. She's playing hard to get, but I'm working on it."

"Well, work harder, little brother. I haven't heard you this excited about a girl in—" Heath cut off his sentence. "Well, ever. Reese and I will be praying for you. If this is the woman God has planned for you, I pray you'll soon be successful in getting that first date. And a lifetime more thereafter."

"Thanks, Heath. I'll see you soon. Send my love to Reese."

Heath chuckled. "Shouldn't you be saving that for— Hey, you haven't told me her name yet."

"Julia. Julia Delpont."

After cutting the call, Hudson sank his palms into the sand behind him. Arms straight, he leaned back to enjoy the sunset. But the magnificent gold and blue hues above the watery horizon soon morphed into the same beautiful image that had filled his mind for the past five days.

Much as he wasn't anxious to meet up with Bill Patterson again, he couldn't wait for tomorrow night.

CHAPTER EIGHT

HUDSON HAD been at a loss for words since picking up Julia at her house. Thankfully, she'd talked most of the short distance to The Fisherman's Hook, briefing him on Bill Patterson.

As they sat in the restaurant, waiting for her boss to arrive, he still could not keep his eyes off her. The weather wasn't the only thing hot tonight.

Julia looked incredible wearing a black, off-the-shoulder cocktail dress that just covered her knees. She'd swept her hair up in a braided up-do, the style highlighting her beautiful face, back, and neckline. With a light application of makeup, the healing scrape on her chin was barely noticeable.

No doubt about it—this girl had gone to a lot of trouble tonight. For him? Or was this just the way she dressed when dining at the fanciest restaurant in town?

Julia's laugh made him realize he was staring.

Again.

She touched the side of her mouth. "What? Do I have toothpaste or something on my lip?"

He shook his head. "Have I told you yet how amazing you look?" he said, his voice low.

"Yes. If I recall, it was the first thing you said when I opened my front door."

Shifting her gaze past Hudson, Julia waved and rose. "Bill."

Hudson glanced over his shoulder to see a tall, gray-haired man heading their way. Briefcase in hand, Bill Patterson, still just as imposing, looked every inch the property-tycoon in his charcoal-colored suit. Hudson breathed a sigh of relief that he had dressed almost equally suitable. Except, instead of a suit, Hudson had chosen smart, dark blue trousers and a cream-colored linen jacket. But unlike Bill Patterson, he'd ditched the idea of a tie.

The waiter hurried to pull out a chair for the third guest at their table.

Bill Patterson nodded a greeting to Julia as he sat down then turned to Hudson. He held out his hand. "You must be the new doctor?"

In the past two decades, Bill's hair—still a short, neat comb over—had grayed and a few wrinkles had formed on his face. One big difference Hudson noticed was that the man now sported a peppery, neatly-trimmed beard and mustache. But apart from that, Hudson would still have recognized him if they'd passed each other on the street. For someone nearing his seventies, Bill Patterson was still in good shape.

"Guilty as charged, sir." He shook the man's hand. "Hudson." He'd forego his surname for as long as possible, just to be safe. Didn't want this business dinner to come to a grinding halt before it even got started.

"Is Dr. Johnson joining us?" Bill Patterson asked.

Hudson swallowed. After all these years, the man still appeared formidable in his eyes. But unlike Hudson's teen years when Bill Patterson had darkened the door of their trailer and threatened their father to keep Hunter away from his daughter, the dread he felt for Olivia's father was now mixed with feelings of awe and admiration. The more he'd learned from Julia earlier, the more he realized that Bill Patterson had played an important part in shaping Chapel Cove. Hopefully the same would soon be said about Hudson's proposal.

Lord, please let him agree to part with the land at a reasonable amount. Please do more than I could think or imagine. Help Chapel Cove to get the hospital it needs. Bring the investors that I so desperately need to make this happen.

"Um, no he won't." Hudson grasped the menu that had been set down beside him earlier. "Shall we order?"

Bill Patterson chuckled. "An excellent idea. I'm starving. And I only have an hour and a half to spare. Promised my wife and daughter I wouldn't be home late. Plus, I do like to say goodnight to my grandson and he's usually in bed around eight thirty." He waved away the menu the waiter tried to hand him. "I'll have the usual, thank you, Thomas."

Grandson? Hudson couldn't recall that Olivia had any siblings. Could it be *her* child? Was she married? No reason that at forty, the daughter of a wealthy man, she wouldn't be.

Hudson's eyes skimmed the menu as he hurried to make a decision.

Julia seemed to do the same because they both shut their menus simultaneously and looked up at the waiter who still hovered beside their table, seemingly eager for them to place their orders. Probably so that he could rush to do Mr. Patterson's bidding.

Once they'd ordered, Thomas scurried toward the kitchen.

Bill Patterson leaned forward, clasping his hands together. "So Julia tells me that you have a business proposition."

Proposition? More like a request.

Lump rising in his throat, Hudson forced out the words before his tongue could seize up. "With the help of government and local investors, I'd like to see Chapel Cove get its own hospital."

Bill Patterson's brows, the color of the rest of his facial hair, rose. "A lofty ambition. And so soon after arriving in town."

"I believe this is long overdue, Mr. Patterson, and I'd like to get the ball rolling sooner rather than later." Refusing to be intimidated, Hudson kept his gaze focused on the man. "I would like to purchase a portion of the riverfront property closest to the existing clinic up to the step-down facility. It's the perfect location to build the hospital—the current clinic could be linked to the hospital in some way; the fire station with the helipad is already there, perfectly situated between the old and the proposed new building; and the step-down facility would be on the hospital's doorstep. And with grounds overlooking the river, the tranquility would be so healing for Chapel Cove's patients."

Bill Patterson shook his head. "That's not possible. The land that you're asking about is earmarked for a holiday resort." His gaze shot to Julia. "Didn't you tell him that?"

"I did, Bill, but—"

"It's not Julia's fault, Mr. Patterson," Hudson defended. "I insisted on meeting you as I hoped to be able to share my vision with you, and in doing so, that you'd get as excited about this as I am. This town will owe you a debt of gratitude if you're able to help make Chapel Cove's hospital a reality."

"I applaud your zeal, son, but it will have to be at a different location. There are many other pieces of land that can do the job equally well. Let Julia take you to see some of the properties. Then we can talk. In the meantime," Bill Patterson leaned to the side, unlatched his briefcase and slid his hand inside. When he straightened, he placed his checkbook on the table. "I'd like to make a sizeable contribution to the hospital building project. Plus, I'll put the word out to all the influential businessmen in town to get in touch with you."

He slid a pen from his top pocket and readied to write the check. "Now, who do I make this out to?"

When Hudson hesitated, Julia answered. "Dr. Hudson Brock."

Bill Patterson lowered his pen, and Hudson's heart sank. "Brock? Did you grow up here?"

There was nowhere to hide the truth of who he was. Hudson could feel that contribution, and the hope of someday convincing Bill Patterson to part with that land—any land—slipping away. "I did, yes."

"You had two older brothers, didn't you? Heath and—"

"Hunter."

"Yes... Hunter." The name still seemed to be poison to Bill Patterson as his lip curled. He shoved his pen back in his jacket pocket and his checkbook in his briefcase then rose. "I'm sorry, this meeting is over. I will *never* do business with a Brock."

Hudson shoved to his feet. "Mr. Patterson...wait! Please."

"Bill..." Julia hurried to her feet too.

Bill Patterson screwed up his eyes and glared at Hudson. "Never."

He turned to Julia. "As for you, young lady, I will talk to you tomorrow." Grabbing his briefcase, he whirled around and stormed out of the restaurant.

Julia eased back into her chair, watching Hudson's shoulders droop. He brushed a hand across his neatly-trimmed beard before glancing at her, dejection written all over his handsome face.

"I–I'm so sorry to have dragged you into this. I hope you don't get into trouble tomorrow," he said.

Seeing the disappointment in his eyes, she reached for his hand, surprised that his hurt, hurt her too. "Don't worry. I'll be fine. I know a thing or two about handling Bill Patterson. And tomorrow, I'll contact a few other real estate agents in town. I'm sure one of them will have a suitable piece of property. I know it won't be the one you'd set your heart on, but perhaps God has a better location. Don't forget that when He closes a door, usually it's because He's about to open a better one."

Ha, she should listen to her own advice. What if James was the wrong door, and Hudson the right one? What if *this* was the man who *was* prepared to choose her, warts and all? And be resolute in that choice. Her fear of being hurt again could rob her of happiness.

But she couldn't ignore the fact that Hudson was a really nice guy, and someone who deserved to have all his dreams fulfilled.

She could never deny him that.

The smile he offered her seemed pasted on. "You're right. I guess this idea and dinner was doomed from the start."

She smoothed her thumb over his skin, surprised at how soft his hands were. But as a doctor, they naturally would be.

Reality struck home at what she was doing and how long her hand had lingered on his. Slowly, she pulled her hand away. In an attempt to lift his spirits, she said, "It's not totally wasted. We can still enjoy our dinner together, and you'll have a seafood platter to take home for tomorrow night's meal." If Bill hadn't been in such a hurry to leave, he might've boxed his order and taken it with him.

Hudson exhaled. "Care to share it with me?"

Share? Oh how she relished that idea, but she wouldn't act on it.

So instead of answering him, Julia changed the subject. "To be honest, I really didn't expect that kind of reaction from Bill when he figured out who you were. Exactly how much bad blood was there between your families?"

Hudson lifted his glass and swirled the sparkling water around. His gaze locked on hers. "Obviously way more than I realized."

Thomas and a second waiter returned bearing three large plates. Both Julia and Hudson had ordered the wild king salmon with roasted poblano pepper, Oregonzola cheese, pan-seared vegetables, and linguini in a tomato saffron sauce. Strange how they had the same taste.

The waiters set the plates down, Thomas looking a little concerned at the absence of Bill Patterson.

"He had to leave," Julia explained. "We'll take that to go."

Golly, that seafood platter looked good—fried fish, oysters, calamari, clam strips, lobster, and tiny Pacific shrimp along with some golden fries and a side salad. Julia couldn't help hoping that Hudson would make the offer to share it a second time.

Hudson's eyes widened. "That's a *lot* of seafood. Definitely going to need help with that tomorrow. Can't keep it for more than a day or so."

"Okay." The words were out of Julia's mouth before she even had time to think them. Seemed, subconsciously, she wasn't taking a chance of him asking for a third time. Well, *this* was a business meeting and not a date, she justified—she might as well have that one-date with Hudson, then they could both go their merry, separate ways. "What did you have in mind?"

"Hmm, for what I have in mind, I'll need your help. All my stuff is in storage, and as I currently stay in a bed and breakfast, I don't have any of the things we'll need."

"I'm sure I can help." Plates, knives, forks, a place to eat... They wouldn't need more than that. "Just let me know what you require."

Once Julia and Hudson had navigated through the upset of Bill storming out of the restaurant, the rest of the evening had been amazing. What an interesting person Hudson was to talk to, although Julia had already gotten a glimpse into that last Thursday. He was the perfect dinner date...not that this was a date. That would be tomorrow. One time only.

When they'd finished their desserts—both having chosen homemade Marionberry Cobbler, another surprise that made them chuckle at their common taste—Hudson asked for the bill, refusing Julia's offer to pay her way.

"I asked you to accompany me tonight," he said when she insisted.

Julia dropped her wallet back inside her handbag. "All right. So long as that doesn't make you think this is a date."

A lopsided grin curved his mouth on one side. "Oh no, that's tomorrow night. Or is that not a date either?"

Julia closed her eyes for a moment, feigning thought. "Um, we'll see tomorrow. It might just be one friend helping another out. Again." She chuckled.

"Oh, so we're friends now. That's good. We're definitely progressing in the right direction." Hudson viewed the bill then handed his credit card to Thomas. The waiter soon returned with the card and the slip for him to sign.

Julia watched, intrigued. Even viewing it upside down, he had a lovely signature. Could he be the antithesis of the norm? Didn't doctors usually have illegible handwriting?

He looked up at her and smiled, and Julia couldn't tear her gaze away.

Never mind his handwriting… Could he be the antithesis of so much more? The opposite of James? The opposite of any man she'd ever dated?

"Shall we go?" Hudson started to rise.

So their wonderful evening had come to an end.

A heaviness slam dunked the pit of Julia's stomach. Should have skipped dessert after such a big meal. Or was that sinking feeling disappointment?

Heaven forbid!

And yet, Julia couldn't fool herself that she wasn't… disappointed.

Neither could she fool herself that she wasn't half curious and just a little more than excited to see whether Hudson would make good on last night's proclamation of walking her to her front door after driving her home, and then kissing her goodnight.

A fuzzy warmth seeped through her as she rose.

As Hudson picked up the two takeout food boxes—way too much seafood on Bill's platter to fit into one—Julia turned to Thomas and thanked him for his excellent service.

Outside, the temperature had dropped considerably. Julia brushed her hands up and down her arms. She should've brought along a jacket, but it had been so warm when Hudson collected her earlier. Amazing how much could change in the space of a few hours.

"You're cold." Hudson stopped and handed the food containers to Julia. He took off his jacket and wrapped it around her shoulders. "That should help a little."

"Thank you." Julia breathed in the woodsy cologne that she'd caught whiffs of all night. Not good for her already racing heart.

When Hudson indicated that she hand him the food, Julia said, "I'll hang onto these. No point in giving them back, just for you to pass them to me again once we get to the car."

He chuckled. "Right. And as you'll be taking them home and refrigerating them until tomorrow, best you hold onto them."

The drive home from the restaurant was way shorter than Julia wanted it to be. Before she knew it, Hudson had parked his SUV outside her modest two-story, two bedroom home with its light blue clapboard walls, white window frames, and dark blue shutters, gutters, and eaves. She'd come to love this little furnished rental. Most of all, she loved the bay window in the front that overlooked her neat little yard. It was her favorite place to curl up and relax with a good book.

Speaking of, she really did need to get another one, or two, novels to read, otherwise this coming weekend would be as boring and uneventful as the last. She hadn't ventured back to Ivy's since the scene she'd caused with Violet. But she'd have to. It was either that, or a visit to the library. Yes, she'd do that instead on Friday afternoon. But just this once. She did like to support Ivy's bookshop and hoped to continue doing so.

Hudson cleared his throat. "You're pretty lost in thought."

"Sorry. Thinking about the weekend, that's all." She opened the car door and slid out.

Hudson followed her lead, hurrying to join her as she stepped onto her front walk.

Julia glanced at Hudson, strolling beside her. "You don't have to worry. I can manage getting to the door." She laughed. "Except, I guess you should take your jacket."

She paused and turned her back to him so that he could slide the jacket from her shoulders.

Hudson lightly grasped her shoulders. "Keep it on. I'll get it from you tomorrow," he whispered in her ear, his breath warm against her neck.

Julia's heart beat faster. Any second now he was going to try to kiss her goodnight.

But instead, he placed his hand in the small of her back, gently encouraging her forward as he continued walking.

After she'd opened the front door and her feet touched the oak floor inside, Hudson pivoted, ready to leave. For the second time in the space of less than twenty minutes, Julia felt disappointment again, finding it hard to comprehend that she'd actually *wanted* him to kiss her. She watched his back retreating.

"I'll see you tomorrow afternoon," he called over his shoulder as he waved. "Five thirty okay?"

"Perfect." She started to close the door then stopped. "Wait! You haven't told me yet what you need me to supply."

"I tell you what, you just keep those little oysters, fish, and crustaceans refrigerated tonight. I have a plan to take care of the rest."

She wanted to protest again, but instead offered a final smile and nod before closing the door behind her. Leaning back against the inch of wood separating her from Hudson, Julia closed her eyes and touched her fingers to her lips, unable to curb her racing thoughts.

If he *had* kissed her, what would that kiss have been like?

CHAPTER NINE

ON THE way to the clinic the following morning, Hudson made a call to Heath. As his brother answered, Hudson anxiously said, "I need your help."

The call hands-free, Heath's low chuckles filtered through the car's speakers. "Good morning to you, too, little brother."

"Yep, morning, sorry. I'm running late. Overslept." And all because he hadn't wanted to wake from the dream he was having about a certain dark-haired, dark-eyed woman. "I have a date with Julia tonight—"

"Seriously? Well done! So we'll get to meet her soon?" Heath sounded really excited, and Hudson's heart warmed.

"As soon as I think she's ready to move on to the next level of our relationship—meeting family—I promise, we'll get together."

"Great. Reese and I will look forward to that. So, how do you need my help?"

By the time Hudson pulled into his designated parking space at the clinic, he'd rattled off the list of things he needed Heath to buy for him and drop off at the clinic before five.

"No problem. I'll ask Reese to help me. Women are good at this stuff," Heath said.

"Thanks. I'll pay you back later. Bye." Hudson ended the call and clambered out of his vehicle, ready to get this day over.

Even though the hours were filled with non-stop appointments, the day still dragged by. When Hudson finally waved his last patient goodbye ten minutes after five, he breathed a relieved sigh. Now he had to hope his brother had come through for him and dropped off everything he'd asked for. Running behind on time, Hudson would have to hurry to get that brand-new picnic basket filled with everything he'd asked Heath to purchase then scoot on over to Julia's house. He did not want to be late for this date.

Doctor's bag in hand, he shut his consulting room door and dashed to Marylin's desk.

She glanced up.

"Did my brother drop off anything for me?" he asked.

Marylin's bright smile spoke of approval for whatever he was up to. "Just a few minutes ago. Said he couldn't stay but to tell you to have fun. Oh, and that with the mercury in the upper eighties, God was smiling down on you. And I couldn't agree more. If you're planning what I think you are, you couldn't have asked for more perfect weather."

Marylin rose and set the four-person wicker picnic basket down on top of the reception counter. On one side, a red, plaid blanket was attached to the basket by leather straps. Hudson had specifically asked for a bigger size so that it would suffice for the day he had a family.

But where were all the bags of food he'd asked for to fill the basket? He was about to ask Marylin as he opened the twin lids. Oh wow, he didn't have to do a thing. The basket had already been neatly packed, no doubt thanks to Reese.

Fastened to one lid were plates and red and white checkered napkins that matched the interior fabric. On the other lid, held secure by similar leather straps were four glasses and knives, forks, and spoons for the same number of people. Even a corkscrew.

But it was what was *inside* the basket that interested him most. He poked around. A carton of fruit juice, bottle of sparkling water, fresh ciabatta bread—thankfully sliced—a tub of hummus, and...

Hudson lifted the tin to read. *Aubergine pâté with honey and cumin.* Oh yum. Good choice.

There was also a small box of crackers and a carton of crudités. The assortment of colors of the cut capsicum peppers, cucumbers, carrots, baby corn, cherry tomatoes, snap peas, and asparagus popped on the white surface. Lastly, Hudson spotted a bunch of bright green grapes. With all of this, plus the seafood platter from last night, they might have to consider another sunset picnic on the beach tomorrow night.

"So who's the lucky lady?" Marylin waggled her eyebrows and grinned. "Or don't I even need to ask?"

Hudson couldn't contain his own wide smile, excitement racing his pulse as he closed the lid and wrapped his fingers around the basket's handle. "I think you know."

He turned to leave.

"So, where are you taking the lovely Julia for your sunset picnic, if you don't mind me asking?" Marylin's laugh rushed toward him. "I promise not to tell *or* to spy on you."

Hudson glanced over his shoulder. "Angels' Cove. Where else?" There wasn't a more romantic spot in the whole of Chapel Cove. And because of the numerous steep stairs down to the beach from the cliff where the tiny chapel the town derived its name from was perched, not many ventured there. But the secluded, white-sanded cove with its pristine views across the ocean was the best place to watch a sunset with that someone special at your side. And staying long enough rewarded adventurous romantics with a star-studded show as the tall, white lighthouse with its red roof cast its long, golden beam across the dark waters, adding a mesmerizing end to a perfect date.

Pleased with himself, Hudson strode out of the clinic, whistling a love song whirling around his mind. He had no doubt this was going to be the start of something beautiful.

Wanting to get out of the office and the tense atmosphere caused by her altercation with her boss earlier that morning, Julia grabbed her bag and announced her departure to a coworker.

"See you tomorrow, Tamarin."

Nobody had to know that she didn't have any houses to show that afternoon. She couldn't bear sitting there any longer, counting down the remaining three hours until Hudson picked her up.

She slid into her car with no clue how to while away the time.

Ivy's on Spruce!

Yes. She'd pop into the bookshop. But not to search for her next novel. She'd been shocked to hear from Hudson last night that Ivy had recently suffered a heart attack. Despite not relishing the thought of facing Violet after how horrible she'd been with the woman, she needed to visit Ivy, see how she was doing.

Julia made a quick stop at the florist to pick up some flowers. She couldn't go there empty-handed, even though it had been almost three weeks since Ivy's heart attack. Knowing the bookshop owner to be more a practical than a romantic person, Julia decided against a bouquet, rather choosing a small hanging basket. This would look lovely out on Ivy's porch.

As she examined the wire container, Julia recognized some of the plants. Sweet alyssum... Trailing ivy geranium... The purple flowers made her think of Violet once more.

Inside the bookshop, Julia was surprised to see Ivy sitting in an armchair near the check-out counter.

Ivy looked up as Julia walked toward her. "Julia, my dear. How wonderful to see you again."

Julia bent down to kiss Ivy on the cheek. "I'm so sorry I didn't come sooner. I didn't know—only heard last night what had happened to you."

She set the flower basket down on the small table beside Ivy's chair. "These are for you."

Ivy smiled. "At last, flowers that will last, that I can do something with besides send to the local hospice."

Julia gently touched her aging hand. "How are you feeling?"

"Oh, you know you can't keep a good woman down." Ivy started to rise. "Do you have time to catch up? It's been a while since I last saw you. I'd love to hear all about what you've been reading."

Julia stepped back. "That's what I'm here for. While we talk, I thought I'd treat you to some tea and cake."

"Well, I'm not supposed to have cake, but maybe I'll sneak a thin slice."

Holding Ivy's arm, Julia walked beside her to the café, Ivy moving far slower than Julia was accustomed to seeing her do. She must've been through quite an ordeal.

Julia pointed to a table beside the window that looked out onto the small garden. "Should we sit over there?"

Ivy nodded her head. "Perfect."

After helping Ivy into her seat, Julia placed an order at the counter for two teas, a slice of apple custard pie, and a thin slice of carrot cake as per Ivy's request.

"I'll bring your order to the table when it's ready," the young girl on the other side of the counter said as she grabbed two teapots from the shelf behind her.

Returning to the table, Julia sat down. She stared at Ivy. "Goodness, but there have been a lot of changes around here since your heart attack. A new lady in the café…"

Ivy smiled. "That's Cas, Fern's friend. She's been a godsend."

"And Fern… Was that really her I spotted as I walked in, fussing about in the bookshop, seemingly doling out instructions to Violet? She looks sooo different."

Soft chuckles tumbled from Ivy's mouth. "Yes. She's barely recognizable these days in her more conventional, businesslike clothes. Except, of course, for her clunky ankle boots. She seems loathe to give those up. Nai shifting her to manage the bookshop was probably the best thing ever. Fern is thriving in her new role with all its responsibility."

Julia raised a brow. "Nai?"

"My niece from Austin. She came to look after me, my animals, and the business after I suffered my heart attack, but she'll be staying in Chapel Cove now that love is in the air. She and Mateo have rekindled their childhood attraction."

At the mention of love in the air, Julia's thoughts rushed to Hudson. Could whatever was going on with Ivy's niece be contagious? Feeling her cheeks warm, she cleared her throat. "Is Nai the tall woman with long, dark hair I saw here a week ago?"

Ivy nodded. "That would be my Nai."

Cas approached carrying a tray. She set their order down on the table and smiled. "Enjoy, ladies."

Julia poured the tea, first Ivy's then hers.

Ivy took a sip of the hot drink before breaking off a corner of her cake with the dessert fork. She looked up at Julia, her gray-blue eyes intense. "Speaking of love, what about you? Anything happen in the romance department since I last saw you? After all, it definitely does seem to be catchy—it's not only Nai who has fallen in love over the past few weeks, but both of her childhood friends, Kristina and Reese. And they've all landed themselves some good-looking and wonderful men."

Certainly seemed as if love *was* sweeping through Chapel Cove. How much did she dare tell Ivy?

Nothing. Because nothing had happened yet. She hadn't even been on a date with Hudson, although that was about to change.

What else would change?

Julia shook her head.

"Well, if love does come knocking at your door, Julia, do open it, please. Don't be like me who has lived a life thinking it wasn't important—wasn't supposed to be a part of my life. You're young and beautiful, and I'm certain that Mr. Right is waiting just around the corner for you."

Julia inhaled deeply. Could God be using Ivy the spinster to speak to her?

Lord, do you really have someone for me? Is Hudson that special guy You chose for me from the beginning of time, the one who will stay no matter what I tell him?

A flash of purple drew Julia's attention.

Violet stood beside the table, clutching the book with its bloody knife image on the cover that Julia had been looking at last week. Was that really only a week ago? A week in which she'd amazingly given very little thought to James Miller.

"Miss Julia, I was wondering…would you like me to package this and add it to your bill? I–I'm so sorry I interrupted your purchase of it last Thursday."

Julia gave the book one look, suddenly repulsed and with no desire to read its contents.

She offered Violet a soft smile. "Why don't you rather find me that romantic suspense book you had suggested? I think I'd like to try it."

Back home, Julia took a shower to freshen up then dressed in a pair of white shorts and a white chiffon blouse with thin pinkish-brown stripes that hung halfway over the shorts. Under the blouse, she wore a white cotton camisole.

After pulling on a pair of ankle socks, Julia slid her feet into her comfortable walking shoes. Hudson had said in his text message earlier to dress that way. Well, not exactly *that* way...he hadn't mentioned shorts at all, but it was far too hot today to think of putting on a pair of long pants. And if she could've chosen, she would have worn open sandals. But he'd been very specific about the walking shoes. Maybe he was just afraid she'd take another tumble while on his watch.

Julia brushed her hair and tied it up in a high ponytail. Once she'd applied some light makeup to her face, she stared in the mirror, praying she was suitably dressed for whatever Hudson had planned.

Glancing at the time on her cell phone, she exhaled. Still another hour to go. Might as well relax on the sofa and start reading that new book she'd bought. She was rather curious to see what Violet's recommendation was like.

The blurb on the back cover intrigued Julia almost as much as the image on the front—an attractive couple embracing amidst a background of flames. She certainly hadn't read anything like this in a very long time.

By the end of the first page, Julia was hooked, and she almost regretted hearing the knock at her front door.

Almost, but not quite.

Heart racing, she sprang from the sofa, dropping the paperback onto the soft beige cushions where she'd been sitting.

She shouldn't be feeling like this.

It's all the book's fault. And the romantic suspense being set in a small town didn't help either. Or the fact that she'd kept visualizing herself and Hudson as the hero and heroine...after all, there were similarities between them and the cover models.

Yes, that was it, that's all.

Despite her conclusion, Julia flung the door open, her grin just as wide. "Hi."

Hands behind his back, Hudson stared at her. "Wow. You look great."

So did he in his navy Bermuda shorts and gray T-shirt that seemed to hug every muscle it covered—and it covered a lot—unwilling to let go.

He smiled. "You ready?"

Swallowing hard, Julia nodded, not trusting herself to speak.

He tipped his head slightly to the side. "And the seafood platter?"

Julia palmed her forehead. "Oh, right. I was leaving it in the fridge until the last minute. I threw the fries away and put the seafood and fish into a plastic container, the salad in another. I'll go grab them. Come inside."

Heart pounding, legs trembling, she whirled around and dashed to the kitchen. "Do I need to heat the food?" she called.

Hudson's voice drifted from the front of her house. "Where we're going, it'll just get cold again by the time we eat."

Where was he taking her? Well, at least one could eat the fish, crustaceans, and mollusks cold.

When she returned, Hudson stood just inside the hall, a paper bag dangling from his fingers. "Swap?"

She handed him the two plastic tubs and took the bag from him. "What's this?"

"Just something you left in my car."

Julia peeked inside then squealed. Excited, she pulled out the pair of high-heels she'd worn the day she met Hudson. "You've had my heel repaired! I can't believe it's the same shoe. Wow, whoever fixed this has done an excellent job. I thought for sure I'd have to throw this pair in the trash. How much do I owe you?"

"Only the pleasure of your company." A slow smile curved his mouth as he held her gaze. "Shall we go?"

Julia dropped the shoes back into the bag and set them down by the front door, her heart swelling. What an incredible gesture. The more time she spent with this man, the more incredible he became.

They stepped outside and Julia locked the door.

As they strolled down the path, Hudson slid his free hand into hers.

She didn't pull away. Might as well enjoy this date to the fullest. She'd promised herself it would be the only one.

But could she keep true to herself?

Honestly, she didn't want to. She wanted to break all the rules she'd made for herself over the past few years. She wanted to find happiness and everlasting love. Like Ivy, maybe she'd wasted far too much time believing it could never be within her grasp.

And maybe it was time to step out in faith again.

Trust God.

Trust Hudson and the undeniable chemistry between them.

CHAPTER TEN

HUDSON GLANCED back over his shoulder at Julia, lagging a few steps behind. "You okay there?"

Pausing, she gripped the wooden railing and puffed out a breath. "Whew, I didn't realize I was *this* unfit."

"It is quite a climb, and of course, going down is harder on the knees." His gaze drifted to the dressing still covering her kneecap. "Are you absolutely sure that leg of yours is all right?"

He'd double-checked with her before they'd set off down the zig-zagging staircase, warning her that three hundred steps lay between them and the beach. But Julia had insisted that she was up for it.

His arm muscle quivered, and he shifted the basket to his other hand. Ha, even he was taking some strain. At least his load would be immensely lighter on the way back up. And the air would be cooler too.

"I'm fine. Besides, we're almost there. Only another fifty-eight stairs to go." She grinned and took another step down. "Or thereabouts. I've been doing my best to count."

The beach was deserted, just as he'd hoped it would be. Most who ventured down here did so on a Saturday or Sunday so as to make the most of a full day in this exquisite location. Very few attempted it for mere hours.

Julia kicked off her shoes and socks and headed for the water's edge.

Standing in the low surf, the ocean rising and falling around her ankles, she turned to Hudson as he spread out the picnic blanket a little farther back. "How did I not know about this place? Property is my game, for crying out loud."

"It's not your fault, Julia. Angels' Cove is probably one of this town's best kept secrets."

"Well, I can see why it's a secret." She ambled back to him, kicking her feet in the shallow water as it followed her up the beach. Tiny droplets spread out toward him, a sprinkling of cool surf landing on his arm. "I've been to the tiny white chapel a number of times, and I never knew that just a short way off into the dense forest, lay this stairway to heaven. It's incredible here."

She eased down onto the blanket then gazed up at Hudson. "Thank you for sharing this with me. This view is worth every step down that cliff."

Yes! He'd made the right decision in bringing her here. His backup plan if Julia felt she couldn't handle the stairs, was the beach in front of Heath's camper. But that, although a fabulous view, could not compare with this place, the seclusion of this cove unbeatable.

"You hungry?" Hudson sank onto the blanket opposite her. He lifted both lids on the basket and began unpacking the food.

"Starving." Julia's smile spread across her face, lighting up her eyes.

She helped him unpack, setting out plates, flatware, napkins, and glasses for each of them.

The meal and conversation stretched effortlessly into hours as they chatted away while nibbling on the food. A grape here, a cracker with pâté there.

As the sun sank closer to the horizon, painting the sky with a palette of sunset colors—shades of orange and gold seamlessly blending into the darker blues of the ocean on one side and the heavens on the other—Hudson began to return what was left of the food to the basket.

Once again, Julia lent a hand. In doing so, more than once their hands brushed against each other, sending jolts of joy each time through every nerve in Hudson's body.

He was falling for this woman. Hard and fast.

Correction.

He *had* fallen hard and fast for this woman.

The blanket free of everything except the two of them, Hudson straightened his legs and leaned on one elbow. He looked to the left side of the cove where the lighthouse cast its beam across the water. "This is my favorite time of day here."

"It's beautiful. I can see why they call it Angels' Cove." Julia twisted around to Hudson and gazed down at him. "Have you brought many girls here?"

He didn't want to spoil their date and prayed she wouldn't be offended by his answer.

"One or two, but that was a lifetime ago, before I left Chapel Cove for med school." He sat upright and reached for her hand, slowly threading his fingers between hers. His gaze held Julia's. "Being here with you right now…those previous few visits so very long ago pale in comparison to the beauty before me."

He leaned forward and brushed his fingers lightly over her cheek, praying that she realized he wasn't referring to the view, even though that, in itself, was spectacular.

Julia seemed to freeze with the action. Did she need reassurance of his intentions?

His voice low, he said, "I know you've been hurt in the past—"

She drew in a breath as if to refute his statement, her searching gaze questioning how he knew.

"I can see it in your eyes." Best to explain first and save Julia from opening herself up to that discussion. "But I want you to know that I will never hurt you. Ever."

Her eyes moistened, and she closed them only to have a tear escape from the corner. And then another.

Gently, Hudson wiped them away with his thumb as he whispered, "Hey… Do you realize how deeply in love with you I'm falling?"

Julia's eyes fluttered open. "Really? So soon?"

He smiled and drew her closer, lowering his lips to hers. "Really. So soon."

At first, Hudson's kiss was gentle, but as Julia responded, undeniable passion exploded between them, leaving her a little more than dizzy and her heart thudding in her chest. At times she had to remind herself to breathe. Yet, despite the ardor between them as they lay on the blanket, nobody around for miles, Julia knew she didn't have to fear that Hudson would take advantage of her as they kissed beneath the stars. Despite his obvious desire, all those feelings remained between their lips alone.

Drawing away, he gazed down at her. "I know it's crazy, but I love you, Julia Delpont, with every part of me."

How she would've loved to repeat the same sentiment to him, because in truth, she was falling for him too. But she couldn't. Not yet. Hopefully someday soon she'd find the courage, not only to tell him that she loved him, but to share her life's story with him. And that would be the day she'd get an inkling of how deep his love for her really ran.

She eased up. Hugging her knees to her chest, she stared across the ocean as the lighthouse beam swept across the water. "We should go. It's dark and the air is getting cooler." She really should've thought to bring along a sweatshirt and something to cover her legs.

"You're right. Much as I would love to stay here forever, kissing you." Hudson shoved to his feet then held out his hand and pulled Julia up. He shook the sand from the blanket before wrapping it around her shoulders. Already she felt warmer, but was it because of the blanket or his loving ways?

"You ready for the steep climb back up?" he asked.

She nodded. "How will we navigate those steps in the dark?"

"Well, we might not have a full moon tonight, but a three quarter moon is definitely better than no moon at all." He grinned. "*And*, you might not have noticed…Heath buried two small but powerful flashlights at the bottom of that basket, just in case we needed them."

Hudson circled his arms around Julia's waist and drew her closer. "This has been the most incredible night. Thank you."

Julia reached up and planted a light kiss on his cheek. "No, thank *you*. I really had a great time. Thanks for bringing me to such a special place."

"Can I see you tomorrow night? And the next, and the next?" Hudson rushed to ask.

Yes. Yes. A million times yes. It was time for her to get out of the boat called "Never Break My Heart Again" and walk on water.

Sink or swim, she would never know until she tried.

CHAPTER ELEVEN

THE PAST two and a half weeks had been bliss. Hudson had seen Julia every night. And on the weekends, day and night, except when he'd worked, then he only got to visit her and take her out in the evening. Every time he'd gazed into those dark brown eyes, Julia had managed to steal a little more of his heart. If that was even possible. Surely she already owned it all?

Hudson relaxed into his chair and closed his eyes. Ah, Monday. He loved Mondays. Didn't always, but now it heralded the start of yet another week with the woman he loved. The only problem was trying to concentrate on work.

He glanced at the time on his cell phone. Only another fifteen minutes left of the hour he always set aside at the beginning of the week to catch up on admin work and prepare himself for the week that lay ahead. He needed to focus.

Lifting his pen again, Hudson returned to the report he'd been writing. He didn't get much further when his cell phone rang.

Seeing his brother's name on the screen, he grabbed the device and answered. "Morning, big brother." Well, technically middle brother, but as Heath was older than him, Hudson referred to both his siblings as 'big brother'.

"Hudson. Hi. You're never going to believe what I have to tell you." Without waiting for Hudson to ask what, Heath rambled on excitedly. "I proposed to Reese this morning. And she said yes! We're engaged. Reese and I are finally engaged!"

"Well it's about time. But seriously, I couldn't be happier for you both. Congrats." If Heath had been standing in front of him right now, Hudson would've given him the biggest bear hug ever. Instead, he asked the burning question. "So, have you set a date?"

"Not yet, but it'll probably be toward the end of summer. Much as we hate waiting, I'd like Hunter to be at my wedding too. I'm praying hard that he'll be granted an early release. Reese and I figured we'd waited so long, another three months wouldn't hurt us."

"Don't put your plans on hold any longer than that for Hunter," Hudson cautioned. "You've waited too many years for this day. And chances are he'll no sooner be out when he'll screw things up again. I'd be surprised if Hunter ever made it back to Chapel Cove."

"Hudson! That's our big brother you're talking about." Heath reprimanded. He softened his voice and said, "Have a little faith."

Hudson twirled his pen around on the desk with his finger. *Yeah, yeah.* "I have faith, Heath. Just not in him. I stopped believing Hunter would change about eight years ago when he messed up so big it landed him in the slammer again with a decade sentence to look forward to."

"Well, when he does get out, he's going to need all the support we can give him. Until then, I'm going to trust that he'll make it to my wedding."

Hudson sucked in a breath, about to argue again, but Heath had continued talking. "However, if it's not possible, I won't postpone."

Hudson paused the pen mid-circle. "Promise?"

"I promise. Before this fall, I want to be married to the woman of my dreams." Heath chuckled. "Speaking of... Don't you think it's about time you introduced us to Julia? Why don't you come around to Uncle— I mean, my house tonight for dinner to celebrate our engagement. The weather is perfect to throw a couple of steaks on the barbecue."

"Sounds great. I'll check with Julia and get back to you." Hudson ended the call, then immediately made another. He had just enough time before his first patient.

The phone clicked as Julia answered. "Hey there."

A smile stretched wide across Hudson's face. "Good morning, beautiful lady. I hear from a very reliable source that the perfect weather of yesterday is spilling over to today. And we just got an invitation to a barbecue at a place with the most incredible view. Feel like going?"

By the time Hudson drove his SUV over the bridge crossing Sweetwater River, the sun had slowly sunk lower. In another two hours it would set.

Her heart beating faster the closer they got to Heath's house, Julia turned to Hudson. "Can I make a confession?"

Hudson eyed her, tiny creases marring his brow. "Sure..."

"I don't know if I'm more excited about meeting your brother and his fiancé or seeing his house. I've always admired Bliant's

Bluff, but as it's never come on the market, I couldn't exactly just knock on their door and say 'Hi there, would you mind if I took a look around this beautiful, historic property?'" She sighed. "I can't believe that house belongs to your brother and that I'll finally get to see inside."

Hudson reached for her hand and squeezed it. "Jules, it's totally understandable for you to be excited about the house. After all, it is what you do. I'm just glad that you're excited about meeting my family, too, and that I'm the one getting to make your dream come true."

He smiled. "And I intend to continue doing so."

Oh, Hudson. If only you knew that some dreams will always remain just that. Some things are beyond even your control.

And it wasn't fair to Hudson keeping the truth from him. She needed to tell him—sooner rather than later.

But she was so scared. She didn't want to lose him. Neither did she want to keep him under false pretenses.

One or two turns later, Hudson pulled the SUV to a stop outside Bliant's Bluff.

Up close, the white Cape Cod-style home with its wrap-around porch and matching picket fence that bordered the property was even more impressive.

As Hudson knocked on the front door, Julia realized she wasn't only excited about meeting his family, she was anxious too. Not quite ready to plunge into meeting his friends and family, Julia had ensured they kept to themselves on dates. And for the past three Sundays, Hudson had attended morning services with her at the small church she'd frequented since moving to Chapel Cove.

It had taken the allure of being able to see inside Bliant's Bluff to make Julia willing to finally meet Hudson's brother. Maybe now, she'd be more inclined to go with him to his church.

The door cracked open, and Julia's heart whacked against her ribs.

Hudson spread his arms wide toward the tall man standing on the threshold. "Hey... The man of the hour. Congratulations, brother." The two men bear-hugged for a few seconds before Heath broke away, his green eyes sparkling.

"You must be Julia. I can't tell you how excited I am to finally meet the woman who has stolen my little brother's heart." Heath wrapped Julia in a warm embrace.

Just then a strawberry-blonde stepped beside Heath, nearly matching his height.

Reese, the supermodel. The bride to be. And she was more beautiful than Julia had imagined. Any one of those factors was enough to intimidate Julia. Yet, when Reese took Julia in her arms and told her how happy she was to meet her, that she couldn't wait to get to know her better, all apprehension simply melted away with her friendliness.

Julia wished that she had come bearing more than a box of chocolates for their hosts. But Hudson hadn't told her until they were in the car that they were actually going there to celebrate Heath and Reese's engagement. She would just have to apologize and find a suitable gift for the next time they met. On the upside, at least this way she'd get to see what their taste was, enabling her to purchase something appropriate.

The house was just as welcoming as its owners with its glossy, Oregon pine floors, tasteful furnishings, and a to-die-for view over steep, rugged cliffs, an azure ocean, and the marina where boats bobbed on the water.

Once Hudson and Heath had grilled the steaks and some corn on the cob, and Reese and Julia had carried out the sides—potato salad, a tossed green salad, and one Julia couldn't wait to taste...a watermelon, tomato, and feta salad—the four sat down at the table in the garden. Heath blessed the food and, after they'd toasted

Heath and Reese's engagement with sparkling grape juice, they began to eat.

Halfway through the meal, Reese set her knife and fork down and eyed Hudson and Julia. "So, tell us your love story. And we want to hear *everything*."

Hudson turned to Julia and smiled. "Well, I have to start by saying that Julia fell for me the moment we met."

Julia's jaw dropped open and her eyes widened. Even though that was true, probably in more ways than one...this was game on. "Oh really. Don't forget to mention that we'd barely met five minutes before you were groping my leg."

Reese threw her head back, laughing. "Oh my. This does sound interesting."

"That's because I needed to play doctor," Hudson counteracted in his defense. He grinned, his eyes twinkling with mischief. He shifted his gaze from Julia back to Heath and Reese. "Not long after, she fell into my arms. Held my leg too. Not once, but twice."

"Oh..." Heath added, widening his eyes, his mouth oval.

They all burst into uncontrolled chuckles.

Setting the jokes aside, Hudson elaborated on the finer details of their first meeting, and the next, and the next, culminating with the beach date at Angels' Cove that had sealed their feelings for each other—minus all the juicy details, of course.

Heath voiced his surprise at Bill Patterson's behavior during that first business dinner she had shared with Hudson. That family history was discussed at length, but when Heath offered to meet with Bill in order to attempt to bury the hatchet and talk some sense into him of the town's need for a hospital, Hudson encouraged him not to.

"But we could've lost our beloved Ivy," Heath argued, "because this town doesn't have a hospital."

"These things have a way of working themselves out," Hudson

reassured.

Finally, their plates were empty, talk of Julia and Hudson's romance and Bill Patterson's grudge against the Brocks, exhausted.

For a while, silence descended as they watched the sun sinking beneath the horizon, the skies bursting in varying shades of blues and pinks and oranges. It was like fireworks without the noise and some scriptures came to mind, warming Julia's heart.

The heavens declare the glory of God; the skies proclaim the work of his hands.

Be still, and know that I am God.

When the colors became darker, Reese rose. "I think it's time for something sweet, don't you think? Let's move inside to the living room and enjoy a cup of coffee and chocolate cake."

Standing beside her Keurig in the kitchen, Reese filtered one cup of coffee at a time, all the while chatting to Julia. What a lovely, down-to-earth person she was, not the stuck-up super-model Julia had initially imagined.

Wanting to do her part to help, Julia meticulously sliced the cake, making sure the pieces were all the same size. She ran her tongue over her lips as she carefully placed a piece on each plate. That cake looked so delicious, she couldn't wait to sink her teeth into all its chocolatey goodness.

Reese looked up at Julia as she set the last cup on the tray. "You and Hudson seem quite serious."

Julia offered her a half smile and shrugged. "It's early days. Time will tell if this relationship will go anywhere."

Lifting the tray, Reese replied, "Oh, I believe it will. You two are perfect for each other. Heath and I couldn't be happier that Hudson has found such a wonderful woman to love. And he *is* very much in love with you, Julia. That much is pretty obvious."

Hudson and Heath were examining some photographic artworks on the living room wall when Reese and Julia entered with the coffee and cake. The men hurried to take the trays from them.

Julia and Reese each plopped down on a separate part of the L-shaped couch, and Heath and Hudson served them before taking their own coffee and cake. Sitting down beside Julia and Reese, the men wasted no time in enjoying the cake.

Julia watched Hudson closely as his eyes slowly shut. He gave a soft moan before opening them again and looking at Reese. "Mmm, this is the best chocolate cake ever."

His gaze shot to his brother. "Make sure you don't let Reese get away this time."

Reese burst out laughing. "Much as I'd like to take credit for this incredible cake—melted chocolate inside and out, plus almonds, pecans, and a secret ingredient—I can't. When Heath told me this morning that we were entertaining you tonight, I dashed down to Aileen's Pastries. Aileen only makes one cake like this a day, and I was determined to be the one to snatch it up. Got there just in time too."

"Thank you, Reese." Julia wrapped her mouth around the piece of cake on her fork, eager to see what all the fuss was about.

Oh…

Oh my…

Ooh, this *was* good.

"So, talking about sweet things, are you guys planning to start a family?" Hudson asked.

His question jolted Julia, making her suddenly feel ill.

"Oh yes," Reese answered on Heath's behalf, partly because her fiancé's mouth was still stuffed with cake. "A honeymoon baby for sure. At least, that's what we'll be praying for. Right, honey?" She combed her fingers through Heath's hair.

Heath quickly swallowed. "Definitely. We've lost so much time, and we'd like at least two, maybe three kids if possible. We have a big house to fill—"

"And my biological clock is ticking," Reese added. "Fast."

Clasping Reese's hand, Heath drew it to his mouth and pressed a soft kiss into her palm. Adoration shone in his eyes. "My love, hopefully, God will bless us with twins so we can make up some time."

Julia's gaze flicked to Hudson beside her, and her heart squeezed. She would never have a moment like that with him.

No longer able to enjoy the sweet dessert, she set her plate down on the coffee table, barely two bites taken from the slice. Leaning into Hudson's shoulder, she tilted her head to whisper in his ear. "I'm so sorry, but do you mind if we go home? I suddenly don't feel very well."

When he whispered his concern to her, Julia blamed it on overindulgence.

They bade a hurried farewell, and soon Hudson's SUV was crossing the bridge again to her side of town. Julia gazed out of the side window. Grateful for the darkness, she allowed her tears to find a resting place in the softness of her blouse.

Instead of turning right toward Julia's house, Hudson made a sharp left and brought the vehicle to a halt in the parking lot right outside the small amusement park on the beachfront. The soft glow of lights from the various rides filtered through the windshield. Suddenly there was no place to hide her distress.

Hudson twisted in his seat and reached for her hand. "You're upset. What's wrong?"

Without looking at him, Julia bowed her head, resting her forehead in her free hand. How could she tell him?

How could she not? She knew the signs all too well.

It was time.

"Talk to me, Jules. Please..."

Hearing the desperation in Hudson's voice, Julia slowly turned to him. "Y–you don't know my s–story... And—" She released a heavy sigh. "I–I'm so scared to tell you."

Wrapping his arm around her shoulder, he drew her close. "There is *nothing* you can tell me that will make me love you less. *Nothing*."

Julia looked up at him, her eyes misting over once again. "Don't be so sure."

He smiled at her. "Hey, everyone has a story. The thing we need to remember is that it's all about allowing God to use our stories to bring glory to His name."

Glory? How could her situation bring glory to anything?

She began to sob softly against Hudson's shoulder. All she had done with her story was allow herself to be unhappy, to not be vulnerable to falling in love again.

Until now.

Until Hudson.

Her trembling voice barely a whisper, she began. "Eleven years ago, I was diagnosed with cancer. I was only twenty-three."

"Oh, Jules…" Hudson tightened his embrace and pressed a long kiss to her head. "But you're cancer free now, aren't you? And even if you weren't, I would still love you—in sickness and in health."

"I'm cancer free, yes, but that freedom came at a great cost." Her next words stuck in her throat like cardboard, but she had to speak them. She'd come this far; she couldn't turn back.

Forcing herself to look at Hudson, Julia made herself tell the rest of her story.

"Late stage 1 ovarian cancer, they removed my ovaries, and to be safe, my womb as well, followed by chemo. I–I can't have children, Hudson. I can *never* have children." She swiped at her wet cheeks, the tears coming faster than she could dry them. "And I know how desperately you want a family."

Heartbroken, Julia watched that reality dawn on Hudson as his bottom lip quivered. She cupped a hand to his cheek and whispered, "I can't do that to you. I just can't."

Hudson stared at Julia. He'd been in some hopeless situations during his tenure in Afghanistan, but never before had he felt *this* helpless. He was a doctor, for crying out loud. He healed things…or at least tried to. But this? This was way out of his control, and there was absolutely nothing he could do. All he could do was either walk away from the woman he loved, or accept her reality and love her through it. He wanted to choose the latter, desperately, but could he face a childless future? What if he came to resent her one day as he played with Heath and Reese's children, knowing the same joy had been denied him?

Sadly, even though he was a surgeon, and a brilliant one at that, there was no surgery in the world that could fix the woman he loved. Another's scalpel had seen to that.

And yet, it had no doubt saved her life.

He began to weep with her. Soft tears that soon turned to sobs that racked his body. He had not seen this coming. And he had to make a choice: grow old with a Julia who couldn't bear his children or with no Julia at his side?

The answer was simple.

He pulled a handkerchief from his pocket and dried his face, knowing what he had to do.

Gently, he tipped Julia's chin so that she faced him.

She slowly raised her gaze, the anticipation of him walking away, ending things right there and then, written in her eyes.

Hudson drew in a deep breath. "Marry me."

"What? But—"

"There are other ways for us to have a family, Jules. We can adopt... When we're ready, of course."

She eased away from him. "Adopt?"

She shook her head and a bitter laugh spilled from her mouth. "That's what the last man I loved said. Stupidly, I believed him…right until the moment he ended things at the altar, realizing he'd been wrong."

Hudson gripped her arms. "I would *never* do that to you. And to prove it, before we walk down the aisle together, we can get married at City Hall. Nobody around…just you and me. And the two witnesses we'd need. We can apply for our marriage license tomorrow. Or the next day. Or next week. Whenever you're ready."

Drawing her close once again, Hudson kissed her, fresh tears wetting her cheek, salty as they reached his lips.

"I don't want to lose you, Jules. I *won't* lose you."

CHAPTER TWELVE

JULIA PULLED the quilt over her head, annoyed at the ringing in her ears.

Argh. Didn't help.

She stretched out her arm and slammed her palm onto the twin bells of her vintage alarm clock, her fingers fumbling between the ringers that reminded her of ear muffs. She shifted the tiny hammer to the off position, but the ringing persisted.

Pushing the covers off her face, she reluctantly moved herself into a sitting position and forced her eyes to open. She glanced at the nightstand and the other source of noise.

Groan, her phone was ringing, and whoever was on the other side, seemed persistent. If she left it to ring a few seconds longer, the call would go to voicemail, and she could go back to dreaming about Hudson.

She missed him so much. Oh why had she told him to take some time to think about her situation…their situation…asking him to allow her the same to consider his impromptu proposal. Although it appeared he'd already thought it through by the very next day. The bouquets of roses that had arrived at her office every morning since bore testimony of his love.

But she still hadn't made a decision on whether she could see herself being that vulnerable again. She'd never imagined she'd walk down an aisle for a second time. Or in this instance, wait at City Hall for a groom who may just decide at the last minute not to show. It hurt every time someone she'd cared for walked away from her. But what James had done hurt more than the measures that had rendered her barren, more than the treatment that had saved her life. She couldn't go through something like that again.

Just couldn't.

Her mind drifted to the colorful bouquets dotted around her small home, each one reminding her of how many days had passed since she'd last seen Hudson, how long ago she'd heard his voice.

Late Tuesday morning, red roses had arrived, the note on the card written in his handwriting. *"To have and to hold, from this day forward. Always yours, Hudson."*

Wednesday brought pale pink ones and a *"For better, for worse,"* signed once again with all his love.

Thursday's blooms were bright yellow. *"For richer, for poorer, you will always have my love."*

What a guy…he had taken the time, likely every day, to go down to the florist and hadn't just called in his order.

Yesterday's white roses and card once again had her in tears— not only because they hit home, but because she missed Hudson so much, even though it had only been four days since she'd last seen him. *"In sickness and in health, until death parts us. I will always love you."*

This card had one difference to the others—there was a postscript beneath his name. *"Please, call me."*

Julia snatched up her phone, only then realizing that it had stopped ringing. How long ago, she couldn't tell.

She didn't recognize the number from the missed call. Who had been trying to contact her this early on a Saturday morning? Not that eight o'clock was *that* early. Unless she called back, she might never know.

As if tuned to her thoughts, the ringing started again.

Julia answered. "Hello…"

"Julia! Good morning." Reese's bright voice burst through the phone. "I hope I didn't wake you."

"No… Not at all."

Liar.

"Listen, I managed to reserve a table for two at 9 a.m. at The Pancake Shoppe—quite an achievement for a sunny Saturday morning at this time of the year. I was wondering if you would join me. I thought it would be good for us to get to know each other better…seeing as we're practically family, dating two brothers."

What had Hudson told Reese and Heath?

She clenched her jaw, then relaxed. Did it really matter if he'd confided in them? Heath wasn't just Hudson's brother and the only family he had in Chapel Cove, but he was a man of the church too. So it was highly possible that he'd sought Heath's counsel.

The thought of drowning her sadness in chocolate once again at Melanie's was very tempting, the endorphins calling to her, promising to make her feel better.

"Sure. I'd love to."

Reese squealed. "Fabulous. I'll see you in forty-five minutes."

Forty-five minutes? Didn't give her much time to get ready, seeing as she still needed to take a shower. She'd been too tired last night and had barely made it shifting from her spot on the couch in front of the TV to her bed upstairs.

Julia said goodbye and ended the call.

Bounding out of bed, her feet hit the floor running.

One of the first things Hudson had implemented at the clinic since arriving in Chapel Cove six weeks ago was to open the medical center every second Saturday morning for walk-in patients—eight until noon. Many people couldn't see a doctor during the week due to work, or school, so this afforded them the opportunity to do so. And Marylin didn't complain about being able to earn an extra day's wages for the two mornings that required her to man the front desk, or to assist with minor procedures. At times, an extra pair of hands went a long way.

Today things were rather quiet, which wasn't good because his mind had time to dwell on Julia and how much he missed her.

A knock at his office door drew Hudson's attention. "Come in."

The door cracked open, and Marylin popped her head inside, a wide smile on her face. "Today is not all lost, Dr. Brock—you have a patient."

He returned her smile. "Well what are you waiting for? Bring the patient in."

Marylin disappeared, reappearing moments later, a pretty girl in her late teens with long, curly blond hair at Marylin's side. "Dr. Brock, this is Zoe Hammond." Marylin slid the new patient file onto Hudson's desk.

Rising, Hudson greeted the young woman. "Please, sit down." He gestured to one of the chairs on the other side of his desk before sitting back down himself.

Still wringing her hands—something Hudson had noticed Zoe doing from the moment she'd stepped into his office—his new patient eased onto the seat.

Patient file in his hands, Hudson relaxed into his own chair so as not to appear intimidating to the obviously nervous girl. "So, Zoe, how can I help you?"

Remaining silent, Zoe stared at her hands.

Just as Hudson was about to speak again, she looked up, her brown eyes moist. "Can you deliver a baby?"

Well, he'd certainly had no need to do so on the battlefields of Afghanistan, or in his prestigious Dallas practice, but he had done baseline training in pregnancy, labor, and delivery in medical school plus an OB term and assisting with a handful of emergencies during his residency years in Seattle as a general surgeon. And it seemed in Chapel Cove, either he or Dr. Johnson would be called to help should a baby decide to come early when the town's lay midwife was away or in the event of serious medical problems or emergencies. Certainly something that hadn't entered his mind when he'd decided to make the drastic change to Chapel Cove, from city surgeon to small town doctor, but something that Dr. Johnson had cautioned Hudson about soon after he'd arrived in Chapel Cove. Said it didn't occur often, but it had happened to him a few times. He'd told Hudson to make sure he brushed up on his obstetrics. Which he'd yet to do.

He smiled. "In an emergency, I could. Why do you ask?" Instinctively, his gaze drifted lower, but his view of her midriff was hidden by his table.

Zoe drew in a long, deep breath then blurted out, "Because I'm pregnant, and I need help."

"I see." She couldn't be more than three or four months, because in that T-shirt he would've noticed if she was showing when she'd walked in. "Wouldn't it have been better to see Trudy Westmacott, the lay midwife?" Dr. Johnson said he'd worked with Trudy for nearly two decades. He respected the English midwife's abilities.

"No way! She delivered me, and my brother and sister. I just can't see her."

Hudson could treat Zoe for a while, make sure the baby was developing well, but sometime down the line, he'd have to hand over her care and delivery to Trudy.

He glanced down to check Zoe's personal details in her file. She'd turned eighteen in November. At least her conception wasn't statutory rape. Hopefully it was consensual or he might have to encourage his new patient to get the police involved and lay charges.

"When was the first day of your last period, Zoe?"

"J–January thirty-first. I–it was only the one time." She burst into tears, burying her face in her hands. "What am I going to do? I can't have a baby."

Was she considering an abortion? Hudson couldn't stop his brow from creasing at the thought. "Zoe, I'm pro-life. You need to know that I wouldn't be able to help you if you were seeking to terminate your pregnancy."

Zoe's jaw dropped, her eyes widening. "Abortion? No…never!"

"I'm glad to hear that. What *do* you want then, Zoe?"

She lifted one shoulder in a shrug. "I–I don't know. Give the child up for adoption, I guess. There are many people out there wanting to adopt, aren't there?"

An ache formed in his chest as his heart squeezed.

"Yes, there are." And he and Julia would certainly be one of those couples. But ethically he couldn't suggest that to his patient. "I can put you in touch with the right people to talk to."

Placing her hands on Hudson's desk, Zoe leaned toward him. "I'm not a bad person, doctor. If you knew my story, you would know that."

Everyone had a story, as he'd found out earlier that week. It wasn't his place to judge her. How much better the world would be if everyone could take the time to listen and understand what other people were going through.

Or had been through.

Setting the file down, Hudson smiled at his patient. "I have absolutely no doubt that you're a wonderful person, Zoe. You're just someone in trouble, that's all, and I'm going to do everything I can to help you."

He eased forward. "Have you spoken to your parents about this?"

She shook her head. "Not yet. M—my mom passed away when I was thirteen. I live with my dad and my younger brother and sister at the trailer park. But I was top of my class for the past three years," she hurried to add as if ashamed of her circumstances, "and received a scholarship to study Business in Portland in the fall."

Good for you kid, not allowing where you come from to determine where you're going.

"It's in my power to make something of myself, Doctor Brock, provide a better future for my little brother and sister. I can't mess that up. I just can't. And a baby—" Tears carved their way down Zoe's cheeks.

Poor girl. He knew all about growing up on the wrong side of the tracks, about losing a mother at thirteen, and about wanting to take full advantage of every opportunity to better one's life. He'd done it. But talk about a rock and a hard place for poor Zoe. If her situation was different, Hudson was certain she wouldn't be thinking of giving up her baby.

But it wasn't.

"What about the father of the child?" he asked softly.

"Pfft." Zoe fell back in her chair, her earlier upset giving way to obvious anger. "The moment I told him I was pregnant, he broke things off with me. Said he was too young to be a father and that it was fun while it lasted. Well, he certainly wasn't too young when he took advantage of Valentine's Day romance, promising he'd love me forever."

Anger broiled in Hudson's gut. Some youngsters... How he'd love to knock some sense into them. He knew all too well the regrets of a Valentine's Day gone wrong. Not personally, but he'd seen Heath beat himself up his entire life over his mistake with Reese. Fortunately, they had come full circle, Heath wasting little time to pop the question. But his brother's youthful mistake had cost Heath and his soulmate over two decades apart, not to mention Reese landing in a bad marriage for far too long.

Hudson rose. "Shall we take a look?" At least the clinic had an ultrasound machine. Not one of the fancy 3D ones, but he'd be able to check how far along Zoe was and whether the baby was healthy.

As his office used to be Trudy's, the machine naturally stood in his examination room. At least until the extra offices and examination rooms were built for Trudy and an additional doctor sometime in the future. Maybe a pediatrician...the town could do with one. But until that building project was complete—hopefully in two or three months' time—Trudy used Hudson's office twice a month on a Wednesday afternoon for ultrasounds on her maternity patients. Because Hudson and Dr. Johnson each worked a Saturday morning a month, they took one Wednesday afternoon off a month. Hudson used Dr. Johnson's office when both he and Trudy were working at the clinic.

"Have you been to any doctor before this?" he asked as they walked toward the examination room.

"N–no. I've been too afraid...too ashamed. But I knew I couldn't put it off forever because soon I'll start showing." She hopped up onto the examination table as Hudson shut the door behind him. "So when I woke this morning, I decided to head on down to the clinic as I'd heard that it was open twice a month. I'm glad you were the doctor on duty and that I didn't have to see old doc Johnson. Not that he's a bad doctor—he's great. It's just…he knows me and my family too."

While Zoe stretched out, Hudson typed her details into the ultrasound machine.

Wearing hipster jeans, her pants were well out of the way, so he only had to shift her T-shirt up a little to expose her pelvis. He tucked a paper towel along the edge of her jeans to protect them from the gel then squeezed a small amount of the lubricant onto her skin before placing the transducer on her abdomen. Thankfully her bladder was full—he should be able to get a good image.

Quickly, the black and white image of the fetus appeared on the screen. Hudson checked several measurements.

"You're just over fifteen weeks pregnant, Zoe." As he'd suspected. "And the baby appears healthy and well formed."

Turning on the sound, he moved the transducer around until a whooshing sound echoed from the machine. "That's your baby's heartbeat. A hundred and fifty-two beats per minute. Strong and healthy."

The yearning to have a family of his own burned in Hudson's gut as he watched and listened to that baby's heart beating. Even if that family wasn't his own flesh and blood. If Julia had to live with the knowledge that biological children were beyond her reach, he could do so too. For her.

Zoe stared at the screen, mesmerized. She shot Hudson a brief smile. "Sounds like a freight train belting down the railway track. Or a dog panting after a long run."

Hudson chuckled. "It certainly does."

"Can you tell what it is?" she asked, her wide eyes expectant.

Hudson moved the transducer again, trying to get a better look at the baby's genitalia while digging deeper into the recesses of his mind and what he'd learned during his time at med school. "Do you want to know?"

She shook her head. "Probably better not to. I think."

"Well, I wouldn't be able to tell you anyway. At least, not today. Your placenta is lying too low, and the umbilical cord is between the baby's legs." And maybe it was still a little early to tell.

Hudson wiped the gel from Zoe's stomach then folded her shirt down again. He pressed a key on the ultrasound's keyboard and printed off an image of the fetus, Zoe's name and the baby's measurements at the top of the picture. He handed it to her. "You know, you *can* always change your mind and keep the child."

"I won't. Too much is at stake." She pressed the photo back into his palm. "And someone else out there needs this baby."

Yes. Me... Julia...

But that wasn't possible.

Hudson set the photo down on top of the keyboard. "Have you spoken to anyone yet about your situation, Zoe? Your pastor? A school counselor?"

Sitting upright, she swung her legs around, allowing them to dangle over the side of the narrow examination table. She stared at her feet. "I can't. My pastor and church will judge me."

Raising her gaze, she stared at Hudson. "As for the school counselor... I'm practically done there—might as well leave with my good-girl reputation intact."

"What about a youth pastor?" They were more equipped to deal with the problems young people faced, weren't they? He was certain his brother could give this young girl some good advice and guidance.

Zoe pursed her lips, shaking her head once more. "Our church doesn't have a youth pastor."

Well that answered those questions. She attended church; just

116

not Heath's. Maybe in a way that was a good thing because she might be more open to confide in someone she didn't know.

"My brother, Heath Brock, is the youth pastor at Chapel Cove Community Church, and a great one at that. If you like, I could give you his number. You can call him any time if you need someone to talk to. He could help you get clarity on your decisions, because you do have important decisions to make, Zoe, and I really don't want you to make them hastily, only to regret them later."

Zoe hopped off the table. "Thank you, doctor. I'd like that." The first real smile since she'd walked into his office lit her face.

"And if you need Heath to be there when you tell your father, I'm sure he'd be happy to assist. It could help ease any possible tension between you and your dad." Or repercussions if her father were to lash out in anger at his teen daughter having gotten pregnant.

Hudson opened the examination room door, allowing Zoe to exit first.

Back behind his desk, he wrote out a script and handed it to Zoe, once again seated opposite him.

She took the paper, her hand trembling. "W–what's this for?"

"A multivitamin containing folic acid," Hudson replied.

"I–is it really necessary?"

"Yes. Those pills are very important to take throughout your pregnancy. They help aid your baby's development." He wished she'd come to see him earlier in her pregnancy, when she'd first suspected...not this far along. Although, he wouldn't have been in town then, and she would've been Dr. Johnson's patient. Maybe God had kept Zoe from seeking help until now because He wanted her to be *his* patient.

"A–are they expensive?" Clearly she was concerned, and rightly so. She was still so young, and from one of the poorer families in town. Probably any money she did make with an after-school job, she was saving for her little siblings or her time away at college.

Hudson shook his head. He'd said he would help her, and he was a man of his word. "You get them for free. As well as your consultations with me. Why don't you let me have that script back? Stop by on Monday afternoon before five—I'll, um, have stock. This way you can get your medication directly from me." He'd pop by the pharmacy later and pick up some supplies for Zoe. She was probably not ready yet for small town talk about her condition, fearing that if any customer in the pharmacy saw what she was purchasing, rumors could spread, no doubt as quickly as some of the forest fires this town had seen.

"Please, you must take them," Hudson urged. "They can help prevent numerous problems."

"Like?" Zoe jutted out her chin as if challenging him to convince her that the medication was necessary.

"At the risk of sounding like a pharmaceutical pamphlet, I'll just say neural tube defects and poor growth for starters." He wouldn't scare the poor girl with images of cleft lip and palate, premature birth or miscarriage. "Not to mention the risks of various diseases you could be spared."

Zoe's mouth skewed as she worried one corner of her bottom lip. "Pregnancy sounds quite scary. I wish I'd never—" She cut her words short and shrugged. "Well, you know."

"Hey, it's going to be all right. Things have a way of working out." He scribbled on a piece of paper. Rising slowly, he leaned over and handed it to Zoe. "My brother's number. Call him. Talk to him."

Looking up at him, she nodded.

"And I'd like to schedule an appointment for a month from now. June nineteenth okay?"

Zoe nodded as she stood. "The date sounds good. I'm not going anywhere just yet."

"Great. In the meantime, where possible, try eating fortified cereals, dark green vegetables, lentils, and citrus fruits. They're good sources of folic acid." Did her father even stock food like that in their house? Judging by her slender build, pale skin, and the darkish circles beneath her eyes, he suspected not.

Zoe tucked the paper with Hudson's number into her jeans' pocket. Her hand drifted over her belly. "W–when is the baby due?"

Hudson lifted the pregnancy wheel from his desk, compliments of the drug reps, and adjusted the one disk to Zoe's last menstrual period. "The seventh of November is your estimated due date."

"I–I guess I'll have to miss my first semester at college. Not sure what that'll do to my scholarship."

"There's no need to do that, Zoe. When you leave for college, I can find a good OB or CNM in Portland for you to transfer to."

Zoe scrunched up her nose. "OB? CNM?"

"Short for obstetrician—a physician who delivers babies. And CNM is a Certified Nurse Midwife," Hudson explained.

"Ah. Wow, it's as if doctors have an entirely new language of their own made up of abbreviations."

Hudson chuckled. "I guess we do."

Hudson walked Zoe out of his office and to the front desk. "Marylin, Zoe will need another appointment on June nineteenth."

He turned to Zoe. "I'll leave your medication with Marylin on Monday, all right?"

Zoe tipped her head.

Whirling around, Hudson made his way back to his office, his mind consumed with one crazy thought—if only he and Julia could adopt this baby; wouldn't that be just the perfect solution to three people's problems?

CHAPTER THIRTEEN

REESE HADN'T been kidding about being fortunate to secure a reservation—The Pancake Shoppe was packed. Outside, the cooler weather Julia had woken to, had given way to a warm sunny day.

For nearly an hour, she and Reese made small talk over food and coffee. As she finished her meal, she was thankful that she'd changed her order from a sweet pancake and hot chocolate to the cheesy pancake with bacon and eggs and bottomless coffee that Reese had ordered.

Julia dabbed her mouth with a paper napkin. "Mmm, that was delicious." She wouldn't mind starting all over again, working her way through the layers of pancake, spring onions, cheese, guacamole, bacon, and soft, poached egg. Thankfully, she didn't have the space.

Reese pointed at the food, only three-quarters of the way

through her meal. "This has become my favorite breakfast in all of Chapel Cove."

Julia laughed. "And this has become my favorite place to drown my sorrows in copious amounts of chocolate."

Ugh. Why had she said that?

Reese raised one of her perfect eyebrows. "All must be well then between you and Hudson because I see no sign of chocolate anywhere."

If only.

Not that they'd had a fight, and the ball was clearly in her court as to what the next move would be. Pick it up and continue playing, or leave it where it fell and withdraw from the game.

Reese reached over and squeezed Julia's hand. "Heath and I were concerned when you left so suddenly on Monday night. We were worried that perhaps we'd said or done something to offend either of you. Hudson assured us that wasn't the case when Heath called him the following day. However, I wanted to make sure for myself that we're okay." She waggled a manicured finger between herself and Julia.

So that's what this breakfast was all about. Hudson hadn't run and told her secret to the world.

Julia smiled at Reese. "We're okay."

She worried her bottom lip. If only she and Hudson were okay.

"Then what is it?" Reese asked, her voice laced with concern. "Because right now it looks as if you desperately need one of those chocolate sin pancake stacks you almost ordered."

Julia closed her eyes and shrugged. Did she offer her story to this woman she'd only just met? Not even Melanie knew what she'd been through. Nobody in Chapel Cove had known until she told Hudson on Monday night.

But if she were to take a chance on Hudson, this beautiful woman—not only on the outside but the inside too—would soon be her sister-in-law. She'd always wanted a sister to share things with. Was God answering a lifelong prayer of hers right now?

Taking a deep breath, Julia told her sad tale for the second time in just a few days, and somehow telling it again was just a tiny bit more liberating, as if more of that burden she'd carried for so long was lifted from her.

Tears streamed down not only her cheeks, but Reese's too.

"Oh, Julia. I'm so sorry for what you've been through. But Hudson loves you so much, and clearly from the messages and flowers you said he sent this week, he wants to make this work. You've got nothing to lose and everything to gain by walking on water with him, Jesus at your side."

She was right.

She was so right!

Julia fumbled in her handbag for her phone and rose. "I–I need to call Hudson. Will you excuse me for a moment?" Outside on the jetty, she'd have the privacy to speak with Hudson, to tell him that she loved him and that she wanted nothing more in this world than to be his wife.

Reese fist pumped the air and whooped. "You go girl. Go get your man."

The day had been off to a slow start. Besides Zoe, Hudson had seen only one other patient. He would rather have had the day busy—at least busyness would keep his mind from dwelling on how much he missed Julia while he sat behind his desk waiting for patients.

On the upside, the quiet day did give him time to wrap his head around the situation. Of course he was disappointed, heartbroken that he would never have children of his own—nor would the woman he loved—but parenting was about more than just genetics. Deep down inside he had an excitement brewing that somewhere out there, God had a child—or children—set aside to join their family. So many babies and children were unwanted, and he and Julia could give them a loving home, become a father and mother to them.

And even if God chose not to answer his prayers about adopting, he and Julia would still be a family. A family of two, yes, but nevertheless a family.

Hudson shifted the papers on his desk around for the umpteenth time that morning, wishing he'd had more time with Julia on Monday night to talk about what had happened to her at the altar. Maybe she'd open up to him about that in the future. At least, from the little she'd told him, he knew that she was open to adoption. Or at least, had been in the past. Surely, once they were married and she knew he wasn't going to let her down or disappoint her as well by walking away, she'd be open to entertaining the idea once again?

His cell phone rang, and Julia's name appeared on the screen. He snatched up the device. "Jules…thank God."

A moment's silence ensued before he heard her suck in a breath. "I—I miss you, Hudson. I love you. And nothing would make me happier than to be your wife."

What? His heart and mind wanted to explode.

"Where are you? I'm coming there now." Hudson was already out of his chair and heading for his office door.

"At the boardwalk, but I'll be on my way home in a few minutes," Julia replied. "Meet me there?"

"I'll be waiting." He ran across the reception area toward the clinic's exit.

"Hey, doc, where's the fire?"

Hand on the door handle, Hudson glanced over his shoulder to see Marylin standing behind the reception counter. "I need to go, Marylin. If any patients happen to stroll in within the next hour, call me on my cell phone. I can be back here in a few minutes."

He didn't wait long for Julia to arrive back home. Seeing her car pull up in the driveway, he clambered out of his SUV and jogged toward her. She hadn't even shut the driver's door before he scooped her up in his arms and twirled her around.

"Marry me, Julia," he said as he set her down.

She gave him the widest smile he'd ever seen, and he knew that something had changed in her during the past few days. Maybe the roses and notes he'd sent had done their job; and maybe God had used something or someone else to get through to Julia that he wasn't going anywhere. He loved her and wanted to spend the rest of his life with her.

Julia threw her head back, laughing. "Yes! Yes!"

First thing they did once they got inside was spend time making up for all the kisses they'd missed out on during the past week. A large amount of time. Thankfully there were no calls from Marylin because it would've been well-nigh impossible for Hudson to tear himself away from Julia and return to the clinic.

Seated beside each other at the small kitchen table, they enjoyed an iced tea together while Hudson wolfed down the sandwich Julia had made him. He paused between mouthfuls and stared at his beautiful Julia. "So here's what I think we should do. On Monday we can go down to City Hall and apply for a marriage license. Are you able to find a spare hour from work in which to do that?"

Julia smiled. "I'm literally my own boss, Hudson. I come and go as I please, so any time that suits you, will be fine with me."

Reaching out, he smoothed a hand over the side of her head. "In that case, let's go at lunchtime. It only takes three days to process the license—I already checked. What if we arrange our civil wedding for Friday? That way we can take off somewhere romantic for the weekend. There's no way I'd be able to take leave now for a honeymoon, but I promise to give you one as soon as I can get a week or two off."

"You really don't want to wait, do you?" Her smile lit her eyes.

Hudson shook his head. "Not a minute longer than I have to. You're my soulmate, Jules. There's no doubt in my heart and mind. So why wait? I want you to feel safe and secure in my love as my wife."

"And I want to. It's just—" Julia lowered her gaze, clasping her fingers around her empty glass.

Hudson tipped her head to face him then slid a hand around the nape of her neck. He pressed his forehead against hers and whispered, "What is it?"

Sighing softly, she eased away from him. "As awful an experience as it was being told by my fiancé at the altar in front of a church filled with family and friends that he could no longer go through with it, I still dream of the perfect wedding—the white dress, the veil, the celebrations after the vows are said and done..."

"And we can still do that. But it will take time to plan a church wedding and reception, not to mention that it might be weeks, even months, before we can get a date that's free at a venue." His eyes searched hers. "I don't want to wait that long to make you my wife. So let's do the City Hall wedding this week, and in the meantime, we can start planning the dream wedding with all the trimmings that you desire. Just name the place where you want to walk down the aisle, sweetheart."

Rising, Julia took their glasses and Hudson's empty plate and dropped them into the sink filled with soapy water. "That's easy. At the lavender farm."

Hudson raised a brow. "The lavender farm? They do weddings there now?"

Julia nodded. "Yes. I believe the wedding venue and chapel

were only added two years ago. I saw the set up when I visited the farm one day, and it's stunning." Julia washed the dishes and set them down on the drying rack.

Hudson rose and stepped across to where Julia stood at the sink. He slid his arms around her waist. "Then we'll do the big wedding there. Should we see if they'll take a call from us? It's only early afternoon—you never know, the office might still be open."

"Yes!" Julia quickly dried her hands, and they made their way to the living room. Once she'd found the number online, she dialed the farm and switched her cell phone to speakerphone.

After a few rings, a woman answered, her voice indicating she was in her forties or fifties. "Good afternoon, Lovender Hill. This is Ruth Anderson speaking. How can I help you?"

Lovender Hill...clever play on words. He liked the place already.

Hudson gestured for Julia to speak.

"Hi there, Ruth." *I can't believe we're doing this*, she mouthed to Hudson, smiling. "This is Julia Delpont speaking. My um, fiancé and I—"

Julia lifted her left hand, her gaze lowering to her empty fingers. Shoot, he'd have to get a ring. As soon as possible.

"Well, we'd like to get married at your venue, and were wondering when your first open date is." Raising her shoulders, excitement plastered over her face, Julia shot Hudson a wide grin.

"Oh..." Ruth's tone didn't sound very encouraging, and Hudson's heart sank. How long would they need to wait to be married there? "Lovender Hill has taken off with such a bang this year. Seems suddenly everyone knows about us, and everyone is getting married. We have bridal couples coming from as far away as Portland."

Great, that's all they needed.

"I'm afraid that at this time we only offer weddings on

Saturdays," Ruth continued, "and we're already fully booked until end October. I can fit you in for November third, if you can wait that long. How does that sound?"

How did it sound? Awful. He would've liked to have their church wedding way before then. November was the rainy season, but if this was where Julia had set her heart on to be married, he'd take what they could get. Anyway, wasn't there a superstition that it was good luck for it to rain on your wedding day? Not that they needed any luck when they had faith, but Julia might still feel that any additional help in making sure her groom said "I do" was welcome.

Seeing the disappointment on her face, Hudson spoke up. "Hi there, Ruth. It's Dr. Hudson Brock speaking."

"The new doctor in town that I've heard so many good things about? The one who bought the property next to the farm?" Ruth suddenly sounded excited.

A chuckle spilled naturally from Hudson's mouth. News travelled fast in this small town. But what *were* the townsfolk saying about him? "The only new doctor in town that I know of, Ruth. And yes, I'm your new neighbor."

"So you're the—?"

"Fiancé, or bridegroom-to-be," Hudson finished Ruth's sentence. Let this little town talk. He wanted everyone to know that he was in love with Julia Delpont.

"Listen, Ruth, I know that sometimes things don't work out for couples…" Argh, he should've thought before saying that. But in all honesty, he was glad things had gone south for Julia and the man she'd planned to marry.

He covered Julia's hand with his, his thumb smoothing over her skin. "Not that I would wish any bad luck on any bridal couple, but *should* you get any cancellations, will you please consider us first for that date."

"Of course I will, Dr. Brock. But just in case we don't get a cancellation, I'll pencil you in for that first Saturday in November. And I will personally see to it that you're contacted if anything becomes available earlier." Ruth sounded genuinely eager to please them.

"Thank you, Ruth. We'll be in touch closer to the time, then. But hopefully we'll hear from you sooner." *Please, Lord, let that happen, for Julia's sake.*

After giving Ruth his number and saying goodbye, Hudson ended the call.

He twisted around to face Julia. "Just as well we decided on that civil wedding first."

"Absolutely." Turning her hand over, Julia twined her fingers between Hudson's. "Speaking of which, don't we need witnesses?"

Hudson sucked in a sharp breath.

Of course.

He nodded. "We certainly do."

"Heath and Reese?" they both said at the same time then burst out laughing.

"I'll give them a call later," Hudson said. "But first, do you think that little jewelry store on the square will still be open?"

Julia glanced toward the hall and the clock hanging there. "Nearly two o'clock. Hmm, maybe. Maybe not. Why?"

"Because we have some rings to buy. Three if I count correctly."

"Three?" Julia frowned. "Last time I checked one plus one equaled two."

Hudson lifted his hand and straightened his fingers one at a time. "Two wedding bands and an engagement ring."

"Y–you want to buy me an engagement ring?"

"Of course I do. But Chapel Cove's only jewelry store is so small, it's entirely possible we might need to take a trip to Portland tomorrow to have a better choice. However, I'm hopeful. Heath got an amazing diamond ring, *and* pendant, there merely weeks ago."

Julia shoved to her feet, holding out her hand for Hudson. "What are you waiting for? Let's go."

Nearly seven hours later, Hudson and Julia drove back to her house. After they had finally settled on the rings, they'd taken a stroll along the boardwalk and the beach, then coffee and later, dinner. Julia had frequently stretched out her left hand to gaze at the diamond ring on her finger. As they walked to her front door, she did so again, even though it was almost dark outside.

Hudson chuckled softly. She was so cute, constantly looking at her hand as if to convince herself that this was actually real.

He'd been pleasantly surprised at the stunning choices the jeweler had set before them. "I wonder how many people don't even give The Velvet Box a second glance," he said as he took her keys from her, unlocked the door and swung it open wide. "You almost miss the small shop. Really doesn't look like much from the outside. But maybe that is Chapel Cove's best kept secret, frequented by an elite few alone. What do you think?"

Julia laughed softly. "I thought that Angels' Cove was our town's best kept secret. But I do agree with you. I certainly have always given it a wide berth. Not that I've been shopping for jewelry since moving here."

She stepped inside, and Hudson followed her. "Coffee?"

"I'd love some." He grinned. "Fiancée."

"Oh, as much as I don't think I could tire of hearing that, I can't wait until we can change that to wife."

Inside the kitchen, Julia opened one of the cupboards above the counter and retrieved two cups. Placing one under the Keurig's spout, she pressed a button. The machine began to grind the beans then filter water through them. Dark, aromatic liquid filled the cup.

While Julia placed the second cup under the spout, Hudson topped off the first cup with creamer. Then the second.

Before he could wrap his fingers around the cups' handles, Julia slid her hands around his neck and kissed him. "Thank you for a perfect day. I love the rings we chose. I loved the romantic stroll down the boardwalk and along the beach, the coffee date at The Pancake Shoppe. And that dinner at the steakhouse was to die for."

Hudson screwed up his nose as his arms circled her waist. "I really wanted to take you to the seafood restaurant again, but we weren't exactly dressed for the place."

"That's okay. Been there, done that. But believe it or not, I've never been to the steakhouse. Dining alone at a restaurant in a small town isn't exactly appealing."

"What? No way. You haven't been out on a date since moving here?" Wow, her hurt went even deeper than he could've imagined. She'd practically become a recluse the past eighteen months. Now he understood why she'd kept telling him in the beginning that he didn't want to date her, didn't want to take her out for dinner. But she couldn't have been more wrong.

"I did. Three dates...with three different guys." Julia held up the same number of fingers. "You see, I had a one-date policy. That is until you came along."

"Seriously?"

Julia tipped her head to the side and laughed. "Actually, I had a NO-date policy with you."

"Hmm, I remember." Hudson tucked her hair behind her ear, kissed her softly on the cheek then whispered. "I'm so glad you changed your mind."

"Me too."

"B–but surely you went out on dinners with friends?" His hand smoothed her back in slow circles.

Julia pursed her lips and shook her head. "I cut myself off from getting close to anyone, although I did visit Ivy's bookshop fairly often. I enjoy chatting with Ivy. But you're my first real friend in Chapel Cove. And boyfriend. And fiancé. Although I do intend on changing that…the girl friends' bit, I mean. In fact, I had breakfast with Reese this morning."

"You did?" That he didn't know. He was surprised Reese or Heath hadn't called and told him.

"Yes. And she's invited me to go out with her and her best friends, Nai and Kristina, sometime soon." Julia twisted around for a moment before turning back to him, her fingers curled around the cup handles. "Should we move to the living room and relax on the sofa?"

Oh yes, he'd love to move back onto that sofa with her.

Hudson tried not to smile too widely. "Good idea. And I'm glad that you're opening yourself up to letting more people into your life."

Grinning, Julia stepped forward. "Me too."

"Here, let me carry those." Hudson tried to take the cups from Julia, almost making the coffee slosh over the rim in the process.

"It's okay, I've got it. But you *can* turn on the radio. And a lamp." She waggled her eyebrows. "A little romantic ambiance would be good, don't you agree? We still have some catching up to do. I believe we only got to Thursday, so we still have yesterday's kisses to enjoy."

Hudson's head bobbed up and down. "I like the way you think." He hurried ahead of her to shed some light on the dark living room, bathing the room in a soft glow.

Julia set the cups down on the coffee table then gently pulled the table a little closer to the couch before sitting down. "I'm sorry

I don't have any romantic CDs. I'm afraid I got rid of my collection before moving to Chapel Cove."

"We'll create our own collection, my love." Kneeling in front of the stereo, Hudson turned it on then fiddled with the tuner until he found a station playing romantic songs. He adjusted the sound so that it filtered softly through the living room before joining Julia on the couch.

Once they'd finished their coffee, she curled up in his arms, and they more than caught up on Friday's kisses. How good it felt to have her back there.

Soon her breathing changed, and he gazed down to her closed eyes. Was she falling asleep?

Pressing a kiss to her head, Hudson offered up yet another silent prayer to heaven. *Thank You, Lord. Thank You for bringing my Julia back to me. I love her so much. Please, never let her doubt that.*

Julia stirred and twisted in his arms. She opened her sleepy eyes and looked up at him. Craning forward, she kissed him on the lips.

"I love you so much, Hudson Brock. You're amazing," she whispered before stifling a yawn with her palm. "I'm sorry, it's been such a busy day, and I was up earlier than I'd planned."

He should go. It *was* getting late. But he didn't want to. And thankfully, very soon he wouldn't need to.

CHAPTER FOURTEEN

THE FIRST thing to enter Julia's mind when she woke that Friday morning was, *I'm getting married today!* As she stretched lazily in her bed like a cat, her toes and fingers arching as only a feline's could, she smiled. She was in love. And she was loved.

Lifting her head from the pillow, she glanced at her trusty alarm clock, the short hand on seven and the long hand just shy of the eleven. She reached across and turned off the alarm before it triggered. Would those slender clock hands still herald in her mornings at 16 Lavender Lane? Or would her gorgeous husband wake her every day with coffee and kisses?

She hoped so, but preferably not in that order.

At the thought of Hudson, her hand touched the empty sheets beside her. Her heart wanted to burst at the thought that the other side of her bed would not be empty for much longer. After three nights away, where she didn't know because Hudson wanted to keep their very short honeymoon weekend a surprise, he would move in here with her until they could take occupancy of the house he'd just purchased. Hopefully that move shouldn't be more than ten days or so away. She still couldn't believe that she was the one who got to spend the rest of her life surrounded by the most magnificent views—her husband and the lavender fields. She couldn't wait to be Mrs. Brock. How had she fallen for Hudson this quickly?

Easy. He was every woman's dream, and she was one lucky lady.

Well, she would be if they made it all the way through the civil ceremony. The last time she'd walked up an aisle had been a disaster. But thankfully, City Hall had no aisle—just a door leading into the judge's chamber.

Giving one last contented stretch, Julia threw the covers back and rose. She had just over three and a half hours to get ready. More than enough time.

Reese had offered to come over and help her dress and do her hair and makeup, but as much as Julia would've loved that bonding time with her future sister-in-law, not to mention the expertise of a supermodel on this special day, she wanted solitude more. Just time to allow everything to sink in, because it all still felt so surreal. Everything had happened so fast.

After a light breakfast—a bowl of cereal and a cup of calming chamomile tea—Julia ran a hot bubble bath then sank beneath the white foam to relax, her thoughts drifting to the past few days.

On Sunday, she'd joined Hudson for the morning service at Chapel Cove Community Church. All through the service, she'd kept her engagement ring hidden by turning the diamond to the inside of her hand. Although Hudson had wanted to shout it from the rooftops that they were engaged and getting married in a few days, they'd agreed not to let anyone know until the wedding was over. She and Hudson knew the reasons they were marrying this fast, and that was all that mattered. They did tell Reese and Heath later that afternoon though. They had to—they were the witnesses Julia and Hudson both wanted.

Julia had loved everything about the church, and she looked forward to becoming a part of the congregation. She'd also met Reese's friends, Nai and Kristina. They were warm and friendly, and the four of them had promised to get together soon for a pancake date.

After church, Julia and Hudson had taken a drive to Lovender Hill. After seeing the place—the chapel, the reception hall, the gardens—*and* meeting Ruth, Hudson had agreed wholeheartedly with Julia about getting married there.

"Pity the lavender won't be in bloom in November," he'd said as they'd gazed across the fields that were slowly changing color. He'd squeezed her hand and smiled. "But, I'll keep praying and trusting God for an earlier date."

Julia had returned to Lovender Hill on Tuesday and the small wedding dress shop that had opened there at the beginning of the year—Lovender & Lace. Although a relatively small selection of wedding gowns to choose from, what they had was incredible. Julia had already earmarked one for their November wedding. Of course, she'd seen a few she would've loved to get married in right now. If only their date at Lovender Hill was in the summer months.

There hadn't been too many dresses suitable for a City Hall wedding, but Julia did manage to find one—a knee-length, A-line, sweetheart-neckline dress in the softest white chiffon. She loved the flowing movement of the cap sleeves and the way the pleated bodice crisscrossed down to her waist, shaping her figure.

For fun, she'd grabbed a lacy garter with a tiny blue ribbon.

Even though the day promised warmer temperatures, Julia had

opted to wear sheer stockings. Not only did they make her legs look good, but they would almost hide the pink remains of the graze she still sported on her knee.

She bolted upright in the bath, soap suds running down her arms as her initial excitement quickly gave way to fear and regret. What was she doing getting married? And she hadn't even told her mom and dad. Worse still, they didn't know about Hudson. Next time they heard from her, she'd be married.

She hoped.

She felt so bad not telling her family or friends that she was getting married at City Hall today to the most wonderful man on the planet, but she just hadn't been able to face that task. They'd be invited to the church wedding soon enough, she reasoned—November wasn't *that* far away. And as soon as she and Hudson had tied the knot, she'd give her parents a call. Once they met Hudson, they'd forgive her and love him as much as she did.

Well, almost as much.

Still, her well-laid plans did little to quell the panic threatening her peace.

Just take a deep breath. In. And out. In. And out. Focus on Hudson and his promises never to hurt you or let you down.

Calm began to seep through her body, and for a blissful half hour she managed to draw strength from the bond between her and Hudson. Until, while styling her hair in front of her mirror, bathrobe fastened tightly around her waist, another wave of doubt threatened to ruin her day. Unable to quell the thoughts, Julia's mind cast itself back two years to another room, another dress, another wedding. And the groom who had broken her heart.

No! Hudson's wasn't like James. He wouldn't hurt her.

Are you absolutely sure?

Dropping her hairdryer onto the dresser, Julia turned and fell to her knees at the end of her bed.

"Father God, help me not to listen to the lies of the evil one. Help me to trust in Hudson, that he won't do to me what James did. I firmly believe that You have brought this wonderful man into my life, and that You have an amazing future planned for us, a future filled with hope and love. Lord, please get me through this ceremony with my sanity intact because I know the devil would love nothing more than to break me again.

"I pray this in the precious name of Your son, Jesus."

As she said 'Amen', the doorbell chimed.

She pushed to her feet and peeked through the bedroom window. Down in the road stood the florist's van that she'd become so familiar with at her office last week.

Oh, Hudson…

He'd told her that he would take care of the necessary flowers and have them sent to her house this morning, leaving her free this past week to find the right dress.

Still wearing her cozy bathrobe, she hurried downstairs to the front door and cracked it open.

The young guy who had delivered four bouquets to her last week, smiled. "Ah, Miss Delpont, good morning. I have more flowers for you."

Julia greeted him and signed for the delivery—two men's corsages, a single red rose with a red ribbon, and a beautiful bride's bouquet, too many red roses to count, although she'd guesstimate at least three dozen, if not four. The dethorned, deleafed rose stems were tightly bound with a white, satin ribbon. Here and there, tiny diamanté were somehow fastened to the center of a rose, making the incredible bouquet flash and sparkle.

Wow. She was truly marrying a gem of a man, and for the first time she realized just how glad she was that James had broken things off. Hudson was so right for her. She could see that now.

She placed the box with the corsages into the refrigerator and

Reese's rose and her bouquet into a vase with a small amount of water, taking care not to get the ribbon on her bouquet wet. Then she headed back upstairs to continue styling her hair, painting her nails and toenails, and applying her makeup.

At ten thirty, her hair swept up into an elegant side bun and the garter carefully positioned on her stockinged leg, Julia stepped into her dress. She slipped her feet into the new pair of pointed-toe, cross-strap high heels with a crystal embellishment at the back. She leaned forward to grab the small, diamond earrings from the dresser—a gift from her late grandmother given to Julia several years ago, shortly before her grandmother passed away. Finally, Julia slid the shell bracelet Reese had loaned her, insisting she needed something borrowed, onto her right wrist.

With a few sprays of her favorite perfume—and Hudson's—she was ready. And she'd managed something old, something new, something borrowed, and something blue, even if the blue bow on the garter was tiny.

She was about to leave her room to wait downstairs for Reese and Heath who had said they would pick her up, when her cell phone rang beside her bed. She'd planned to leave the device at home as she had no need for it, or its interruptions, today.

Julia hurried back to her bed and snatched up the phone. Her pulse raced at seeing Hudson's name and number on the screen.

Please don't be calling to say you've changed your mind. I couldn't bear it.

"Hey," came his baritone voice with its beautiful, rich timbre. "I wanted to catch you before you left just to tell you how much I love you and how much I can't wait to marry you."

"I love you too, Hudson." *With all my heart.*

"Did you get the flowers?"

Julia nodded, even though they weren't on video call. "I did. And they're so beautiful. Thank you. You'll make a wonderful wedding planner." She laughed. "*If* you ever decided to change professions."

"Well, at the rate people seem to be getting married, it's a lucrative business to be in, I think. I still can't believe we have to wait five months for our church wedding."

"Maybe we'll be fortunate enough to have a cancellation long before then. Let's not stop hoping and praying because I would rather get married there when the lavender is still in bloom."

Hearing a car outside, Julia moved to the window and eased back the lace curtain with her free hand. A silver sedan had pulled up in her driveway. The driver's door opened, and Heath's tall frame emerged, so easily mistakable as her beloved Hudson from this distance.

Her heart longing to be with him, she let the curtain fall back in place and stepped back to the bed. "Heath's here. I should go."

"And I am going to let you go because I can't wait to marry you. I'll be leaving shortly."

"Are you still at home, or at the clinic?" Hudson was so dedicated to his patients, she wouldn't be surprised if he'd get dressed at work and come straight from there.

"I'm at home, at the B&B. I took today and Monday off, remember?"

Julia chuckled softly. "Just checking. I'll see you soon. I love you, Hudson, and I can't wait to be your wife."

She ended the call, set her phone back on the nightstand, and headed downstairs, offering up a final prayer to calm her fears. Given her past experience at getting married, it was probably only natural for her to be waiting for something to go wrong.

Please Lord, get Hudson safely to City Hall. And please, don't let this man change his mind.

After slapping cologne onto his neck and neatly-trimmed beard, Hudson tugged the ivory colored linen jacket over the pale blue collared shirt. He'd once again opted to forego a tie—he hated the things—complementing his jacket instead with a navy silk handkerchief carefully tucked in a pyramid shape into the breast pocket. Silvery lines waved across the dark fabric of the small piece of cloth.

Light beige linen pants and brown, pointed-toe, formal shoes completed his wedding outfit. He hoped Julia remembered to bring the corsage he'd ordered to go in his lapel.

Ready to meet his bride, he shut the door to his room at the B&B and made his way downstairs, then outside to his SUV.

Inside the car, he was tempted to call Heath, just to make sure his brother had the two wedding rings. He stared at the phone then turned it off and dropped it into the console. Wouldn't need that until Tuesday. And, of course, Heath had the rings.

The road into town ran parallel to the Sweetwater River before crossing the river close to where it flowed into the sea. Hudson peered through the windshield at the blue skies. What a perfect day to get married.

He glanced to his right through the passenger window. Just across that expanse of water, lay the ground he so desperately wanted for Chapel Cove's hospital. What would it take to make Bill Patterson change his mind?

The sudden squeal of tires jolted Hudson. His head snapped back in time to see a kid on a bicycle hit the side of the car that drove a little way ahead. Both small bike and body flipped through the air and over the car before hitting the sidewalk.

Oh no! That didn't look at all good.

Hudson sped up and screeched to a stop behind the vehicle. He dashed to the back of his SUV and grabbed the first aid kit before sprinting to where the child lay sprawled across the path, the twisted bicycle in the grass nearby.

He fell to his knees beside the child and unzipped the first aid kit. The boy couldn't be more than eight or nine. Blood oozed onto the concrete from a gash on his head. Anger mingled with his fear. Why didn't this child have a helmet on? And where was his mother or father? Why was he riding out here on a main road alone?

A hysterical woman ran toward them, crying. "H–he came out of n–nowhere. I couldn't avoid hitting him." Must be the driver of the car. "Is he d–dead?"

Hudson hoped not. But if he didn't act quickly, depending on the extent of the boy's injuries, that could soon be true.

"Do you know who he is?" Hudson asked as he felt for a pulse on the unconscious child. Thank God there was one, albeit slow. He pulled one eyelid open. Then the other and his heart squeezed. This wasn't good. One pupil was dilated. He had to get this child to the clinic immediately.

"No. I'm here on business. Arrived this morning," the middle-aged woman replied.

Packing the gash with gauze and securing it with a makeshift bandage, Hudson spoke as calmly as he could. "I'm a doctor. Do you have a phone on you?"

The woman nodded, pulling her cell phone from her jacket pocket.

"Good." He held out his hand.

The woman handed over her phone and Hudson dialed the clinic. He didn't wait for Marylin to give her usual friendly "Chapel Cove Clinic, good morning," before lunging into his requests.

"Marylin, Dr. Brock here. I'm bringing in an emergency patient with a suspected acute subdural hematoma. You and Dr. Johnson need to be ready to assist in my examination room. Prepare for a burr hole trephination. I'll be there in two minutes."

He ended the call and handed the phone back to the woman. He zipped the first aid kit closed and swung it over his shoulder. Then he scooped the child into his arms and hurried to his car.

The woman followed him and opened the passenger door at his request. Hudson laid the boy on the seat beside him, quickly releasing the back of the seat and easing it down so the child lay nearly flat.

Hudson hopped behind the wheel, put on his hazard flashers, and pulled away at high speed. In his rearview mirror, he spotted the woman keeping up with him in her car.

He shot a glance at the child, his face so familiar. Was he one of the many patients he'd treated over the past few weeks? He couldn't recall seeing any boys his age though. Hopefully they'd know soon enough who the child was.

"Just hang in there, buddy."

Chapter Fifteen

STANDING ON the steps of City Hall, Reese and Heath beside her, Julia twirled the rose bouquet in her hands. Any minute now, Hudson's blue SUV would pull into a parking space. But he was cutting it close.

She gazed down at the bouquet, the blooms' deep red a stark contrast to her white dress. A familiar scripture from Isaiah sprang to mind. *Though your sins are like scarlet, they shall be as white as snow; though they are red as crimson, they shall be like wool.*

She raised her eyes heavenward. *Thank You, Jesus, for your sacrifice.*

Pondering sin and forgiveness and redemption, Julia's thoughts turned to another scripture, this time in the New Testament. *If you do not forgive others their sins, your Father will not forgive your sins.*

Reality hit home that she'd been living with unforgiveness for two long years, harboring resentment toward James. No wonder she'd struggled so to move on. She *had* to forgive him for what he'd done.

I forgive you, James. I truly do.

She dabbed a finger at the corner of her eye. As she did, an arm slid around her back and a soft hand squeezed her shoulder.

"Hey, it's going to be all right," Reese said. "He'll be here any minute. Maybe there's traffic."

Right... In Chapel Cove?

Wait a minute... Hudson was late? She'd been so lost in thought she hadn't realized how long they'd been waiting. It only felt like a few minutes.

Her heart squeezing tightly, Julia's pulse began to spike, each beat in discord to its predecessor.

"What's the time?" she asked.

Heath glanced at his wristwatch. "It's just past eleven. I'm sure he'll be here soon. Something must've delayed him. I'll give him a quick call." He reached into his jacket and pulled his cell phone from the inside top pocket. He dialed a number and waited. And waited.

Without leaving a message, Heath ended the call and returned the phone to his pocket. He looked up at Julia. "He must've already put his phone on silent for the ceremony."

Maybe, but Julia just couldn't shake the feeling that once again, she'd been made to look the fool.

Could you forgive Hudson if history repeated itself today?

Julia inhaled deeply then released a heavy sigh. *I don't know, Lord. I just don't know.*

Hudson rushed into the clinic, the boy, still unconscious, lying limply in his arms.

Dr. Johnson and Marylin ran behind Hudson to his examination room.

"What happened?" Dr. Johnson asked.

"Rode his bicycle into a car. GCS score is 8." Hudson lay the boy down on his back on the examination table, already moved into the center of the room in order to give them space to work around the child. Immediately, he strapped a neck brace on the boy, and then an oxygen mask, barking orders to Dr. Johnson to set up an 18-gauge IV cannula with Ringer's lactate.

He snapped on the pair of nitrile gloves that Marylin handed to him, as did Dr. Johnson, then removed the bandage from the child's head, leaving the blood-soaked gauze packed against the head wound.

Dr. Johnson moved to the other side of the table and gazed down at the boy. He gasped.

"What is it?" Hudson asked his colleague. Had he missed something vital?

"That's Bill Patterson's grandson, Huntington," Dr. Johnson replied.

What? "A–are you sure?"

Dr. Johnson's steely gaze bored into Hudson. "I delivered this child and have been his doctor his entire life. Of course I'm sure."

Hudson glanced up at Marylin, standing at the foot of the table, ready to assist where she could.

"Marylin, contact Mr. Patterson and inform him about his grandson." He shifted his attention back to Dr. Johnson as Marylin dashed out of the examination room. "I presume his mother is Olivia Patterson?"

Dr. Johnson nodded.

"And his father?"

"To my knowledge, his father doesn't feature in his life. Never has. Olivia is a single mother," the older doctor replied.

No father?

He looked down at Huntington, his name so similar to that of his own brother, Hunter. Was this why the boy looked so familiar? Could this be his brother's son? Hunter had been in jail for nearly eight years now. However, if the boy was younger than Hudson had initially estimated, it was possible. Perhaps he only looked older because he was tall. Hunter was tall—all the Brock boys were. Could Hunter and Olivia have met up shortly before he was arrested? If they had, then it was entirely possible that this was his nephew's life he held in his hands.

Hudson peered up at Dr. Johnson. "How old is he, doc?"

"He turned seven almost four months ago. I know because I treated him for the flu in January, and he didn't miss the opportunity to tell me that he was turning seven in two more weeks and that his grandfather was buying him the bicycle he so badly wanted."

The child stirred then groaned. He turned onto his side and retched.

Vomit splashed onto the floor, splattering Hudson's pants. For a moment his gaze took in his bloodstained shirt and jacket. So much for getting married today.

Julia.

He needed to let her know what had happened. But more importantly, he needed to save this child's life.

"Huntington… Can you hear me?"

Huntington's eyes flicked open and closed, and he mumbled. Hudson leaned in closer but the boy's confused speech was too slurred for him to make out what he was saying.

"Don't worry. Everything is going to be all right," Hudson reassured the boy.

146

Dr. Johnson held out a filled syringe to Hudson. "Lidocaine." The elderly doctor was one step ahead of Hudson, knowing exactly what needed to be done in this emergency.

"I'll take that as soon as I've prepared the area for burr hole placement."

Hudson grabbed a sterilized razor from the surgical tray. He gazed at the location of Huntington's head wound then shaved a two inch strip of the boy's scalp a little farther down, midway between the top of his skull and his right ear. A lock of straight brown hair, the color of his brother's, fell to the floor.

Marylin entered again just as Hudson took the syringe from Dr. Johnson.

"Bill and Alison Patterson, as well as the boy's mother, Olivia, are on their way," she said.

"Thank you, Marylin. You'll need to keep them outside and calm until we're done here. But first, call the fire station. We need an ambulance immediately to transfer the patient to the children's hospital in Portland once he's stabilized. And the police will need to come and take a statement from the woman whose car Huntington rode his bike into. Is she still outside?"

Marylin nodded. "She seems rather shaken. I'll make her a cup of tea the moment I can."

"Oh, and when you do get a chance, please call Julia, tell her what's happened and that I'll be at City Hall as soon as I can." Bloody suit and all.

"Will do, Dr. Brock." Marylin disappeared from the room again.

Hudson stared at the bald spot, hoping and praying that he'd chosen correctly. A little too high or too low and he could cause more damage. If only they had a CT scan, he could be absolutely certain of where to drill. But they didn't, and this boy couldn't wait to be transferred to Portland. He had to perform the procedure now.

He closed his eyes for a second. *Lord, please guide my hands. Help me save this child.*

Taking the syringe from Dr. Johnson, Hudson inserted the needle into the spot where he needed to drill, drawing on his instincts and the numerous times he'd performed this procedure, and worse, in the dusty deserts of Afghanistan. He was certain the hematoma was located in the parietal region.

The child flinched and then relaxed as Dr. Johnson, holding Huntington's head still, spoke softly to the confused boy to keep his attention away from what Hudson was doing. In five or ten minutes he'd be able to drill into Huntington's skull to relieve the pressure on the brain. When Huntington's head hit the concrete, blood vessels between the skull and the brain had ruptured causing the bleed. Once the immediate danger was alleviated, Hudson could attend to cleaning and stitching the gash on the child's head.

And then, he'd have to face Bill Patterson and Olivia. First thing he'd love to ask them was whether this boy was his brother's child. But this was neither the time nor the place to do so.

Hudson cleaned the bald patch with chlorhexidine then marked an inch-long incision line. Whipping off his gloves, he dropped them in the medical waste can then snatched up the sterile pair waiting on the tray. He ripped open the packaging then snapped the blue nitrile onto his hands. No time to scrub in first—the seconds ticking by felt like minutes.

He was about to cut into Huntington's scalp, when he heard Bill Patterson's booming voice on the other side of the drywall, demanding to see his grandson. Any moment now he expected the imposing man to burst into the examination room and see him drilling into his grandson's head.

That would go down well.

And then Marylin's firm yet compassionate voice came,

calming the man.

He smiled to himself, *good girl*, then cut into Huntington's scalp, down to the bone. Red blood followed the scalpel's path. Holding the incision open with a self-retaining retractor, Hudson began to drill the burr hole.

Dr. Johnson held Huntington's head still, all the while talking to the boy telling him about when he'd had to deliver him in an emergency at his grandfather's house because Huntington had made his entrance into the world three weeks early and the midwife was out of town.

Hmm, you learn something every day.

When the bit stopped spinning, Hudson removed the drill then opened the dura carefully using a sharp hook and scalpel. Fresh red blood squirted out, splattering Hudson, Dr. Johnson, and the examination table paper beneath Huntington.

Thank You, Lord. God and his instincts had not failed him.

Once the blood stopped oozing from the small burr hole, Hudson packed the site as well as the gash Huntington had sustained in the accident with wet gauze, ready for a neurosurgeon in Portland to take over. He wrapped the small head with a pressure bandage to keep the gauze in place. As he did, he gazed down into two large green eyes staring up at him.

Same color as Hunter's. This *had* to be his brother's child. Now that he was looking for them, the similarities were hard to ignore.

"What a good patient you are," Hudson said. Thanks to Dr. Johnson's calming ways, no doubt. "I'm almost done. Soon you'll be as good as new. But first, you're going for a ride in an ambulance. Isn't that exciting? Have you ever been in an ambulance before?"

"N–no."

"Well, don't you worry about a thing," Dr. Johnson added. "There will be great EMTs taking care of you until you get to the hospital. You might have to stay there for a few days, just to make sure everything's all right, although I can already tell you it will be because Dr. Brock is one of the finest doctors that I've seen."

Huntington flexed his arm to scratch his chest. "W–will my mom be there?"

"Of course," Hudson replied, thankful that Huntington's Glasgow Coma Scale scores had improved to 13, his eye, verbal, and motor responses good. "In fact, I know that she and your grandparents are waiting in the clinic, anxious to see you. Dr. Johnson is going to stay with you while I go out and speak to them as well as check if the ambulance is here. Then I'll bring your family in to see you. All right?"

Huntington nodded.

Once the boy was on his way to Portland, Hudson needed to find Julia and explain. He could only imagine what she must be going through, thinking that he, too, had stood her up. Hopefully Marylin had managed to contact her.

CHAPTER SIXTEEN

"WHAT'S THE time?" Julia asked Heath for the third time since he'd told her it was just past eleven.

"Almost eleven thirty." Heath looked as dejected as she felt.

"There must be a really good explanation why he hasn't shown," Reese said brightly, trying to defend Hudson.

Of course there was an explanation. The same one as always: the reality of a barren wife had finally hit home, and he realized he couldn't go through with marrying her. At least James had told her to her face. But Hudson had stayed away like a coward, despite declaring his undying love to her only minutes before not showing.

So much for Hudson being a man of his word. She should never have trusted him; never have believed a man's lies again. She was done. Soon as she got home, she was contacting Bill and pushing for that move to California.

But first, chocolate at Melanie's.

Julia eased the diamond ring from her finger and placed it on top of the box that sat on the wall beside her containing Hudson's corsage. She handed the box and ring to Heath. "Clearly he's had a change of heart. Please give these to your brother."

She whirled around to leave but before she took a step, a hand touched her shoulder.

"Julia, please don't go," Reese begged. "Not until we've found out what's happened to Hudson. He loves you, and he wouldn't deliberately stand you up unless there was a good reason."

Twisting away from Reese's grasp, Julia shook her head. "I–I can't. I can't do this. Not again." She dumped her bouquet into the nearest trash can and started to walk away, her feet hastening with every step.

"At least let us give you a ride home," Reese called after her.

Julia shot a look over her shoulder. "No. Please, just leave me alone." She began to run, high heels and all, and the memory of running up the aisle in the chapel at Echo Bay flooded her mind. Why was this happening to her again? Why was God punishing her so?

Concerned she might trip and fall, or break another heel, Julia slowed her pace once she was far enough away from Heath and Reese. The last thing she needed was a visit to the clinic.

Soon Julia found herself at a quiet corner table in The Pancake Shoppe, a large chocolate milkshake and a sinful pancake stack between her and Melanie, and for the second time in less than a week, she poured her heart out to another woman.

Melanie kept on plying her with paper napkins to dry her tears. She probably didn't have a stitch of makeup left on her face. Either that or her black mascara had smeared across her cheeks. But Melanie would surely tell her if that happened.

"What I need to do is find myself a sugar daddy, someone who is beyond wanting to have children and just needs a wife to care for him in his golden years." Julia mustered a bitter laugh through her tears. California was looking more and more attractive. She was bound to find someone like that in Hollywood, surely?

Alternatively, she could opt for a future filled with cats. Lots of cats.

Not that either thought excited her. In truth, she really couldn't see herself being a sweet old lady to a clowder of cats, or an old man's sweetheart.

"Oh honey, you're just not that kind of a woman," Melanie said as if to reinforce Julia's thoughts. She patted Julia's hand. "Don't sell yourself short for any man. And don't give up on Hudson just yet either. I agree with Heath and Reese—something big must've come up for him to let you down. I saw how he looked at you on Sunday at church—the man is crazy about you."

When Julia finally finished her milkshake and pancake stack—promising to settle her bill the next day because she'd only realized she didn't have a dime on her when it was too late—she gladly accepted Melanie's offer to drive her home. It was way too far to make it on foot in these heels, and she wasn't about to take them off and ruin another good pair of stockings because of Hudson Brock.

But that was the least of her problems. How was she going to get inside her house? She'd stupidly left her purse with her house keys in Heath's car, and she couldn't even call for a locksmith because her cell phone was up in her bedroom. Of course, she could ask Melanie if she could call from her phone, but she didn't want to load the young mother with any more of her problems. Melanie was bound to want to get more involved than just loaning Julia her phone, and her friend had a business to get back to. She'd just figure it out once she got home. Hopefully she'd left a window open somewhere that she could clamber through.

Hudson was fifty minutes late by the time he got to City Hall. Nobody was outside. But then, did he think that everyone would still be there waiting for him to show? Heath and Reese? The judge? Julia?

Well, maybe he'd thought his brother might stay until he showed, but even he had gone.

He pulled into an open parking space and left the car idling. Snatching his phone from the console, he turned it on. His only thought once Huntington was in the ambulance and on his way to Portland was getting to City Hall. He hadn't allowed a thing to stand in the way of that goal. Not even a phone call.

He hoped he'd be successful in contacting Julia. Marylin hadn't been.

Three missed calls from Heath and a voicemail message. He should've thought to ask Marylin to try Heath, but he'd never given it a second thought that Marylin wouldn't be able to get in touch with his fiancée.

His heart sank. Nothing from Julia. What must she be thinking of him right now?

He listened to the message.

"Hudson, I don't know what's going on, but I'm sure you have a pretty good reason for not showing. Julia, however..." His brother's sigh whistled softly through the phone. *"Well, let's just say we couldn't convince her to stay. She left on foot at eleven thirty. We waited fifteen minutes more, hoping you'd show. Call me as soon as you get this. We're praying for you both."*

He'd just missed Reese and Heath.

He tried Julia's number first. It rang several times before going to voicemail. He cringed inside as her sweet voice came over the line.

"This is Julia. You know what to do." A moment's silence ensued and then the last part of her greeting he knew so well because he didn't always get her when he called. Sometimes she was in the shower; other times she'd left her phone on silent after a business meeting. *"Leave a message."*

"Jules, it's me. Please tell me where you are. We need to talk."

He cut the call then phoned Heath.

His brother answered on the first ring. "Hudson. What happened?"

"There was an accident, a little boy. It was an emergency. I had to attend to him or he could've died." He'd tell Heath later of his suspicions about Huntington. He didn't have time now to have that family discussion.

"We must've just missed you. After leaving City Hall, we drove past the clinic but didn't see your car so we figured you were elsewhere. I'm sorry for the child, but glad it wasn't a case of your getting cold feet or having a change of mind."

Cold feet? Changing his mind about marrying Julia?

Never.

"Where are you now?" Heath asked.

"Outside City Hall." If only he'd worked a little faster, spent a little less time with the Pattersons, he might've caught up with Julia. But he *had* worked as fast as he could. And he *had* spent as little time with the Pattersons as he could, especially after Bill Patterson threatened to ruin Hudson should anything happen to his grandson.

"Heath, do you know where Julia went?"

"No. She just took off down the road. Reese tried to stop her, but we realized she probably needed some time alone."

"I have to find her...to tell her what happened." How hard could it be to spot a bride walking the streets of Chapel Cove?

Unless she caught a cab and went straight home.

An awful thought hit him. What if she decided to up and leave Chapel Cove after this? Go back home to Gig Harbor? Or elsewhere? He couldn't lose her. Surely once she saw him, heard his story, she'd understand. But what if she didn't? What if she realized that patient emergencies would always come above her needs? Not that he wanted it to be that way, but if a crisis arose—as it had today—he couldn't just walk away, no matter what. She might not be prepared to live that way.

"I'll try her house first." If she wasn't there, it might be safer to just sit outside and wait for her. She'd have to come home sooner or later. He didn't want to run the risk of missing Julia because he was scouring the streets looking for her.

"Hudson, before you go, hang on a few minutes more, will you? Reese and I are on our way back to City Hall. We have Julia's purse. She left it on the back seat of our car. And I have her engagement ring—she asked me to return it to you."

The electric blue SUV parked in Julia's driveway was hard to miss. Her heart thwacked against her ribs and her stomach lurched at seeing Hudson sitting on the step at her front door. Part of her wanted to ask Melanie to keep on driving—beg if she refused. The other part wanted closure, and not knowing why Hudson hadn't shown up at City Hall earlier, she'd always wonder.

Melanie pulled up behind the SUV. She smiled at Julia. "Looks like you have company."

Julia swallowed hard and offered her friend a wobbly smile in return. "Best get this over with as quickly as possible, I guess." Like ripping off a Band-Aid.

"Or get things going again." Melanie smiled and patted Julia's hand. "Again, I'm sure that he has a perfectly good explanation. He's shown up, hasn't he? Granted almost two hours late and at a different venue, but he's here. Just give him a chance to tell you what happened."

"I–I'll try my best." Julia stepped out of the car. "Thanks for giving me a ride home."

As she trudged toward Hudson, blood whooshing in her ears, drowning out the sound of Melanie's car driving away, he rose. Julia gasped. What had happened to him? He looked a mess. Red stained his blue shirt, creamy jacket, and beige pants. Had he been in an accident?

She glanced back at his SUV, not a mark on its metal surface.

Certainly not in that car, anyway.

Arms open, he neared. "Jules, I'm so sorry. There was an accident on the way to City Hall. I–I couldn't come. I had to save a young boy's life. Bill Patterson's grandson. And my nephew, I think. I got to City Hall as soon as I could, but I was too late. You'd left twenty minutes before."

Julia shook her head, confused. Her boss's grandson was Hudson's nephew? "I don't understand…"

"I'll explain later. But first—" He was about to draw her into his arms, and oh how she wanted him to. Then he seemed to think better of it and his hands fell limply to his sides. "I'd hug you but… Even though all this blood has dried, it's probably best not to risk marking that beautiful white dress."

"And I'd ask you in so that we can talk, but I'm afraid I left my keys in Heath's car."

Hudson dug in his pocket then dangled two keys hanging from a keyring in the air. "Heath brought them to me at City Hall."

Her house keys. Yes!

She took them from him.

"He also gave me this…" Hudson's hand disappeared into his

jacket once more. When he opened his fist, her diamond ring lay in his palm. "Please, allow me to put this back on your finger. We'll set another date—and this time I'll have someone drive me there blindfolded."

She stared at the ring in his hand, remembering the promise she'd made to marry him. Without warning, the question God had asked of her merely hours ago rushed into her mind.

Could you forgive Hudson if history repeated itself today?

Yes, she could. Especially now that she knew he hadn't deliberately not shown up at City Hall.

However, if he hadn't shown up for other reasons, her answer might be very different.

But God hadn't asked if she could forgive Hudson if he'd decided he couldn't go through with marrying her, or couldn't go through life not having his own children. He'd merely asked if she could forgive him if history repeated itself. And it had. Once again, she'd walked away from the altar alone.

"I forgive you," she whispered, stretching out her left hand.

As Hudson slid the ring back on her finger, his hands trembling and his eyes tearing up, Julia leaned forward and kissed him, taking care not to get too close. She didn't know how soon she'd have to put this dress on again.

Grabbing his hand, she led him to the front door and unlocked it. "Let's get those clothes of yours into some cold water. Maybe we can still salvage them. And you'll need to take a shower—you have blood splattered everywhere, even on your cheek."

"A shower would go down well seeing as I've been puked and bled on, but what am I supposed to wear while I wait for my clothes to dry?" He chuckled. "I know the weather's warm today, but I still don't fancy the idea of waiting for hours with nothing more than a towel around my waist."

He flashed a playful grin. "Of course, once we are married, that would be a different story entirely."

Julia's cheeks warmed at the thought of being husband and wife. She'd fan herself but didn't want to draw attention to her blush. "Don't worry, I have a baggy T-shirt and sweatpants that I'm sure you'll fit into. Once you're clean and these clothes are soaking, we can talk." She'd like to hear exactly what had happened and why he thought Bill Patterson's grandson was his nephew.

Hudson had dropped his stained clothes just outside the bathroom door. While he showered, Julia changed into a pair of jeans and a cotton blouse before heading to the laundry to rinse the blood and vomit from his clothes. Then she placed them in a bucket of cold water to soak. And she'd better get used to it. As the wife of a doctor, she might be doing this sort of thing often.

Hearing Hudson trotting down the stairs, she carried the two cups of coffee she'd just brewed to the living room, as well as his cell phone. Fortunately she'd found that in his jacket pocket before soaking the item of clothing. As she sank down on the couch, Hudson entered.

"That feels better." He plopped onto the cushion beside her, raking his fingers through his damp hair, the brown darker with it wet.

Leaning forward, Julia retrieved the cups and handed one to Hudson. "Are you hungry?"

He took a sip before answering her. "Hmm, a little peckish, I guess. It's been a rather eventful morning, drilling into a child's skull when I should've been saying 'I do'."

Julia's eyes widened. This sounded way more serious than she'd envisaged. "I'll make you something to eat, and then I want to hear all about what happened."

"I've a better idea, I'll order in a pizza, and while we wait for the delivery, I can fill you in." Hudson reached for his phone on the coffee table. "Glad you found that and it didn't end up in a bucket of water."

So was she.

He was about to call the pizza place, when his phone started ringing.

He answered. "Hello."

As he listened to the caller on the other side of the line, his brows began to rise. "Ruth, wait a minute, let me put you on speakerphone so that Julia can hear too." He touched his phone's screen and a woman's chuckles floated from the device.

Ruth? Lovender Hill Ruth?

Well, how many other Ruths did she know?

None, that's how many.

"Hello, Ruth," Julia greeted. Why was she calling them now?

"Julia. I didn't think that I'd be speaking to you and Dr. Brock so soon, but I have good news for you. We've had a cancellation. You and Dr. Brock can get married here sooner."

What? That was amazing news. "H–how much sooner?" Julia asked.

"Is two weeks too soon? I know you didn't wish anything bad on anyone, but the bride was in New Zealand this week for a conference, and she foolishly went snow-skiing with some colleagues."

Skiing? Snow?

"You know they're in the middle of winter down in the southern hemisphere," Ruth explained as if reading Julia's mind. "Anyway, to cut a long story short, according to the bride's mother, her daughter fell while slaloming down a slope and managed to break both her legs. She had to be operated on and it's going to be a few weeks before she'll be able to fly back home, let alone walk down the aisle. So, June ninth is open if you want it."

Did they ever!

"Yes!" Julia squealed before looking at Hudson. "We do want it, don't we?"

Hudson slid his hand behind her neck and pulled her into a quick kiss. "Of course we do. As long as you can pull off planning a wedding in so short a time."

Ruth laughed. "Oh, don't you two lovebirds worry about a thing. We're experts at that."

"I—I'll need a new dress." She'd given today's dress a second thought as she'd washed the blood from Hudson's clothes and realized she couldn't use it again—for a court or church wedding. Hudson had seen it. And besides, she wanted the train and the veil for her church wedding, the whole nine yards.

She knew exactly which dress she was going to choose.

Well, one of three, anyway.

More laughter spilled through the phone. "Come and see me at four and we can go through some menus and ideas. And afterward, you can try on a few more dresses, Julia, although I do remember you had your heart set on two or three."

"We'll definitely do that," Hudson said. "Thank you, Ruth."

"It's my pleasure, Dr. Brock. What are neighbors for?"

CHAPTER SEVENTEEN

DRESSED IN an Aegean blue two-piece suit, this time with a tie—burgundy, Julia had insisted—Hudson took in the view from the balcony of his bedroom at 16 Lavender Lane. He would never tire of the sight of these purple fields.

Excitement filled him. In little less than an hour, he would watch his bride walk down the aisle. And he couldn't wait.

The past week had been long, unpacking and settling into his new home. Not that he'd brought that much stuff from Dallas— some rugs, a bed, couch, chairs, coffee table, bookrack, a few kitchen items, and loads of medical books.

Julia wasn't bringing much to the house either. According to her, only her clothes, a few books—including her Bible—and an infamous alarm clock. The bulk of her book collection she was donating to Ivy's on Spruce, where she'd bought them originally—

said her tastes had changed.

They were excited about furnishing the rest of the house together in the coming weeks.

Hudson breathed in deeply of the fresh morning air, the earlier mist having lifted. The warmer temperatures of the past week had given way to light rain shortly after he'd risen. Fortunately, that had subsided. Now, scattered tufts of broken clouds painted the skies. He prayed the rain would stay away for the rest of the day.

Thankfully, his new medium-weight wool suit guaranteed to keep him cool in summer and warm in winter, but what about Julia? Most summer brides he'd seen had bare backs, arms, and shoulders. Was Julia going to declare "I do" through chattering teeth?

Hudson glanced at the time on his wristwatch. Ten minutes past ten. Any moment now, Heath would arrive. Even though the lavender farm was right next door, his brother had insisted on picking him up. And a good thing too. If he'd walked, as he'd originally intended to, those shiny brown shoes would be a muddy brown by the time he got to the tiny chapel where they were getting married.

In the distance, Heath's red pickup approached, and Hudson headed downstairs. Julia's parents and her maid of honor, Reese, were driving to the chapel in Heath's sleek Tesla.

Hudson had met Julia's mom and dad for the first time two nights ago. They seemed like lovely people, although her father *had* pulled Hudson aside during their dinner at The Fisherman's Hook, promising to break both Hudson's arms and legs if he hurt his daughter as that good-for-nothing James Miller had done.

Hudson had assured his future father-in-law that his only intention was to make Julia happy for the rest of her life.

Before Heath could knock, Hudson swung the door open. On the other side of the threshold, Heath stood grinning, hand still raised to the door.

"Morning, brother," he greeted. "Eager to get married, I see."

"You have no idea." But soon Heath would know the angst of counting down the minutes until one saw one's bride.

Heath cocked his head. "Hmm, I think I do… Forty-five minutes early for the church?"

Hudson stepped outside and shut the door behind him. "I want to make absolutely sure I'm inside that church long before Julia, so that *if* anything goes wrong—" He raised his eyes heavenward. "Please, Lord, don't let it. But, should something happen, I'll have plenty of time to give her fair warning. *And* someone at my side to make sure I do."

Heath slapped Hudson on the back as they headed toward the truck. "Relax. It's not even a quarter of a mile from here to the chapel. What could possibly go wrong?"

Pausing, Hudson raised a brow. "I am taking no chances." He opened the passenger door and clambered inside. "Besides, I want some time to pray too."

"And I'll be right there beside you, praying. After all, what's a best man for?" Heath started the truck and reversed out of Hudson's drive.

Ruth had offered Hudson and Julia a choice of two chapels and reception venues—one for extravagant affairs; the other for small, intimate gatherings. But no matter the size of the wedding, Ruth had assured them that Lovender Hill only did one wedding on Saturdays, thereby ensuring undivided attention and perfection at every event.

So, even though the wedding originally planned for today had been a large, extravagant affair, he and Julia had been able to plan something smaller. They didn't know many people in Chapel Cove. Including themselves, Julia's parents, and Pastor Don Keller and his wife, they'd only managed a total guest list of twenty-five people, and that suited them just fine. Others attending were, of course, Heath and Reese, then Nai and Kristina with their respective fiancés, Dr. Johnson and Ivy, Marylin and her husband, Violet and a plus one, and Melanie, her mother-in-law, and little Alia who was the flower girl.

Hudson and Julia had debated over whether to invite the Pattersons—Bill, Alicia, Olivia, and Huntington. Bill Patterson had threatened Hudson that fateful day at the clinic, despite Hudson having saved his grandson's life. The man's words still rang in Hudson's ears, and he winced at the memory.

If anything happens to my grandson, Brock, I promise I'll make you pay. You'll never practice medicine again. Not in this town, or this state, or this country.

But despite his threats two weeks ago, which Hudson hoped and prayed had been spoken in the heat of the moment out of sheer panic and fear, Bill Patterson was Julia's boss. And Hudson was almost certain that Huntington was his nephew. And so, the invitation was extended, and to his utter surprise, accepted.

The small white clapboard church with its steeple and weathervane welcomed Hudson and Heath inside. Warm air wafted over them as they strolled up the aisle, five rows of wooden benches flanking each side. Good, the heat must be on. At least Julia shouldn't get cold.

Low bouquets placed on the floor in the aisle beside each bench offered a splash of color to the white clapboard interior—pale blue-green silver dollar foliage with daubs of burgundy, cream, and pink peonies and roses. And, of course, touches of lavender.

The same bouquets, only much larger, flanked each side of the small, wooden pulpit.

Hudson and Heath's heels clunked against the pine floor as they made their way to the front row and sat down on the right-hand side bench. Hudson immediately bowed his head and closed his eyes. They had half an hour at the most to pray before guests started arriving.

Father, I want to thank You for bringing such an incredible woman into my life. I promise to be the husband that You expect me to be. I promise to love her sacrificially just as Jesus loved His bride and gave Himself up for her.

Hadn't he already proven how much he was prepared to sacrifice to be with her? Some days it was still difficult to wrap his head around the fact that he'd never father a child. And still, his own sacrifice paled in significance when compared to what God's Son gave up. He suffered so for those He loved.

Thank You, God for the indescribable gift of Your Son.

Hudson continued praying for Julia, that God would remove any insecurities she might be feeling today, and that he would bless their marriage, perhaps even with adopted children one day.

Heath's arm wrapped around Hudson's shoulder, the gesture reassuring. He was so glad to have his brother standing at his side on this once-in-a-lifetime day.

"Can I pray for you?" Heath whispered.

Without opening his eyes, Hudson nodded.

"Almighty God, our Heavenly Father, the One who instituted marriage, performing the very first joining together of a man and a woman on the sixth day of creation, thank You for orchestrating Hudson and Julia's love story. Thank You that You looked down from heaven and said, as you did with Adam, 'It is not good for him to be alone'. We give you praise and glory that You have given my little brother *his* bone of his bones, *his* flesh of his flesh, the one he'll unite with today—his wife.

"You know the challenges and heartaches Julia and Hudson must face in their forward journey together, but You also know the joys and the triumphs that You have planned for them. Give them strength to endure the former and time to enjoy the latter."

Hearing voices at the back of the church, Hudson opened his eyes and peered over his shoulder. Guests were arriving.

"I pray that You will give them their hearts' desires as they seek to serve You and follow Your ways. In Jesus' name I pray. Amen." Heath must've realized the same about the guests because he'd rushed to the end of his prayer.

Agreeing with Heath, Hudson whispered his own 'Amen' then opened his eyes. He turned to his brother. "I guess we'll need to stand in the front of the church now and wait?"

"Probably a good idea," Heath said. "You don't want your bride to enter and find you sitting here relaxing in your seat, not ready for her arrival like the five foolish virgins spoken of in the book of Matthew who weren't ready for the arrival of their bridegroom. Julia needs to walk into this church at any time and find you expectant, waiting, anxious for her arrival. Much like Jesus and His church."

Hudson shot to his feet. "And I am."

As they stood upfront in their matching suits, smiling at each guest as they entered the small sanctuary, Hudson leaned over to Heath. "Thanks for being my best man."

"It's my honor. And I'm going to be calling in the same favor when Reese and I get married in August."

"You've set a date?" Even though surprised, Hudson kept his voice low.

"We have. August eleventh, hopefully. I received a letter from Hunter yesterday and there's still no news about an earlier release. With Nai getting married in two weeks' time, and Kristina in July, Reese and I decided to wait until August. But no longer. If Hunter is out of prison and makes it to our wedding, wonderful. It is what it is if he can't."

Even if Hunter *had* been out of jail now and was able to attend this wedding, Hudson would never have asked him to be his best man. He just wasn't that close to his oldest brother. But Heath…

He wished that Heath could've officiated at the ceremony too, and at one point he'd considered asking him, but with Heath offering to do a private photoshoot after the church ceremony with just the bride and groom *plus* being his best man and chauffeur—albeit for only a very short distance—he couldn't have his brother involved in yet another chore. Having Heath beside him as his best man meant more to Hudson than having him in the front of the church, leading the proceedings.

Although Hudson had hired a photographer to take photos of the bride's preparations, the ceremony, the reception, and the bridal party, he'd informed the man that photos of himself and Julia were not required. Photos from a photographer like Heath were a priceless wedding gift, and an offer he'd never turn down no matter how many wedding photographers he'd have to offend to leave that shoot out of the bridal package.

Hudson glanced up to see a handful of people dotted around the chapel. He did a quick headcount. Sixteen.

Just then, Pastor Don entered and strode up the aisle, beaming.

Seventeen. Still just Julia's mom, who would most likely arrive shortly before Julia entered with her father. And, of course, Reese. Melanie was missing too, but she probably had to remain with Alia to ensure the little girl cooperated.

The pastor paused in front of Hudson. "You ready?"

Hudson shot him a grin. "Absolutely. Let's get this show on the road, Pastor."

Pastor Don stepped behind the pulpit and announced, "Ladies and gents, I know it's common practice to stand when the bride enters, but *this* bride and groom have requested that you all remain seated, please." He chuckled. "I guess they don't want anyone to spoil their view of each other."

Hudson nodded, knowing exactly why he and Julia had decided

to make that request of their guests.

Julia's mother, looking elegant and every bit the mother of the bride in a teal knee-length dress, hurried to the front row and took her place on the left.

Music filled the chapel—a classical piano and cello rendition of "A Thousand Years." Julia had chosen the music that she wanted to walk down the aisle to, and what a fitting choice—for them both.

Melanie tip-toed in, turning frequently as she beckoned Alia to follow her, all the while demonstrating how her daughter was to scatter petals from the basket that swayed on her thin arm as she walked. Finally, Melanie sat down on the left in the second row from the front.

Oohs and aahs surrounded the little girl dressed in a pale pink flower girl dress. Somehow her mother, he assumed, had managed to create soft, gingery curls from Alia's usual long, straight wisps. The curls bounced as her head twisted this way and that as she smiled at everyone. Behind her, she'd managed to leave a dotted trail of cream, red, and pink flowers.

Face beaming, she made it to her mother—not a step farther.

Melanie shifted on the bench so the child could take a seat beside her. They'd all known it would be a long shot getting Alia to stand at the front of the church with the rest of the bridal party.

Reese entered next in a long, sleeveless dress, the same dark sea-green as the men's suits. Her own engagement ring sparkled as she clutched a bouquet of flowers similar to those lining the aisle.

Hudson's pulse thrummed with the knowledge that his bride, his future wife, would be next.

Reese took her place on the opposite side of Hudson and Heath, offering them both the widest of smiles.

And then *she* appeared, bouquet in her hand, her father at her side. Hudson was surprised at first that Julia had opted not to wear white. Almost white, but not quite. But he wasn't in the least bit disappointed at the lace bodice, tinted with just a whisper of lavender, that hugged her figure beneath a matching veil. Her long, dark tresses trailed over one shoulder. Soft chiffon in the same misty hue flowed to the floor, floating around her with every step and reminding Hudson of the morning's vapor that had clung to row upon row of purple bushes.

Hands clasped in front of him, Hudson pinched himself to make sure that he hadn't died and gone to heaven, despite his thumping heart.

CHAPTER EIGHTEEN

SEEING HER handsome Hudson standing in the front of the sanctuary, waiting, Julia tightened her grip on her father's arm lest her wobbly legs caved in.

He's here. He's really here.

Now to hope and pray he didn't change his mind before they both said 'I do'.

Her dad turned to her, leaned closer and whispered, "Don't be scared, sweetheart. He's the right man for you. I don't believe *this* one is going anywhere. I'm afraid you're probably stuck with him for life. Not that I think you mind in the least."

She didn't. Not one bit.

Seeking strength, Julia focused her gaze on Hudson, her doubt and fear ebbing away with every step she took, moving closer and closer.

Hudson walked toward her, looking so dashing in his deep blue suit. Or was that fabric really green, disguising itself as blue? Much like his hazel eyes that couldn't quite decide whether they were green or brown. Eyes that now shone down at her with so much love.

Lost in their depths, she almost didn't realize that her father had lifted her veil. He kissed her goodbye then placed her hand in Hudson's before taking a seat beside her mother.

"You look beautiful," Hudson whispered as they continued on in time to the music. "And I love that color."

Julia smiled at him as they stopped close to the pulpit. "Me too. I figured white hadn't worked out so well for me in the past, hence the not quite white."

The pastor's voice brought a quick end to their whispers.

"Dear friends and family, we are gathered together here in the sight of God to join together Hudson and Julia in the holy estate of marriage, instituted by God and signifying the mystical union between our Lord Jesus Christ and his Church."

Moving out from behind the pulpit, Pastor Don came to stand in front of Hudson and Julia before continuing. "This union is not entered into lightly, but with reverence and discretion, and in the fear of God. If any man can show just cause, why this man and this woman may not lawfully be joined together, let him now speak, or hereafter forever hold his peace."

Julia filled her lungs and waited. Would anyone object? Would Hudson? This was the perfect opportunity for him to walk away. But then, James had gone right through this part of the ceremony, stopping short of his "I do" before speaking his mind.

Hudson squeezed her hand, offering another whisper. "I love you."

Silence had descended on the chapel and Julia was certain that every person gathered there could hear her exhale.

A smile brushed across Pastor Don's lips. "Hudson, Julia, if either of you know any impediment why you may not be lawfully joined together in matrimony, now's the time to speak."

She didn't. Neither were there any secrets between them.

"No reason at all I can't marry my beautiful Julia," Hudson said boldly.

Julia shook her head and answered in a soft voice. "No."

"Then, Hudson, do you take Julia to be your wife, to live together after God's ordinance in the holy estate of marriage? Will you love her, comfort her, honor and keep her in sickness and in health; and, forsaking all others, keep yourself only for her, until death parts you?"

"I will." There was such confidence in Hudson's response to the minister's question.

"And Julia, do you take Hudson to be your husband, to live together after God's ordinance in the holy estate of marriage? Will you love him, comfort him, honor and keep him in sickness and in health; and, forsaking all others, keep yourself only for him, until death parts you?"

Oh yes, she would. For a thousand years and more, if that were possible.

She nodded. "I will."

Pastor Don cast his gaze over Hudson and Julia to those gathered behind them, settling on someone to his right. "Who gives this woman to be married to this man?"

"Her mother and I do," her father's voice boomed.

Tipping his head, Pastor Don acknowledged her father's pledge. "The bride and groom have prepared their own vows, so Hudson, Julia...please continue."

Julia twisted around to hand her bouquet to Reese. As she turned back to Hudson, he clasped her hands between his, his burning gaze holding hers. "Julia Rose Delpont, from the moment we met, you captured my heart. I fell for you…" He smiled. "Or was it the other way around?"

Chuckles rose, and Julia added hers. By now, most people knew the story of the day they'd met.

His face quickly growing serious again, Hudson continued. "Today, tomorrow, always, I will choose you, no matter what. I promise that I will love you with every fiber of my being. I will be your fortress to run to when the world is cruel, because life won't always be a bed of roses. I will be your shield and I will protect you through everything that comes our way. I will be everything you desire me to be and all that God expects me to be as your husband, your lover, your friend.

"I love you, Julia. Today. Tomorrow. Always." Eyes glistening, he reached up and lightly trailed a finger across her cheek. "For a thousand years and more."

It was her turn to speak, but she was so overcome with emotion at Hudson's words. Dare she trust her voice?

Julia clasped his hands between hers this time and sucked in a deep breath. She swallowed hard. "Hudson, literally from the moment we met, you were saving me, patching up my wounds. And you didn't stop. You have reached the very depths of my hurts and healed them all."

A loud sob came from the front row and Julia glanced over her shoulder to see her mother crying. Happy tears, she hoped.

Mom glanced up and offered Julia an apologetic smile.

Happy tears, she was sure.

Relieved, Julia turned back to Hudson, holding his moist gaze. "We were meant to be together, made for each other, and I don't regret an ounce of the heartache and pain I've been through, because that led me to Chapel Cove, and to you.

"Thank you for choosing me, despite my imperfections, to be the one to spend the rest of your life with. I will do everything in my power to make you the happiest man alive. I give you my word."

Julia raised his hands to her lips and kissed them. "I love you, Dr. Hudson Brock, so very, very much."

Heath stepped forward and handed them the rings which they exchanged, along with the words, "With this ring, I thee wed. In the name of the Father, and of the Son, and of the Holy Spirit. Amen."

Pastor Don covered their hands with his. "Father God, bless these rings. May these who wear them live in your peace and favor until their life's end, through Jesus Christ our Lord. Amen."

Joining Hudson and Julia's right hands, he declared, "Those whom God has joined together let no man put asunder. Forasmuch as Hudson and Julia have consented together in holy wedlock, and have witnessed the same before God and this company, and have given and pledged themselves to each other, and have declared the same by giving and receiving a ring, and by joining hands; I now pronounce that they are husband and wife. In the name of the Father, and of the Son, and of the Holy Spirit. Amen."

He grinned at Hudson. "You may now kiss your bride."

And her husband did. It was the sweetest kiss Julia had ever tasted.

One long, stylishly-decorated table seating twenty-five filled the small reception hall. On both sides of the room, windows with tied back drapes allowed every guest to gaze out onto pristine gardens and fields of lavender. Hudson took his place at the center of the table beside his bride. Next to Julia sat her parents, and on Hudson's side, Reese and Heath. Dr. Johnson and Ivy were seated opposite Hudson and Julia, with Huntington strategically placed beside Dr. Johnson so that the old doctor could keep an eye on the boy.

Hudson, too, kept a keen eye on Huntington throughout the luncheon. When he wasn't pouring attention on his wife, of course.

Wearing a flat cap, likely to hide the patch where Hudson had shaved his head—probably the neurosurgeon too—the boy seemed to have his eyes trained on Hudson as well, their gazes often meeting, accompanied by mutual smiles.

He needed to find an opportunity to talk to Olivia. He had to find out if this was his flesh and blood—he and Heath had little enough of that—and this reception might be his best shot to find out the truth.

When Olivia stood and ambled off in the direction of the restrooms, Hudson rose too. He leaned down to Julia. "Excuse me for a moment, my love."

She smiled up at him. "Of course. Is everything all right?"

He nodded then whispered. "Olivia... I need to talk to her about her son."

Understanding filled his wife's gaze. "Go. I'll be praying you find your answer. After all, he'll be my nephew, too, now."

Hudson fastened his jacket's single button then followed Olivia. Seeing her enter the ladies' room, he waited outside for her.

Unease filled Olivia's face as she exited the restroom and spotted Hudson standing there, alone. Her gaze flicked left and right, as if seeking an escape route.

Instead of running from him though, she edged closer. "Hudson. Thank you for inviting my family to your wedding. What a beautiful ceremony. You're a lucky man—Julia is a special girl."

She certainly was. But he wasn't here to discuss his wife or how fortunate he was to be the one to win her heart.

He cut right to the chase, before they were interrupted. "Olivia, I need to know... Huntington, is he my nephew? Is he Hunter's son?"

Olivia looked away and sighed. "Walk with me."

They strolled out into the gardens, Hudson patiently waiting for her to say something.

She stopped at the border of the lavender fields and plucked a long, slender bloom. "Thank you for saving my son's life. I'm sorry I haven't come to see you yet, or called, but we only returned from Portland with Huntington on Wednesday. And then, when I heard from Julia that you two were getting married, and so soon, I knew you'd be extremely busy and that any talking would need to wait. Besides, my father—"

She twirled the lavender between her fingers and gazed out across the purple lands.

What about her father? Would she continue her sentence?

"Eight years ago, Daddy sent me down to California for several weeks to check out some land deals he thought would be lucrative investments," Olivia said, her voice a monotone as if giving evidence at a trial. "As fate would have it, shortly after my arrival in LA, my path crossed with Hunter's. The first time in fourteen years. We started seeing each other and quickly picked up where we'd left off. I–I wanted him to come home to Chapel Cove with me, didn't care for the friends he hung out with, but Hunter…" She humphed. "He wanted to do one last job. Wanted my father to accept him once and for all if he was to return home. He foolishly believed that without wealth, that would never happen—didn't want to listen that I didn't care if my father accepted him or not; I did. Sadly, his beliefs cost him another ten years of his life."

She swiped at her tears.

Hudson reached into his jacket pocket for his handkerchief, still unused, even though he'd been brought to the brink of tears during Julia's vows. He handed it to Olivia and she dabbed her cheeks.

"The day he was arrested for carjacking with aggravated

circumstances, I'd planned to tell him I was pregnant. But he never showed at his apartment. I waited there until the next morning. He never came home.

"When I found out he'd been arrested and faced a lengthy sentence as this was his second offense, I concluded my business in LA and returned home to Chapel Cove as fast as I could. I'd already lost him once to prison; I couldn't stick around to watch it happen all over again. I had a child to think of."

She turned to Hudson and gripped his arm. "Please, don't tell Hunter. He must never know. Huntington must never know."

Hudson shook his head. "I–I can't do that, Olivia. I can't keep silent. Hunter has a right to know that he has a son. It could be the one thing that makes him turn his life around this time."

He exhaled a heavy sigh. "And Huntington… The boy needs to know he has a father, and uncles who can't wait to get to know him. You can't deny us that. You just can't. Neither can you take that away from your son."

Hudson had accepted the fact that Julia couldn't do a thing to give him his own children. But Olivia? This woman had the power to offer him and Heath family—something they hadn't had for a very long time—most of their lives, in fact. He wouldn't allow her to take that away from them. And now that he knew for certain that Huntington *was* his nephew, he needed to tell Heath too.

Eyes brimming with moisture once again, Olivia pursed her lips, pivoted, and hurried back toward the building where the reception was being held.

Hudson followed after her. "I don't want to hurt you or Huntington, Olivia, but trust me, this is for the best. As soon as I can, I'll write to my brother, let him know about his boy. I hope in the meantime that you'll talk to Huntington, let him know who Heath and I are. And who his father is.

"In a few months, two years at the most, Hunter will be out of prison. And when that happens, without a doubt he'll want to see his son, want to get to know him. Prepare Huntington for that day."

"What's going on here?" Bill Patterson loomed in front of Olivia, causing her, and Hudson, to jolt to a stop.

Olivia blinked back her tears. "Nothing, Daddy. Hudson and I were just enjoying the fresh air and the gardens, catching up on old school stories. Oh my, he had me in tears at some of the memories." She placed a manicured hand on Hudson's arm. "I pulled him aside initially because I wanted to thank him for saving my son's life. It was time to offer him that courtesy."

Bill Patterson nodded, his head tipping toward the convivial chatter from wedding guests that permeated the adjoining room. "Huntington is asking where you are. You should go to him. And I need to speak with Hudson, alone."

Hudson? Not Dr. Brock, or just Brock as he'd last called him. Hmm.

"Care to take another walk, doctor?"

"Sure." Why not? Huntington had recovered well it seemed, so the man couldn't be seeking to destroy him. Not today, anyway.

They strolled across the manicured lawn.

Bill Patterson cleared his throat. "I owe you an apology, Hudson. That day in the clinic after my grandson's accident...well, I said some terrible things. I was way out of line. I know it's no excuse, but I was scared, like I've never been scared before.

"But after the neurosurgeon in Portland told me that your quick thinking and surgical skills had saved Huntington's life, I should've come to see you, or at least called. Truth be told, I was ashamed. *And* I needed to sort out some things before speaking to you again."

Well, well, well. This *was* a glorious day. Not only had he married the woman of his dreams, but the great Bill Patterson was actually offering him, a Brock, an apology. Miracles did still happen.

"You were right," Bill Patterson said. "This town does need a hospital—and the sooner the better. Huntington's accident was a wake-up call for me. So, I've spent the past ten days contacting influential people, investors for Chapel Cove's new hospital. Already, I've managed to raise a substantial amount of money. Granted, there will always be a need for more, so it'll be a good idea to get the townsfolk involved in doing some fundraising. And it's important for them to feel they've played a part too."

He stopped walking and turned to Hudson. "And the ground you wanted...it's yours. I'm donating it for the good of the town. Of course, I would expect a seat on the hospital's board in return for my generosity, but I want you on that board too, Hudson. You're a man of great vision. Chapel Cove needs more people like you." He held out his hand. "Shake hands with me as a sign of agreement and burying the hatchet?"

Heck, yes.

Hudson shoved his hand forward and clasped Bill Patterson's, shaking it vigorously. "You won't be sorry, sir."

CHAPTER NINETEEN

JULIA LOOKED up at Hudson as he pulled out his chair then sat down beside her. "What was *that* all about?" she whispered. Her gaze drifted momentarily from Hudson as she followed Bill Patterson striding to his seat a little farther down. "I saw you talking outside."

"You won't believe it, but Bill Patterson has just donated the land near the river for the hospital. *And* he has a bunch of investors lined up." He grinned. "Chapel Cove is getting its hospital, and I have married the woman I love. All in one day! God is good."

Leaning toward him, Julia kissed his cheek. "He is indeed." She eased back, her eyes searching his. "And Huntington? What happened with Olivia? Did it go well?"

Hudson's shoulder lifted in a slight shrug. "Depends how one defines well. Yes, the boy is my...our nephew. But she doesn't want me to say a word to my brother, and I can't do that. No matter what he's done in life, Hunter has a right to know. To deny him his son..." Hudson cupped her cheek. "Oh honey, I'm sorry. I didn't mean that the way it came out."

Julia clasped his hand. "It's okay. I know you weren't talking about us."

Hudson blew out a relieved sigh. "Good. I have *you*, and that's what matters to me. Nothing else."

"Olivia... How did she take it? I presume you told her you can't keep silent?"

"I did. And she wasn't happy about that." Hudson's mouth pursed, his lips narrowing to a thin line. "I feel sorry for her, but the boy needs to know that he has uncles who can't wait to get to know him. And hopefully his father will feel the same way too."

Hudson held her gaze before he nestled his head in her neck and whispered, "Honey, what do you say we skip out of this party and start our honeymoon? Well, I guess we should call it a pre-honeymoon as it's only three nights, but we'll do that longer one as soon as we're able."

"Oh, I would so love to, but we haven't cut the cake yet. We can't leave until we've tasted Aileen's creation." Especially after all the begging it took to get the pretty, redheaded baker to agree to make it. Somehow Julia suspected there was more to Aileen's reluctance than just time. Julia prayed if there was, that the woman would find someone to confide in, just as she had found confidantes in Melanie and Reese.

"*And* we need to throw the garter and bouquet. But I promise, as soon as we've done that, we can go." She grinned. "I'm just as anxious to be alone with my husband."

"What are we waiting for then?"

Hudson rose and tapped a spoon against his champagne flute. "Julia and I will be cutting the cake now, so please make your way to the front of the room. Right after the cake, we'll toss the garter and bouquet, so don't be in a hurry to return to your seats. I know there are several of you here who aren't married...yet." He scanned the table from left to right. "Melanie... Dr. Johnson... Violet..."

Violet's purple head nodded up and down vigorously in agreement with the groom as she shouted to Julia to throw the bouquet her way. Her request brought several chuckles to the room. Julia had other plans though.

Her gaze drifted toward Melanie as she stood.

With her hand safely in Hudson's, they made their way to where the white, two-tier buttercream cake was proudly displayed on a table. In three places, white fondant roses and daisies cascaded like waterfalls from one ribbon-edged layer to the next.

Ruth, who'd been waiting in the wings the entire wedding, making sure that everything was executed to perfection, stepped up and removed the top layer. "That'll keep in the freezer for three months. Save it for the baby announcement," she whispered to Julia and winked. Then she handed Julia and Hudson a large silver knife with which to cut the cake.

Julia gazed down at the knife and swallowed hard. Ruth's words had cut as sharply as this blade would slice through that cake. But the woman, who wouldn't hurt a fly, had no idea how ill-placed her words were. She'd meant no harm. And now that she and Hudson were married, Julia would have to either keep dodging the questions about when a baby would come, or be bold enough to say when people asked that she was unable to bear children. The latter seemed the better option. But not right now.

Julia guided Hudson's hand and the knife to the top of the cake.

When they'd cut a slice, they shared it, feeding each other.

"Ooh, so good," Hudson mumbled through a mouthful.

Julia nodded in agreement, her mouth too stuffed to talk.

That part of the formalities done, Ruth handed Julia her bouquet, a mischievous smile on her lips. "I've seen *that* look on many a bride and groom's face. I can see you're both anxious to be alone now—and who could blame you, my dear, with such a handsome husband. Go, throw that bouquet and garter, and then get out of here. I'll take care of your guests for the rest of the afternoon. Right until the last one leaves."

Julia smiled at Ruth then pulled her into a hug. "Thank you, Ruth. You have made our day perfect. And if it weren't for you..."

"Pfft, if it weren't for that silly bride doing something she shouldn't have done so close to her wedding... But frankly, I'm glad she did and that you and Dr. Handsome," Ruth chuckled, "I mean Hudson got to have your dream wedding so much sooner. I only wish I could've ordered sunshine for you instead of these clouds. Not to mention the occasional drizzle."

Julia rubbed a hand up and down Ruth's arm. "That's okay. You can control many things, but the weather is not one of them. Besides, Heath said it made for fantastic photos. And I trust his eye behind the lens."

"Good. Now, go on girl and let me cut the rest of this cake for your guests while you throw those flowers." Ruth shooed Julia and her bouquet to where Hudson stood waiting for her.

In addition to the many hats Heath had worn today—chauffeur, best man, photographer—he also wore the Master of Ceremonies' cap. Standing beside Hudson, he bellowed out, "Single *and* engaged ladies, we need you up here, please, so that Julia can toss her bouquet."

The eight unmarried women gathered in front of Julia, some more eager than others to be there. Julia noted where Melanie had placed herself on the outskirts of the group then turned her back on the ladies. She only hoped her friend made the effort to reach for the flying bouquet. Fortunately, Violet stood far away from

Melanie, otherwise her friend would stand no chance of getting her hands on that bunch of flowers.

The moment the bouquet left her hands, Julia spun around to follow its path and the actions of the female guests. To Julia's surprise, Melanie lunged toward the flowers. The bouquet bounced off her body and fell to the floor at her feet. Everyone stood rooted, waiting for her to pick it up.

Violet rushed forward as little Alia's voice rang out, "Pick up the flowers, Mommy."

Melanie stooped and gathered up the bouquet, just as Violet ran past her.

"Nooo, so close," Violet wailed.

Laughter followed by cheers and whistles sounded around the room while a deep bass chanted, "Here comes the bride…"

As the women moved out of the way so that the men—all five of them, and that included Heath—could take their place for the throwing of the garter, Paula, Melanie's mother-in-law, brushed past Julia.

"You can thank me later." Smiling, she winked. "I pushed her. My son's widow deserves to find happiness again."

Wow. "Good for you, Paula. Thank you." When it came to matters of romance, some women only needed a gentle prodding, while others, like Melanie, needed a hefty shove. Irrespective, every woman needed a Paula in her life.

Hudson knelt down in front of Julia, smiling up at her. His hands slid beneath her wedding dress and up her leg in search of the garter.

Thrilling at his touch, heat flooded Julia, as did visions of her wedding night with him. *Hurry up and throw that piece of fabric, my love, so we can leave.*

"Got it!" Hudson straightened, holding the garter high in the air, triumphant.

"Make haste, husband," Julia whispered in his ear.

Hudson spun around, his back to the five men, and tossed the garter over his shoulder.

As if pre-arranged, the three younger men lunged for Dr. Johnson and lifted him in the air.

Dr. Johnson, not prepared to waste this opportunity it seemed, stretched for the garter. As his fingers wrapped around it, he let out a loud yell, "Yes!"

Hudson whooped and bolted for his colleague, wrapping him in a bear hug.

Not long after the festivities of the bouquet and garter, and of course another slice of that delicious cake, Julia and Hudson said farewell to their guests then made their way toward Heath's silver Tesla. Hudson's brother had insisted they use the car for their weekend away.

"Travel in style," he'd said, making a quick comeback by adding, "not that your SUV isn't stylish, Hudson—just not stylish enough for a bride." Heath had promised to get Hudson's SUV later—it was only a short walk away—and drive Julia's parents back to the B&B where Hudson had stayed for several weeks.

The air cool outside, Hudson had quickly draped his jacket over Julia's shoulders to keep her warm.

As they reached the car, a voice called after them. Both Julia and Hudson whirled around to see Olivia hurrying toward them, her hand firmly clasped in her son's.

"I—" Olivia began as she reached them. "Huntington has something he wants to say to you, Hudson."

Crouching in front of the boy, Hudson spoke first. "I'm glad you're looking so well, Huntington. The last time I saw you… Well, let's just say you had me, and everyone else, concerned."

Eyes downcast, Huntington reached for his flat cap and pulled it from his head, the stitches on his head only just visible beneath the short growth of brown. Likely Olivia had given him a buzz cut so that the hair could grow out evenly. He held the cap tightly against his chest and raised his gaze to meet Hudson's.

"Thank you for saving my life, Dr. Brock." Without warning, Huntington wrapped his arms around Hudson's neck. "I just wanted to ride my bike on the road, so while my gran was busy in the kitchen, I snuck out. But I forgot my helmet, and I couldn't go back. The road soon became steep and I— I couldn't stop."

The child closed his eyes, as if the memory was painful to relive. "I–I'm sorry I caused so much trouble."

Olivia laid her hand on her son's shoulder. "It's all right, Hunt. We're just all grateful that Jesus placed Dr. Brock at the right place at the right time. But there's something else you should know— you don't have to call this man Dr. Brock anymore. From now on, you can call him Uncle Hudson."

Huntington looked up at his mother, confusion in his eyes.

"This is your uncle...your father's brother," Olivia explained, tears filling her eyes.

Huntington's eyes widened. "Does that mean that Mr. Heath, the best man, is my father?"

His mother chuckled, as did Hudson and Julia.

"No, son," Olivia said. "Heath is also your uncle. And if it's all right with Uncle Hudson, I'll introduce you to your other uncle in a little while."

Hudson nodded. "It's fine. I haven't had a chance to speak to Heath yet, but you can tell him."

"I will," Olivia whispered. She knelt down on the grass beside Huntington. "Your two uncles have an older brother...Hunter. He's your daddy. Hopefully soon, you'll get to meet him too. He's been away for a long time, but I think he'll be coming back to Chapel Cove when he's done what he has to do."

"S–so I'm a Brock?" Huntington asked, his head oscillating

between his mother and Hudson.

Hudson drew him into a tight embrace. "You're a Brock. You're family."

Holding Hudson's shoulder, Julia crouched down beside him. She smiled at Huntington. "And now I'm no longer Miss Delpont to you," as Huntington had called her when visiting the office. "I'm your Aunt Julia."

An hour's drive north of Chapel Cove, Hudson pulled the Tesla to a stop outside an A-frame beach cabin. It was only God's providence that, at such short notice, had secured him this secluded hideaway nestled between the wide-open ocean—large rocks dotting its shore—and forests of ancient redwoods towering into the sky. Here he and his bride could get lost from the world—for three days and nights at least.

Their own piece of paradise, just like the very first couple that God joined together at creation.

Julia peered through the windshield. "Oh Hudson, this is simply breathtaking. And look, the place even has a wrap-around porch." She chuckled and leaned into his shoulder, her touch already lighting the fire he'd tried hard to quell since the day they'd met. No more quelling though. From this day forward his passion for her could burn brightly. Day and night...especially at night.

"Is that why you chose this place?" she asked.

Hudson smiled down at her, sweeping away the dark strands that had fallen across her cheek. "No, my love. I chose this place because there is no one around for miles, and because for the next three days, I want to watch the sun setting with you from that very porch."

"Wait right there." He climbed out of the car and rushed around to her door. He opened it, and as she swung her feet to the ground and straightened, Hudson scooped her into his arms. "Allow me to carry you over the threshold, Mrs. Brock."

Inside the cozy cabin, a fire crackled. The owner had promised to light a fire shortly before their arrival after Hudson had called to say he'd just left Chapel Cove with his wife.

Hudson shut the front door with his foot then carried Julia up the stairs to the loft bedroom with its ocean views. At least, that's what the website had said. The only view he cared about right now was the one in his arms.

Gently he set her down on her feet. His hand brushed over her back before venturing to those tiny buttons running down her spine that he'd eyed all afternoon, eager to loose them.

He kissed her shoulder. Her skin was so soft.

Agreeing with his brother's earlier prayer, he whispered, his voice husky, "Now this is bone of my bones and flesh of my flesh."

The words to the end of the passage drifted through his mind like a soft breeze.

And they were both naked, and they felt no shame.

CHAPTER TWENTY

TAKING HIS lunch break in his office, Hudson gazed at the framed wedding photo of him and Julia as he took a bite of the sandwich his wife had made—ham, lettuce, and tomato on multigrain bread, a spread of Miracle Whip adding creaminess and flavor. Tasty as the meal was, he'd much rather be feasting on Julia's kisses.

He took a few swigs of the freshly brewed coffee Marylin had brought to his desk, as she did every lunch break.

Hard to believe he and Julia had been married for ten days already. Ten incredible days. He loved waking up beside her each morning. And at the end of every day, he couldn't wait to get back home so he could hold her in his arms through the night.

His lunch finished, Hudson washed his hands in the small basin in the corner of his office. As he stepped back to his desk, he glanced at his wristwatch. Ten minutes to one. Only four more hours and he could hurry back home to his wife.

His wife... How he loved the sound of those two small words.

Seated again, he allowed his mind to drift for a moment to earlier that morning. As usual, he hadn't wanted to get out of bed. Neither had Julia. But they both had jobs to do, and so reluctantly they'd left the comfort of the cool linen sheets and each other's warm embrace.

As had become the norm, breakfast was enjoyed together from the nook in the kitchen, taking in the splendorous view over the fields as they ate. With each passing day the lavender bushes turned a little more purple.

A knock at the door drew Hudson's attention from his favorite person and place. "Come in."

The door cracked open, and Marylin poked her head inside. "Zoe Hammond, your one o'clock, is here. Shall I bring her in?"

Ah, the pregnant teen. Between everything that had happened in the last month since he'd last seen her—weddings, accidents, moving, honeymoon, wife—he'd still managed to give Zoe's situation some thought, as well as speak to Heath. His brother had promised to get in touch with Zoe. But caught up in marital bliss, Hudson had forgotten to follow up if this had been done.

"Of course, send her in."

He reached for Zoe's file and slid it closer.

Every morning before he arrived at the clinic, Marylin had his patient files stacked neatly on his desk, ready for the day. What an amazing asset she was to him and to this clinic. He only hoped a new hospital wouldn't change things.

Who was he kidding? Of course things would change around work...in a huge way. For one, they'd all move out of this building and into the new facility, the current clinic planned for a birthing center. Change was inevitable; the hospital a necessity. And even though he loved to dream big, it was better to start small—a proper ER, OR, observation unit, and day surgery unit. Further down the line, as Chapel Cove grew, they could expand to a twenty-five-bed hospital. And beyond, if needed.

But until they moved, he'd cherish the close working relationship that he, Marylin, and Dr. Johnson enjoyed.

He rose as Zoe entered. Her baby bump had grown a fair bit since she'd first walked into his office, but then, she'd be halfway through her pregnancy now. Her condition that noticeable, she must've spoken to her father by now. How had it gone? Had Heath been there to help her through it? Poor girl—what a situation for her to be in. Alone.

"Hello, Zoe, it's good to see you again. How are you?"

"Hello, Dr. Brock. As you can see, I'm just swell." Zoe smiled as she rubbed a hand over her tummy before easing into a chair opposite him. She set her backpack down on the floor beside the chair.

"Good." Hudson reached into the cabinet next to him and pulled out a refill of Zoe's tablets. He set the bottle down in front of her. "Before I forget…your medication."

"Thank you, doctor." Zoe picked up the bottle and dropped it in her backpack. As she straightened, she smiled, her gaze fixed on his wedding photo. "That's a new addition to your desk. What a beautiful bride."

The girl was observant.

"My wife. We were married ten days ago."

Zoe's eyes widened. "Oh wow! Congratulations. But what are you doing back at work so soon, Dr. Brock? Shouldn't you be away on your honeymoon or something?"

"I wish. Although we did go up north for three days. Unfortunately, I haven't been at the clinic long enough to think about taking a week or two off. But Julia and I will take a proper honeymoon as soon as we can."

"Well just don't put it off for too long, doc, or you might have to pack a crying baby into the car as well." She eyed him. "I presume you and your wife *are* planning to have children? Or are you those career types who don't want kids?"

Hudson couldn't prevent a somber expression from wiping the smile from his face.

It would be far easier to move on from this topic if his patient wasn't a pregnant one.

Avoiding Zoe's question, he rose. "Should we see how much your baby has grown in the past month?"

"Yes, we should." Zoe remained seated. "But only after you tell me why you suddenly look so sad."

Teenagers… Always so inquisitive. But if he didn't satisfy Zoe's curiosity, she'd only keep on asking, and he and Julia *had* agreed they wouldn't hide their situation from the world. If people asked, they were to be told the truth.

"M–my wife can't have children." He choked on the words. They were far more difficult to say out loud for the first time than he'd imagined.

His eyes burned, and he blinked.

"Oh. I'm so sorry. I–I shouldn't have pried." Zoe looked as repentant as she sounded.

Swallowing hard, Hudson nodded and rounded his desk. "It's all right, Zoe. Julia and I need to get used to being open about this, and you've just been good practice for me to do exactly that.

"But enough of me and my wife—come, let's see how your baby is doing. Is your bladder full?"

"Yes, doctor." Zoe rolled her eyes, the teenager in this young mother-to-be still evident. "As you'd requested it to be the last time I was here."

She followed him into the examination room and hopped onto

the table.

"You must've started to feel life by now," Hudson said as Zoe lay down.

She smiled. What a different girl she seemed from the frightened one who'd walked into his office a month ago. More at peace, more what he assumed was herself.

"I think so, if that's what those flutters in my stomach are." She chuckled. "Or is that just gas?"

"Oh, I think you can safely say that it's your baby. And soon, he or she will be kicking up such a storm. Then there'll be no mistaking those prods for anything else." Hudson tucked a paper towel into the waist of Zoe's jeans, once again to protect them, before squeezing gel onto her swelling abdomen.

"Your father? Does he know yet?" He must surely know, unless Zoe still hid her pregnancy under bulky clothes. Easy to do in winter—not that easy in the summer, and the weather was only going to keep getting warmer. Today the mercury would almost reach the nineties.

"He does. I told him last week." Zoe gripped his arm, preventing him from placing the transducer on her belly. "Thank you so much for giving me your brother's number. Pastor Heath has been amazing and has given me so much good advice—the best being that Jesus still loves me, no matter what. And that He loves this baby, too, and has a plan and purpose for its life."

She released her hold on Hudson.

"That He does, Zoe. Never forget that." Hudson moved the transducer over her skin. "How did your father take the news? Was Heath there?"

"He was, and I'm so grateful. I think things could've gotten out of hand if he hadn't come with me. My dad was angry at first, but Pastor Heath calmed him down so quickly. Then he counseled us and prayed with us.

"Dad agrees with me that I need to give my baby up for adoption, that a child will ruin my chances of achieving what I'm able to."

"I see." Pausing, Hudson lifted the transducer. "And what does Pastor Brock say?"

"He said it didn't matter whether I kept the baby or gave it away, that God had a plan for this baby's life. If I decided to keep it, God would supply my needs. And if I gave it up for adoption, God would still care for this child. He reminded me that while my boyfriend and I might've made this baby, God had chosen it and loved it before He even made the world. What an incredible thought."

He smiled at her. "Wise words from a wise man."

Zoe's face grew serious as her wide brown eyes stared at him. "Dr. Brock. I know what I want to do with my baby."

Good. Hopefully she'd had a change of heart and wanted to keep the infant. First prize was always for a child to stay with its mother.

"I–I want you and your wife to adopt my baby. That is, if you're open to adopting."

What? His senses reeling, Hudson held his breath. Were they ever... Or at least, he was. But Julia? Would she still want to adopt, and so soon?

But Zoe...was she serious? How much thought could have gone into her suggestion? She'd only just found out that they couldn't have children.

"Dr. Brock, I know my offer may seem sudden to you, but I believe God caused our paths to cross for a reason," Zoe continued. "I almost didn't enter this clinic that first morning I came here, afraid it would be Dr. Johnson on duty. Then I prayed and the next thing I knew, I was inside and being led into your office."

No wonder she'd looked like a deer in headlights that morning.

"And now to find out that you can't have children, and I have a baby I can't keep… I believe we're the answer to each other's prayers. I just know that you and your wife will make wonderful parents to this…" Zoe lifted her head to gaze down at her tummy. She scrunched her nose. "What am I having anyway? It'll be so much easier to say this little boy or little girl."

"Do you want to know?" Hudson asked.

A grin lit Zoe's face. "Ah, the question is, do *you* want to know, Dr. Brock?"

He chuckled softly. "I already do." It was hard for him not to notice the sex of the baby this time as he'd scanned.

"Well then, what are you waiting for, doc? I do want to know."

Guess she wouldn't let up until he told her. And she was the mother; she'd asked to be informed, so it was his duty to do so. "You're having a little girl."

Zoe's mouth circled into an oval as she whispered, "Wow."

She gripped his hand for the second time. "Do *you* want a little girl?"

What man didn't want a daughter?

At his hesitation in giving her a swift answer, Zoe spoke again. "I'm not going to change my mind, if that's what you're worried about. And you don't have to give me an answer now, but please, Dr. Brock, just give it some thought."

He nodded. "I–I'll need to speak to my wife."

"Naturally. How about you give me an answer at my next consultation? And if your wife agrees, bring her to the appointment so that she can see her baby and get as excited as I am right now at the thought of trusting you both with this little life."

CHAPTER TWENTY-ONE

"HUDSON, where are you?" Hudson's phone on handsfree, Heath's voice filled the interior of the SUV.

"Sorry, I know we're running a little late, but we're on the way. We'll be there in a few minutes." They weren't *that* late for the Fourth of July celebrations at Heath's house, were they?

"Huntington, Olivia, and her parents have been here for nearly half an hour already. Your nephew is anxious to get to know his other uncle."

Hudson glanced at the console clock. Eleven fifteen. Meh, they'd only be twenty minutes late, although it seemed as if his brother had expected them to arrive an hour ago.

Heath chuckled. "Secretly, I think the boy hero worships you. I might be just a little jealous of you right now."

"Don't worry about the hero stuff," Hudson said. "Lead our

nephew to Jesus and thereby save his soul and you'll be the better hero for it. *That* salvation lasts throughout eternity; mine's only a temporary fix."

Heath snorted. "Ha, I would've tried, but Huntington already informed me last weekend that he gave his heart to Jesus when he was only five."

"Well that's good news." Hmm, Olivia certainly had turned her life around from the bullying queen-bee she'd been in school and the rebellious teen who had hooked up with his troublesome brother. She was doing a fantastic job of raising their brother's son.

"It is. All right then, I need to get back to teaching Huntington about baseball. Hurry and you can pitch a few balls to him before lunch. I'm afraid his grandfather is no Randy Johnson, even though he may look a little like him."

"I'm driving as fast as Chapel Cove's speed limits permit me. See you soon." Hudson ended the call.

Six minutes later, he pulled his SUV to a stop at Bliant's Bluff, anxious not only to see Huntington, but Heath too. They hadn't managed to get together yet as a family since the wedding. If Hudson wasn't at work or in meetings with Bill about the new hospital's needs and designs, then he and Julia were running back and forth to Portland to furnish the rest of their home. It had been a busy three and a half weeks.

But busyness wasn't the reason he hadn't told Julia yet about Zoe's proposal. He just didn't know how to broach the subject. Couldn't exactly come home from work after ten days of marriage and say, "Guess what happened at the office today, honey? And oh, how do you feel about having a baby in say…twenty weeks' time?"

Julia prodded his arm. "Are you planning on getting out of the car? You certainly are lost in thought this morning. Nervous about getting to know your nephew?"

Hudson shook his head. "I'm excited. Heath had him over last Saturday, took him fishing. Said he's such a great kid."

"Really? You should have joined them." Realization dawned on her face. "Ah yes, we were in Portland shopping for furniture and accessories. Again."

She slid her hand onto his thigh. "Sweetheart, you should've told me. We could have gone shopping another weekend. Bonding with your nephew is important."

Hudson pressed a kiss to her brow. "And bonding with my wife is even more important. Or have you already forgotten that I vowed to choose you every day, no matter what. That means above everyone else too. I'm a man of my word, Jules—I told you that the first day we met."

"I know you are." Her eyes searched his as she trailed her fingers through his hair. "Still, we could've gone fishing and shopped another day. Or is fishing in the Brock family for men only?"

Hudson's laugh filled the interior of the SUV. "I wouldn't know—I've never been fishing. My dad wasn't big on doing things with us boys. He preferred spending time with his bottle. So this would've been a first time for me. But I see no reason why it should be an outing for boys alone. I'm sure Reese would've been there with them, scouring the beach for shells while Heath and Huntington fished from the jetty. Besides, some girls like fishing, don't they?" And if they did happen to adopt Zoe's little girl, he'd certainly want her to hang out with her older cousin. So if Huntington liked to fish, Hudson would teach his daughter to fish too.

His daughter...

Well that wasn't going to happen if he didn't talk to Julia. Soon.

And he would. One of these fine days he'd find a way to open this discussion with his lovely wife. But he couldn't ignore the ticking clock.

Hopping out of the car, Hudson dashed for the passenger side. Julia loved the romantic gesture of him opening the door for her, but sometimes the old habit of doing things on her own was hard for her to break.

After grabbing their picnic basket filled with thick, juicy cuts of steak and a few racks of ribs for the grill, a bowl of coleslaw, and two bags of sweet potato chips, they made their way to the backyard overlooking the ocean. Heath and Reese were supplying the freshly-squeezed lemonade and sweet iced tea, as well as a few hot dogs, corn on the cob, and a chive potato salad. The Pattersons had promised to bring dessert—mini berry pies, homemade ice cream, and a watermelon. Couldn't have a watermelon seed spitting contest without it.

Yum. At the thought of all this delicious food, his stomach growled.

Out on the grass, Heath stood behind Huntington, teaching him how to hold a baseball bat while Bill pitched the ball. Hudson, Heath, and Hunter might've grown up without a mother and not much of a father figure, but this was one little Brock boy who wouldn't suffer the same fate. Even if Hunter didn't return, Hudson and Heath would see to it that they filled that gap in Huntington's life.

It had been three weeks since he'd written to Hunter, and still he'd had no response. Surprise, surprise. Yet again, his big brother had disappointed him.

"Hi everyone," Hudson and Julia greeted everyone as they made their way to the long picnic table in the yard.

Huntington dropped the bat and raced toward them.

"Uncle Hudson…" He slammed into Hudson, wrapping his thin arms around Hudson's waist. "What took you so long?"

Hudson hunkered down in front of his nephew. "I'm so sorry

we're a little late." He leaned closer and whispered, peering up at Julia and speaking just loud enough for her to hear. "It's all Aunt Julia's fault. She couldn't make up her mind what to wear, despite me telling her that she looked gorgeous in everything." He grinned and winked at her.

Julia shook her head then held up her hands. "Guilty as charged."

Julia had gone from jeans to shorts to long pants to a short dress to another longer one, finally settling on the long, white cotton dress dotted with shades of red and green flowers. The dress wrapped around in the front, her shapely, tanned legs and flat, strappy sandals peeking out from the fabric as she walked. She'd tied her hair up in a high ponytail, the off-the-shoulder sleeves revealing more tanned skin. He loved summer, and the extra fifteen minutes she'd taken deciding what to wear had been sooo worth it.

Huntington gazed up at Julia. "You do look pretty in that dress, Aunt Julia."

He gave Julia a hug before turning and tugging on Hudson's arm. "C'mon, Uncle Hudson, let's play some baseball."

Hudson straightened then ruffled his fingers lightly over Huntington's head, unable to tell where the boy had been stitched up beneath the longer growth. "Almost back to normal, I see."

Huntington grinned and slipped his hand into Hudson's. "Still an inch or two before my hair is back to normal. But Mom says she likes the shorter cut. It *is* cooler."

They joined Heath and Bill out on the grass. Hudson took over pitching, and Bill played outfield, while Heath swapped between the roles of catcher for Hudson and coach to Huntington. They had so much fun.

He liked being an uncle.

He'd love being a father.

After a glass of ice-cold lemonade, Hudson and Heath fired up the grill and began cooking the ribs, steak, and corn on the cob while the women set out the hot dogs and salads on the table.

Heath gazed across to where Huntington stood with his grandparents. "Thank you for being astute enough to recognize who Huntington was and to approach Olivia about your suspicions. God really works in mysterious ways. If that accident hadn't happened in front of you, we might never have known we had a nephew. I just wish we hadn't missed out on seven years of his life already."

Hudson wished that too.

And the more he thought about it, the more he didn't want to miss out on that little girl's life that had been promised to him and Julia.

"I can't wait to have a son of my own. Or a daughter," Heath hurried to add. "By this time next year, for sure. God willing."

Hudson nodded absentmindedly, his brother's voice fading to white noise.

Please, Lord, work in Julia's heart. Make her ready to hear the news I have. Make her as excited about the prospect of a baby daughter come November as I am.

Heath nudged him in the side with his elbow. "Hey, you've been pretty lost in thought a lot today. Trouble in paradise?"

"What? Never. Julia and I couldn't be happier." Hudson flipped a steak over, then another. He sighed. He should tell his brother, get his opinion. But mostly, his prayers.

"I… We have the opportunity to adopt a newborn, but I haven't scraped up the courage to tell Julia about it. Every time I want to say something, I clam up. We just got married. How can I drop a bomb like this on her?" Hudson shook his head. "But how can we walk away from this baby either? We may not get another chance like this again."

Heath breathed out a long sigh. "I hear you. That's heavy. Zoe's baby, I take it?"

"Yes."

"A private adoption?"

Hudson nodded.

Heath rested a hand on Hudson's shoulder. "She's a great girl. I had hoped she'd change her mind and keep her baby, but I certainly can understand her concerns as well as her reluctance to do so. She's thinking further than herself—she's taking her brother and sister's futures into consideration, as well as that of her child. And I can't think of two better parents for her to have chosen."

Hudson blinked and brushed the burning tears from his eyes with the back of his hand. "Confounded smoke," he muttered.

"Yeah, blame it on the smoke. I'll do the same." Heath also wiped his glistening eyes. "So, how long have you been carrying this secret around?"

"Two weeks."

"And when do you need to let Zoe know?"

"She said she'd like an answer by her next appointment, which is in another two weeks. I'll have to talk to Julia sooner rather than later." He twisted around to gaze across at Julia as she chatted and laughed with Reese and Olivia. "She'll need time to process this, I'm sure."

"Don't leave it too long, Hudson. In the meantime, I'll be praying for the two of you. And for Zoe and the baby as well."

Hudson smiled as an idea formed in his mind. He knew how he was going to tell Julia. And when. Until then, he'd pray hard this didn't all backfire on him.

CHAPTER TWENTY-TWO

HUDSON LAY awake in the early hours of the morning listening to Julia's soft breathing. And the clock tick, tick, ticking, closer to the time she'd wake to its alarm. He disliked Mondays because they heralded the end of an entire weekend with Julia. Sixty-two uninterrupted hours with his wife, unless he was working on Saturday morning.

Staring into the darkness, time seemed to drag on for as long as the past five days had since the family Fourth of July barbeque. Once more, excitement *and* apprehension broiled in his gut. As much as he looked forward to his wife waking and celebrating their one-month anniversary with her, he would be very glad when this day, or rather morning was over.

Would Julia be excited about his surprise? Or would it rock her world and spin it off course?

He just had no idea.

When the skies began to lighten outside, Hudson lifted his head to glance at the time on the vintage alarm clock. Five forty. He'd snuggle up to Julia for a little longer, get up at six. That would give him half an hour to prepare breakfast before her clock began to chime, its sound so reminiscent of a telephone's ring in a classic movie.

As he slid his arm around her waist, his body curving to the shape of hers, she released a soft moan. But she didn't stir. One thing Julia did well was sleep soundly. He might have to do the night feeds if she agreed to adopt Zoe's baby.

Unless she opted to breastfeed, which was entirely possible for a woman to do, even if she hadn't given birth.

Holding her close, Hudson watched the short hand of the clock moving closer to the six. When it finally reached its destination, he slipped out of bed and headed downstairs.

In the kitchen, he put two coffee cups beside their brand-new Keurig, ready to brew as soon as their breakfast was cooked. He rustled up two of his mouthwatering, to-die-for—as Julia called them—smoked salmon, lemon crème fraîche and dill omelets.

Finally, he placed the plates filled with his tasty omelets on a tray. He added the freshly-brewed coffees, two glasses of orange juice, flatware, and a long-stemmed red rose then headed back upstairs.

He entered the bedroom and set the tray down on his side of the bed. The colors of the food and the rose popped against the background of white linen.

He lifted the rose and quietly moved to Julia's side of the bed. She slept so peacefully, he hated to wake her. But her alarm would do so in a few minutes, anyway. Saving Julia and himself the rude intrusion, he turned off the ringer then knelt down beside the bed. Trailing the rose softly across her cheek, he whispered, "Julia, my love, it's time to wake up."

A smile curved her lips as she stretched her hands above her head. Her eyes flickered open. "What's the time? I didn't hear the alarm." She shimmied up in the bed, raking her fingers through her hair, trying to tame some wayward strands. "Did I oversleep?"

"You didn't oversleep—I turned off the alarm. It's only six twenty-seven." Hudson handed her the rose and started to stand. Unable to resist her, he leaned forward and kissed Julia with ardor. Then he reached for her cup on the tray and handed it to her. "Kisses and coffee. In that order, as always."

"*You* spoil me." She rewarded him with a wide grin as she sipped the hot, dark liquid.

Closing her eyes, she breathed in deeply. "Mmm, what *is* that delicious aroma?"

"Breakfast in bed." Hudson pulled the tray closer then set it down on Julia's lap.

"Omelets? Yum. What's the occasion?"

"Happy anniversary, my love." He placed a kiss on the top of her head then lifted his plate from the tray. He snatched up a knife and fork then moved to sit on his side of the bed beside Julia. He said grace for them and opened his eyes to Julia's dark stare.

"Happy anniversary? Aren't you a little early? Like months?"

Hudson cut off a slice of omelet and shoved it into his mouth as he shook his head. He quickly chewed then swallowed. "Not for our one month celebration, it isn't." He reached for his juice then took a swig before putting the glass back down on the tray. "Jules, this has been the most wonderful month of my life. You make me so happy."

Abandoning her knife on her plate, she reached up and brushed the back of her hand over his cheek. "And you make me happy, even without the coffee and omelets. I love you so much, Dr. Brock."

Hudson sighed. "How did I get to be so lucky?"

"It's God's grace and His blessings, dear hubby. Luck has nothing to do with it." A mischievous grin flashed across Julia's face.

"I know. God is good." Hudson loaded his fork with more omelet, as did Julia.

When they'd finished eating and Julia sat sipping on her coffee, Hudson rose. He removed the tray, placing it on the floor at the bedroom door.

Returning to the bed, he opened his doctor's bag standing beside his nightstand and pulled out the smallish box he'd been hiding in there since Friday. That was the one place Julia wouldn't have spotted it. Between his clothing, she might've seen it when she packed away the clean laundry. His heart beat so hard he thought it might burst right out of his chest. For sure, tomorrow he'd feel as if he'd had CPR.

While he'd been busy, Julia had grabbed her Bible and opened it. She was about to start reading when he set the pink box with its white, satin ribbon down beside her.

She shifted her gaze. "For me? Hudson, I... I didn't get you anything. I never realized we were going to celebrate months."

An affirmative answer is all I need.

Julia picked up the box and untied the ribbon. Lifting the lid off, she peeked inside. Her smile faded like the setting sun, and tiny ripples formed on her brow. "W–what is this? I–I don't understand."

Maybe this wasn't such a good idea after all.

Hudson dipped his hand into the box and pulled out the pair of dusty pink booties for a newborn, hand knitted with organic cotton. The sides of the soft shoes were decorated with an ash wood button. They were so cute that even he hadn't been able to resist them.

Palm up, he held them out to Julia. "Honey, I know this is very sudden, but—" Goodness, what did he say? Honey, we're pregnant?

He filled his lungs and started at the beginning. "Seven weeks ago, an unmarried, pregnant teen walked into my consulting rooms. Zoe Hammond. She was scared and in desperate need of help. Although Zoe comes from the wrong side of the tracks, she's a grade A student with the resilience, and the opportunity, to make something of her life—not just for herself, but for her younger brother and sister."

Julia held his gaze as he spoke, listening. So he continued.

"Zoe lost her mom when she was just thirteen. I–I guess I feel a bond with the girl because I lost my mom at the same age, except my mother didn't die; she walked out on us and never looked back.

"Zoe has received a college scholarship, but keeping her baby would ruin that opportunity. The effect would mean that Zoe doesn't go to college, and if she doesn't go to college, she doesn't get to better her life. There isn't just one child's future at stake here, there are three—Zoe's brother, her sister, and her child. Not to mention Zoe's own future. She's trying to do what's best for everyone."

Hudson set the booties down on the white quilt covering Julia. "From the get-go, Zoe had decided to give her baby up for adoption. She hasn't wavered in that choice. When she heard that we couldn't have children—"

Julia's jaw dropped. "Y–you told her, a *patient*, about our...my situation?"

"Our situation, Jules. And yes, I did. You said we were to be honest with people should they ask. Well, Zoe saw our wedding photo on my desk at her last appointment. She asked why I wasn't away on honeymoon, and when I said we could take one as soon as I could get time off work, she cautioned me not to leave it too long lest we're expecting by the time we *do* take a honeymoon. My face must've dropped because she wouldn't budge and move to the examination room until I told her what was wrong. I think she'd still be sitting there if I hadn't said something to her. So I told her we were unable to have children. Halfway through the consultation, she suddenly said she wanted you and me to adopt her baby—she believes we will make wonderful parents. We can do it through private adoption, if you're ready."

He didn't want to pressure her into a decision, but she needed to see the importance of this decision.

"Zoe firmly believes that God orchestrated our paths crossing. I–I'd like to believe that too." Hudson wove his fingers between Julia's and squeezed her hand. "This could be our one chance, Jules…maybe our only chance."

Julia sniffed then ran a finger beneath one eye, then the other.

"Honey? Are you crying?" Was she happy about this? Or had the enormity and sadness of her barrenness hit home again?

"I… I can't make a decision right now, Hudson. I–I just can't."

Silence descended, as heavy and palpable as their breathing.

He was about to speak when Julia said, "But I'll think about it. And pray."

She lifted the tiny shoes and set them down on the nightstand. "I'll keep those there as a reminder."

Hudson pressed her hand to his lips. "Thank you. I'm praying too. Zoe's next appointment is in ten days' time—July nineteenth,. If you've made a decision by then, she would love to meet you and introduce you to the baby. We do an ultrasound every time."

He wanted to add that it would be a good idea if she *could* make her decision by then, but he didn't want to push. Neither would he talk about this again. He'd grant her the space she needed to think and pray. Maybe Zoe would be prepared to wait another month or two for Julia to decide.

So instead, he said, "Jules, if this is something you don't think you can do, then don't do it just to make me happy. Remember, I chose *you*. Only you. If our little family has to remain just the two of us, that's okay with me. Really."

CHAPTER TWENTY-THREE

JULIA KISSED Hudson goodbye then watched from their front door, waving as he drove off down Lavender Lane. She had a house to show at nine thirty this morning not far from where they lived, so she'd decided to work from home before leaving.

She closed the door and ambled to the study.

Sitting behind her desk, she tried to work, but her mind quickly returned to earlier that morning. She could tell over breakfast that Hudson was anxious about today. Neither of them had spoken a word in the past ten days about the baby elephant in the room. And now, D-day had arrived and her husband had left for work without a decision from her. He had no idea how she felt about the thought of adopting a baby in a few months' time.

But how could she give him an answer when she was still so torn in her soul over what to do? She wanted to say yes. And she didn't. What if God had made her barren because she'd be a terrible mother?

What a ridiculous notion. She'd yearned to be a mother nearly half her life, a good one like her own mom. She'd be an amazing mother to any baby in her care. More importantly, even contemplating such a thought was ludicrous—God was love, and she was His child. His Word declared that in everything He worked for the good of those who love Him. And she did love God.

So did Hudson.

Could it be then that, instead of causing the illness which rendered her unable to ever have a child, God had allowed it because He had chosen *her* to be this little girl's mommy?

If sinful people give good gifts to their children, how much more won't I give to you, My child?

Only a few years ago, she'd asked God, no, begged Him for children.

Hudson's voice drifted into her mind, his words soothing to her soul. *"God is good."*

He *was* good. And she needed to stop being so scared to put her trust in Him. She finally had done so with Hudson, and look how that turned out—she'd married the most thoughtful, caring, sacrificial man on the planet, at least in her eyes. God had known James wasn't good for her, and He had worked that heartache into something far better with Hudson.

She raised her face to the ceiling. "Lord, please give me a sign. Show me what I must do."

An image of two tiny pink shoes drifted into her mind. She flew out of her chair and hurried upstairs.

Sitting on the edge of the bed, she stared at the booties on the nightstand, as she had every morning when she'd woken. Never touching, only looking.

Today she ventured further as she stretched out her hand and picked them up. And for the very first time, she read the small designer label stitched into the back seam.

"Pink Me."

What a novel name.

Pink Me.

Pink me.

Pick me.

What? Julia blinked and peered at the wording again. Had the 'n' in pink just morphed into a 'c' a moment ago?

For a second time in the past few minutes, she tipped her head heavenward. "Lord, are you telling me to pick this child? *This* pink baby girl?"

Silly question. Even though she couldn't audibly hear His voice, she knew exactly what God was saying. And she also knew, without a doubt, that her heavenly Father had guided her husband to that exact pair of pink booties.

Just as He'd guided Zoe to Hudson.

Words from her recent reading in Ephesians once again came to mind. *Chosen before the creation of the world...predestined for adoption...*

God had already shown her days ago what to do. She'd just been too scared to take notice, to believe the words were meant for her.

Peace filled Julia.

God was good indeed.

"She's not coming?"

Lips pursed, Hudson stared across his desk at Zoe. What did he say to this young, disappointed girl who seemed to have placed all her hopes in him and Julia?

He sucked in a deep breath. "It's a lot for her to take in. And her lack of making a decision is partly my fault—I only found the courage to tell her ten days ago. As much as I want to adopt that little girl of yours, give her a home and a family, it was difficult to broach the subject with Julia because we've only just married."

He mustered a smile. "On the upside, she hasn't said no. She just needs a little time, Zoe. Do you think you can give that to her? To me?"

Zoe nodded. "Of course, Dr. Brock. I totally understand. I can wait some more. I guess I'm just anxious to know that my baby has a good home to go to."

"Zoe, you must know that if Julia agrees and we go ahead with a private adoption, I can no longer be your physician. But it's inevitable that sometime in the next few months, I would have had to hand over your care to Trudy Westmacott. Or an OB or CNM in Portland. Have you decided yet if you're going to start college come mid-September, or wait seven more weeks in Chapel Cove until you've given birth?"

Zoe shifted in her seat, her baby bump considerably larger than a month ago. "As much as I'd like to hide my condition from the world, you've taught me that things work out far better if you're just honest and open with people."

Hudson widened his eyes and pointed at himself. "*I* have taught you? When?"

"When you were transparent with me about your wife being unable to have children. If you'd kept quiet, I would never have thought to suggest that you and Julia adopt my baby. And that would've been such a shame for her to miss out on having such a wonderful mommy and daddy."

"I'm glad, but that all depends on my beautiful Julia."

"Yes, it does. But no matter how that turns out, I'm willing to hold my head up high through this. Pastor Heath has taught me that it doesn't matter what other people think of me—all that matters is what God thinks of me. And according to the Bible, well, I'm the apple of His eye. I'm protected. I'm loved.

"So I guess I may have to see Miss Westmacott once or twice, after all, before switching to someone in Portland, because I'll be going to college in September, baby bump and all."

Zoe lowered her gaze and brushed her hands over her stomach. "And while I'm there, I pray that God will use my story to help other young girls not to stupidly allow their boyfriends to take advantage of them. Girls need to realize that if he says he loves you—and really means it—he wouldn't expect you to throw your morals away for a quick roll between the sheets."

Wow, such wisdom garnered from this experience at such a young age. "I'm proud of you, Zoe, that you're willing to allow God to use this for His glory."

Smiling, she leaned forward, holding Hudson's gaze. "Please will you tell me how you told your wife about the baby?"

Hudson lifted his phone then opened his digital photo album. He turned the device to Zoe. "I bought these as a one-month anniversary gift and wrapped them in a box."

Zoe reached for the phone, taking it from Hudson's hands. She drew it closer. "Aw, those are so gorgeous, doc. How can any woman resist those baby shoes?" Zoe gazed wistfully at the phone for a little longer before handing it back to Hudson.

Hudson grinned. "I know. Even I couldn't resist them."

And yet, somehow Julia had managed not to let the tiny pink booties melt her heart.

"Dr. Brock. I have faith that Julia will come around. As you said, she just needs time." Zoe eased out of her chair. "Speaking of time, should we get this scan over with?"

"Yes." Hudson rose and led the way to the examination room.

He'd just started with the ultrasound when a knock sounded on the door. "Excuse me a moment, Zoe."

Hudson placed the transducer back into its holder then rose from his stool beside Zoe. He stepped to the door, opening it to Marylin's face.

"What is it, Marylin? I'm busy with a patient."

"I'm sorry, Dr. Brock, but your wife is here. And she says it's important. Seemed like a matter of life and death."

Hudson twisted around to Zoe lying on the table. "I'll be back in a minute. Julia is here."

Zoe fist pumped the air. "Yes! Thank you, Jesus."

Seeing Hudson emerge from his office and head toward her, Julia's heart beat even faster than it had since she'd raced her car from the show house to the clinic, praying she'd be on time. She had no idea whether Zoe would be gone already by the time she got there.

"You came," Hudson said as he neared.

"I—I'm sorry I'm late. The people I was showing a house to took forever. They wanted to inspect each and every room two or three times. I got here as fast as I could."

Hudson wrapped her in his arms. Holding her tightly, he whispered, "Does this mean—?"

Smiling through her tears, Julia nodded. She leaned back, needing to gaze into her husband's eyes when she told him. "I want us to adopt this baby. God has clearly shown me that this is His will. And His perfect gift to us."

"Come, let me introduce you to Zoe. And our baby girl." Taking her hand, Hudson led her into the examination room. "Zoe, this is my amazing wife, Julia."

Zoe shot upright and hopped off the examination table to hug

Julia. Then she pulled back. "Oops, I hope I didn't get belly jelly all over your beautiful red dress."

Julia laughed, her gaze falling to the place where Zoe's belly had pressed against hers. Hopefully the gel would wash out. "It's all right. Guess I'll have to get used to having my clothes soiled by that baby. There will, without a doubt, be times when I'll be peed on, pooped on, and retched on. So what's a little harmless, odorless gel?"

Zoe's smile widened as she clambered back onto the examination table. "Does that mean you—?"

"Yes. I…we would consider it the greatest honor to adopt your baby and raise her as our own."

Zoe started crying, spluttering through her tears, "I'm. So. Happy."

She reached for Julia and Hudson's hands and placed them on her belly. "Quick, she's kicking."

Feeling those tiny thumps from within the womb, Julia's heart soared. She smiled at Zoe then pressed a kiss to Hudson's cheek as tears rolled down her own face. "We're having a baby."

As if adding her own delight, the baby added a few more kicks.

Thank You, Lord, for showing me the right choice to make. I wouldn't have wanted to miss this for the world. How blessed and favored she was.

Zoe's soft voice interrupted Julia's thoughts.

"Dr. Brock. Show Julia the baby. Let her hear her little girl's heartbeat."

After dinner that evening, Julia and Hudson went upstairs to their bedroom balcony to watch the sun set over the gently swaying rows of lavender. All afternoon, baby names had popped into her head. Each time, she'd quickly Google the meaning of the name then either discard the idea or add the name to the list she was keeping on her phone's notepad.

Hudson's arm had circled her waist and his hand rested on her hip as she stood beside him discussing names.

"As long as it doesn't begin with an H." Hudson chuckled. There are enough of those in our family. We don't need another."

"Totally agree." Julia lifted her head from his shoulder to gaze up at him. She drew in an excited breath. "I know. What about Lavender?"

Hudson gave her that "Seriously?" look, and a nervous laugh spilled from her mouth. "Blame it on the series of love stories I've been reading set in England. Each of the heroines—seven sisters—is named after a flower. I'm thoroughly enjoying the series but do wish the author would write the last two stories. They're not planned to release until next year, unfortunately."

"Um, I don't think Lavender would be a good name for our little girl. Sorry, my love."

Julia shrugged. "You're probably right. Besides, I don't even know if the name has any particular meaning. And a meaning is important, don't you think?"

Hudson nodded. "How about Emma?"

Emma. "That's a lovely name. Emma Brock. I like that."

Hudson turned and leaned against the railing. He drew her closer. "It's Zoe's mother's name. I thought it might be a fitting way to honor Zoe for her sacrifice."

How she loved this man. Always so thoughtful about people's feelings. "I think Zoe would love that," she whispered.

Reaching into the back pocket of the jeans she'd changed into once she got home, Julia pulled out her cell phone. "Let's see what Emma means."

She quickly found the name. "Universal, complete, whole. Or if you prefer the Germanic meaning—healer of the universe."

What a perfect name. Barely a day in their lives—even though she was yet to be born—this little one truly was a healer of their universe. Little Emma would make Julia's world, and Hudson's, whole again.

She shoved the phone back into her pocket before curving her arms around Hudson's neck. Resting her brow against his, she said in a soft voice, "It's perfect."

"It is." Hudson's warm breath against her cheek sent enjoyable tingles down Julia's spine. They should turn in earlier tonight.

"Let's keep the name a secret until she's born though," Hudson said. "I think it'll be a nice surprise for Zoe…brighten what will certainly be a difficult day for her, even if only a little."

Julia's eyes searched his. "I couldn't agree with you more. And now that we've chosen a name, do you think we could choose a color for the nursery? I know I seem like an eager beaver, but we don't have *that* long to sort out the nursery, and Portland isn't exactly around the corner where we can purchase a stroller, crib, car seat, and all those wonderful little knickknacks that we won't be able to resist for the baby room."

"You're right." Hudson lightly tapped the tip of her nose. "I'll be happy with any color you choose."

Julia trailed a finger over his lips. "Even lavender?"

Hudson's hearty laugh filled the night sky. "Even lavender."

CHAPTER TWENTY-FOUR

Three and a half months later...

HUDSON AND Julia had waited on tenterhooks for days now as the estimated birth date of baby Emma approached. Four more days. But Hudson had to keep reminding Julia that babies arrived in their own time. Emma could come earlier, and she could decide to make her grand entrance later, keeping her anxious parents-to-be waiting a little longer than they would like.

Their preparations for the new arrival were complete—in fact had been for three weeks. A small packed suitcase in the car for each of them, and of course one for Emma, bore testimony to how ready and excited they were. They were set to leave for Portland the moment they got word from Zoe that she was in labor.

Seated beside each other at the breakfast table, they gazed out of the window across the lavender farm as rain continued to fall unabated on the now green bushes. Hudson would be happy if the call came today. According to Zoe when she'd phoned last night, Portland was dry and rather sunny. He could do with some drier weather.

Zoe had called to ask for Hudson's medical advice. She was concerned because the baby didn't seem to be moving as much.

"But you're still feeling her move?" he'd asked concerned.

Zoe had confirmed she was.

It was probably because she was almost ready to give birth, but to be safe, Hudson had cautioned her that if she hadn't felt the baby move by the next afternoon, she could contact Dr. Oswald, her obstetrician, immediately.

"I will," Zoe had answered. "And I'll text you and Julia to set your minds at ease the moment this little munchkin moves."

Sipping his coffee, Hudson turned to Julia. "It's a good thing that date in June opened for our wedding. This would've been our church wedding day. Can you imagine getting married in *this* weather?"

Julia smiled over the rim of her own cup before setting it down on the table. "Well, I'm very glad that it isn't, and not just because of all the rain and gray skies. Mostly because I would've missed out on nearly five months of marital bliss with you. It's so true that in all things, God works for the good of those who love Him. We've experienced that so much in the past few months—the accident preventing our City Hall wedding led to you discovering a nephew you never knew you had; a bride injuring herself, led to a date opening up for us and saving us from a washed out wedding; and a young girl's mistake has offered us the opportunity to have a child. God is good."

"Amen."

Hudson's phone started ringing. Seeing Zoe's name and

number, he snatched the device from where it lay on the table. "Zoe?"

"Hi, Dr. Brock…Julia…if you're on speakerphone."

He wasn't.

Hudson quickly switched the phone to speakerphone and set it down on the table again. "It's Zoe," he told Julia.

She laughed softly. "I know. Hi, Zoe. How are you doing?"

"I'm doing great, Julia. I just called…ow, ow, ow…" Zoe inhaled so deeply, Hudson and Julia could hear her take the breath. On her exhale she said over and over. "I'm okay, my baby's okay. I'm okay, my baby's okay. I'm okay, my baby's okay."

"Zoe, what's happening?" He shouldn't be panicking, but he was.

Julia clutched his hand and squeezed it tightly.

A few deep breaths and mantras later, Zoe said, "I'm sorry, but these contractions hurt. Maybe I'm just a sissy when it comes to pain."

"Contractions? A–are you in labor?" Of course she was in labor. She was due, and that didn't sound like a Braxton Hicks she'd just experienced. And she'd said contractions.

Zoe's slightly panicked laugh filtered through the phone. "I–I guess I am."

Both Hudson and Julia sprang from their seats. They'd found several hotels close to the hospital. Julia would make a reservation at one on their way to Portland.

"How far apart are the contractions?" Hudson barked. "How long are they? Has your water broken? Are you still at home or the hospital?"

"Whoa, doc, you're scaring the baby. And me. I'm still at my dorm. My roommate will drive me to the hospital as soon as the contractions are regular and strong—five minutes apart, just as you told me. And before you ask, they're now about ten to fifteen minutes apart. The contractions woke me early this morning. I've been monitoring them since."

Early this morning? Hudson wished she'd called them the moment she thought she was in labor. And now they had to contend with the deluge on the roads. That would slow them down considerably, making their travel time longer. "Keep us posted. Julia and I are on the way."

"Doc, is it still raining in Chapel Cove?"

"Uh-huh. Raining buckets down here," Julia answered as Hudson opened the kitchen door leading into the garage.

"Drive safely, please. The baby and I will both still be here, even if you arrive a little late for her birth."

Hudson chuckled. "Zoe, I'm afraid first births generally don't go that fast." But there were those that were over within a few hours.

Please, Lord, don't let that happen today. Please get us safely to Zoe before she gives birth to our daughter.

"I'm praying my labor doesn't drag on for *too* long, doc. And although I don't like pain, I do hope it's long enough for you to get here. I really want...no need you and Julia at the birth."

Although Julia and Hudson were excited that the day of Emma's birth was finally here, they soon settled into contemplative silence. While Hudson concentrated on driving in the heavy rain, he no doubt pondered on Zoe's labor. His comments every now and then, wondering how far Zoe had dilated, confirmed her suspicions.

Julia's thoughts, however, were consumed with everything they'd done to get to this moment, and whether it could all blow up in their faces. It wouldn't be the first time someone had promised her the world then changed their minds.

After agreeing to adopt Zoe's baby, Hudson had immediately hired an adoption attorney. Thankfully Bill had donated the grounds for the new hospital and rounded up several good and serious investors, because adopting this baby did not come cheaply. It took a significant sum from their savings. But Julia and Hudson knew that Emma would be worth every dollar paid to the lawyer for his fees as well as to cover Zoe's medical expenses.

They were required to undergo a home study—more like a home scrutiny. Praise God, the pre-placement report certified that they were able to provide a suitable environment for little Emma. Naturally, they'd passed with flying colors. What little girl wouldn't want to grow up at 16 Lavender Lane with the kindest man as a father, and a mother who would love her like her very own?

Zoe had assured Julia many times that she wouldn't change her mind about the adoption. Julia believed she meant it, but she couldn't help wondering whether Zoe would still feel the same once she'd given birth, once she'd seen her child.

Julia turned to Hudson. "Remember, the attorney said to contact his office as soon as we know that Zoe is in labor?" According to him, the quicker Zoe signed the consent papers once Emma was born, the better. Even though the adoption wouldn't be finalized for three to six more months, once the consent became irrevocable, Emma would be theirs. Waiting the few days after Zoe signed for that to happen would be the longest time of her life. Already she loved this baby so much it almost scared her. She couldn't survive if something went wrong.

But God willing, in a couple of days they'd return home to Chapel Cove with their newborn daughter wearing the first pair of pink shoes her daddy had bought her.

"As soon as this rain subsides, honey, and I don't have to concentrate so to keep this car on the road, I'll give him a call."

Julia and Hudson often talked about the future regarding Zoe. Chapel Cove was a small town, and her family lived there. Eventually they both agreed they wanted Zoe to be part of Emma's life. It wasn't about them, it was about the child and what was best for her. Once she was old enough, she had a right to know who her birth mother was, to have a relationship with her. They didn't want to deny her that part of who she was.

Julia knew that she'd be the one who'd be her little girl's mommy—the one who nursed and fed her, the one who tucked her in at night and sang lullabies to her, or wrapped her in her arms when she was afraid. She'd be the one who would doctor Emma's scraped knees—although maybe her daddy would do a better job at that—or wipe away her tears. She would laugh with her, and cry with her, through all stages of life.

But after they'd discussed the future as they envisaged it with Zoe, all she asked for was a photo on each birthday and at the start of a school year. A short update if Julia and Hudson found the time to write one. Julia suspected anything more would be too difficult for Zoe.

"I'll be focusing all my energies on my studies going forward, so I don't believe I'll return to Chapel Cove much," Zoe had said. "As soon as I have my business degree and I'm settled in a job, I'll bring my siblings to live with me so that I can educate them and give *them* a chance at a better life. My little girl's future is in your hands, and it is bright. I wouldn't want to tarnish that."

The idea of Zoe not being a physical part of their lives saddened Julia. Her earlier joy at the knowledge that Emma was about to be born, gave way to tears for Zoe and her loss.

Although she tried to hide her crying from Hudson, he noticed. "Happy tears, I hope, my love."

"I am happy," Julia said, "but so very sad for Zoe. While this will be a day of rejoicing for you and me, it will be one of great pain and mourning for Zoe."

Hudson paced the corridors of the hospital like an expectant father. Oh wait, he *was* an expectant father. There was many a time in his life when he'd resigned himself to the fact that "Father" might be a title he would never bear, none more so than the day Julia had told him she couldn't have children.

He glanced at her, leaning against the wall and watching him pace, the faintest of smiles on her lips. He paused, then changed direction and strode over to her. Taking her in his arms, he whispered, "I love you so much, mommy-to-be."

Julia was going to be a great mother. Already, she'd done so much to prepare herself for motherhood. Not long after they'd agreed to adopt Zoe's baby, Julia began preparations to breastfeed little Emma. The daily expressions every few hours with a breast pump and hormones to induce lactation took real commitment on her part. Of course, given her medical history, Julia would face additional challenges, but she was determined to do everything in her power to give their baby the best. And this was more than just about breastfeeding—this was about bonding. He was so proud of her.

Cathy, the labor and delivery nurse, exited Zoe's room. Earlier, she'd suggested Hudson and Julia grab a coffee while she examined Zoe to see how far dilated she was, as well as check on Zoe's blood pressure and the baby's heartbeat.

She smiled at them. "You can go back inside now."

"H–how is she, nurse? And the baby?" Hudson tried his best not to sound as anxious as he felt. Zoe had been in labor for hours now. Poor girl was exhausted.

He was exhausted. What with having to travel slowly on the wet and winding forest roads, the usual ninety minute drive to Portland had taken more than two hours, the first half especially taxing due to the awful weather. Thankfully the rain had stopped once they neared the city, and Hudson was able to make up some of the lost time.

"It's almost time," nurse Cathy said. "She's eight centimeters dilated. Both mother and baby are fine."

"Have you called the OB yet?" Hudson asked.

"I'm about to. Dr. Oswald already knows that Zoe is in labor. He'll be here within ten minutes once I contact him."

Hudson nodded.

Grabbing Julia's hand, he hurried back into the room.

Zoe stood bent over her bed, elbows digging into the mattress. "Oooh, it's so painful…" she groaned, dragging out the last word.

Immediately, Julia rubbed Zoe's back, speaking soft, encouraging words to her. "You're doing so well, Zoe. Not long now. Be brave."

Hudson took Zoe's hands in his and prayed her through yet another contraction. She was so courageous to do this without an epidural. He only hoped the obstetrician hurried, or he might need to deliver this baby himself. Transition could last anywhere between thirty minutes and two hours. During this time, Zoe's cervix would dilate from eight to ten centimeters. But the contractions had been coming fast and furiously since before nurse Cathy examined her—that's why Hudson had called for the nurse.

Ten minutes and six strong contractions later, Dr. Oswald strolled into the room, Cathy following close behind him. Every time Hudson saw the man when they'd come through to Portland for Zoe's appointments, he couldn't help thinking that the OB looked more like a NFL quarterback than someone who delivered babies for a living. But he was one of the best obstetricians in Portland. And the hospital where he practiced wasn't too far from where Zoe lived.

"Zoe, how are you doing? You ready to have this baby?" he asked cheerily.

"Yesss," Zoe groaned determinedly through another contraction, then added an uncertain, "Nooo."

She started crying. "I–I don't know if I can do this."

Hudson hoped and prayed she was talking about giving birth and not about giving her baby up for adoption.

"Sure you can, Zoe." The OB motioned for Hudson and Julia to step aside then he closed the curtain around Zoe's bed, shutting them out. "Many, many women before you have felt like you do right now, and they made it through childbirth. Several times. You will too."

"I'm *never* having another baby…" Zoe wailed.

Hudson heard Dr. Oswald snap on a pair of nitrile gloves, no doubt checking to see if she was ready to give birth.

Moments later, the curtain was yanked open. Dr. Oswald and nurse Cathy stood beside Zoe's bed, preparing to wheel it to the delivery room.

"Come along," Dr. Oswald said tipping his head. "This baby girl is ready to meet you all."

Zoe gazed up at the doctor, her brown eyes wide. "They will be allowed in the delivery room with me, won't they? They need to be there."

Dr. Oswald smiled at her. "Yes, Zoe. They will be, just as you requested at every consultation. I haven't forgotten."

Inside the delivery room, Hudson and Julia stood on either side of Zoe, each holding her hand, wiping her brow as she sweated and grunted through the final stages of labor. What a different feeling it was being on the other side of the delivery table. Definitely far more stressful, he thought. He felt so helpless to take Zoe's pain away.

And then they heard it. Emma's first cry.

"It's a girl," Dr. Oswald announced with a broad smile, holding up the slimy, purply newborn. "But you already knew that."

After the umbilical cord was clamped, Dr. Oswald handed a pair of surgical scissors to Hudson. "You want to cut the cord...Dad?"

Of course he wanted to.

Hudson took the scissors and severed the physical tie between Zoe and Emma.

Soon, their attorney's pen would sever the ties legally.

Tears traced Hudson's cheeks at the enormity, beauty, and sadness of it all. He wiped them away with the back of his hand.

Nurse Cathy quickly wiped Emma down then took her to weigh her and check her Apgar score. Hudson's hand clamped the bed's frame, holding himself back from rushing over to see Emma and hear what her score was.

As agreed prior to the birth, nurse Cathy brought the pink bundle to the bed, covered in a receiving blanket, and placed her on Zoe's left breast. This would allow the baby's birth stress hormones to subside, her serotonin to be maintained. A baby never needed its biological mother as much as during the moments right after birth. As a doctor, Hudson knew this—contact with the left breast, beneath which beat Zoe's heart, would stimulate the five senses, helping the infant to feel safe in this strange, new environment.

Staring down at her newborn, Zoe asked, "H–have you chosen a name for her yet?"

"We have," Julia replied. "Emma. After your mother."

Zoe began to weep, allowing her tears the freedom to fall. "Emma... It's perfect."

She gazed up at Hudson and Julia through moist eyes. "Thank you. Thank you so much."

All eyes returned their focus to the tiny, squirming bundle in Zoe's arms. Soft brown hair covered her tiny head.

Zoe kissed Emma and hugged her before turning her attention to Hudson. "She has her father's hair." Then she shifted her eyes to Julia. "And I've no doubt that even though her eyes are dark blue right now, she will have her mother's brown eyes. I'm glad."

It was hard to tell if Zoe spoke about herself and Emma's biological father, or Hudson and Julia. Somehow, from Zoe's tone, he wanted to believe the latter.

When Dr. Oswald said they were ready to take Zoe back to the ward, Zoe pressed a final kiss to the baby's lips then handed her to Julia. "You should feed her."

As if in agreement, Emma let out a wail.

Julia stood rooted, uncertainty filling her eyes. "A–are you sure, Zoe. Don't you want…need more time with her?"

With a shake of her head, Zoe whispered, "It's better this way."

Zoe's bed was wheeled out of the delivery room.

Hudson swallowed the lump rising in his throat, blinking back the tears that stung. If little Emma grew up even half as wise as her biological mother, they were going to raise a pretty terrific kid. The wisdom and maturity that Zoe had shown astounded him. She would go far in life.

"You should try feeding her." Dr. Oswald's voice drew Hudson back to Julia and Emma. The doctor pulled the surgical gloves from his hands and dumped them in the medical waste can. "A nurse will be back in a while to take the baby to the nursery.

As he walked out of the delivery room, he dimmed the lights.

Sitting down in a chair, Julia placed Emma to her breast. An unearthly silence descended on the delivery room, the tiny baby suckling at her new mother's breast the only thing heard.

Standing there watching his wife feed their newborn, Hudson's heart wanted to explode like the fourth of July fireworks that had recently lit the night sky over Bliant's Bluff.

Julia gazed up at him. "I can't believe this is happening. Is this really true?" she said in a hushed voice.

Hudson pulled up a chair beside her and sat. He wrapped his arm around her shoulder, his other hand lightly brushing Emma's soft head.

"It's true, my love. God is good."

Julia smiled. "Amen. God is very good."

Lowering her head, she kissed the baby's forehead and whispered, "Welcome to our world, little Emma. I promise it will be filled with lavender and lace, and lots of hugs and kisses."

Then she turned her gaze back to Hudson and laughed softly. "Another good thing about not getting married today is because we've just had a baby."

Hudson grinned. For so many reasons, he couldn't agree more. God had certainly held their future—and their pasts—in His powerful, loving hands. As always. He had given them hope and a future overflowing with butterfly kisses.

THE END

GLOSSARY

Apgar score : A measure of the physical condition of a newborn infant, obtained by adding points (2, 1, or 0) for heart rate, respiratory effort, muscle tone, response to stimulation, and skin coloration; a score of ten represents the best possible condition

Flatware : Utensils, such as knives, forks, and spoons, used at the table for serving and eating food

Keurig : A beverage brewing system for home and commercial use

Persona non grata : A legal term used in diplomacy that indicates a proscription against a foreign person entering or remaining in the country—literally meaning "an unwelcome person" [Latin]

Randy Johnson : Randy Johnson, nicknamed "The Big Unit" was arguably the most overpowering starting pitcher in Major League Baseball history

Shiplap : 1. An overlapping joint, as a rabbet, between two boards joined edge to edge
2. Boarding joined with such overlapping joints

SCRIPTURE REFERENCES

Chapter 1:

"You shall not murder."
~ Exodus 20 v 13 (NIV)

"Forgive, and you will be forgiven."
~ Luke 6 v 37 (NIV)

Chapter 2:

But I want you to know that the Son of Man has authority on earth to forgive sins." So he said to the paralyzed man, "Get up, take your mat and go home."
~ Matthew 9:6 (NIV)

"I tell you, get up, take your mat and go home."
~ Mark 2:1 (NIV)

But I want you to know that the Son of Man has authority on earth to forgive sins." So he said to the paralyzed man, "I tell you, get up, take your mat and go home."
~ Luke 5:24 (NIV)

Chapter 8:

Now to him who is able to do immeasurably more than all we ask or imagine, according to his power that is at work within us, to him be glory in the church and in Christ Jesus throughout all generations, for ever and ever! Amen.
~ Ephesians 3:20-21 (NIV)

What he opens no one can shut, and what he shuts no one can open.
~ Revelation 3:7 (NIV)

Chapter 10:

The heavens declare the glory of God; the skies proclaim the work of his hands.
~ Psalm 19:1 (NIV)

"Be still, and know that I am God."
~ Psalm 46:10 (NIV)

Chapter 14:

"For I know the plans I have for you," declares the Lord, "plans to

prosper you and not to harm you, plans to give you hope and a future."
~ Jeremiah 29:11(NIV)

"Come now, let us settle the matter," says the Lord. "Though your sins are like scarlet, they shall be as white as snow; though they are red as crimson, they shall be like wool."
~ Isaiah 1:18 (NIV)

For if you forgive other people when they sin against you, your heavenly Father will also forgive you. But if you do not forgive others their sins, your Father will not forgive your sins.
~ Matthew 6:14-15 (NIV)

Chapter 17:

Husbands, love your wives, just as Christ loved the church and gave himself up for her.
~ Ephesians 5:25 (NIV)

Thanks be to God for his indescribable gift!
~ 2 Corinthians 9:15 (NIV)

So God created mankind in his own image, in the image of God he created them; male and female he created them. God blessed them and said to them, "Be fruitful and increase in number; fill the earth and subdue it."
~ Genesis 1:27-28 (NIV)

The Lord God said, "It is not good for the man to be alone. I will make a helper suitable for him."
~ Genesis 2:18 (NIV)

So the Lord God caused the man to fall into a deep sleep; and while he was sleeping, he took one of the man's ribs and then closed up the place with flesh. Then the Lord God made a woman from the rib he had taken out of the man, and he brought her to the man.

The man said, "This is now bone of my bones and flesh of my flesh; she shall be called 'woman,' for she was taken out of man."

That is why a man leaves his father and mother and is united to his wife, and they become one flesh.

~ Genesis 2:21-24 (NIV)

The Parable of the Ten Virgins:

"At that time the kingdom of heaven will be like ten virgins who took their lamps and went out to meet the bridegroom. Five of them were foolish and five were wise. The foolish ones took their lamps but did not take any oil with them. The wise ones, however, took oil in jars along with their lamps. The bridegroom was a long time in coming, and they all became drowsy and fell asleep.

"At midnight the cry rang out: 'Here's the bridegroom! Come out to meet him!'

"Then all the virgins woke up and trimmed their lamps. The foolish ones said to the wise, 'Give us some of your oil; our lamps are going out.'

"'No,' they replied, 'there may not be enough for both us and you. Instead, go to those who sell oil and buy some for yourselves.'

"But while they were on their way to buy the oil, the bridegroom arrived. The virgins who were ready went in with him to the wedding banquet. And the door was shut.

"Later the others also came. 'Lord, Lord,' they said, 'open the door for us!'

"But he replied, 'Truly I tell you, I don't know you.'

"Therefore keep watch, because you do not know the day or the hour.

~ Matthew 25:1-13 (NIV)

Chapter 18:

The man said, "This is now bone of my bones and flesh of my flesh."

~ Genesis 2: 23 (NIV)

Adam and his wife were both naked, and they felt no shame.

~ Genesis 2: 25 (NIV)

Chapter 20:

Even before he made the world, God loved us and chose us in Christ to be holy and without fault in his eyes.

~ Ephesians 1:4 (NLT)

Chapter 23:

And we know that in all things God works for the good of those who love him, who have been called according to his purpose.

~ Romans 8:28 (NIV)

If you, then, though you are evil, know how to give good gifts to your children, how much more will your Father in heaven give good gifts to those who ask him!

~ Matthew 7:11 (NIV)

For he chose us in him before the creation of the world to be holy and blameless in his sight. In love he predestined us for adoption to sonship through Jesus Christ, in accordance with his pleasure and will—to the praise of his glorious grace, which he has freely given us in the One he loves.

~ Ephesians 1:4-6

Keep me as the apple of your eye; hide me in the shadow of your wings.

~ Psalm 17:8

Chapter 24:

And we know that in all things God works for the good of those who love him, who have been called according to his purpose.

~ Romans 8:28 (NIV)

"For I know the plans I have for you," declares the LORD, "plans to prosper you and not to harm you, plans to give you hope and a future."

~ Jeremiah 29:11 (NIV)

ACKNOWLEDGEMENTS

I don't always get to do an acknowledgements page in my books, but this book needed one! So I'd like to thank the following people, without whose help, this story wouldn't have been as real or as perfect as I hope it is.

- My crit partner, Jan, and my editor, Ailsa—as always, my writing is richer for your polishing.

- My awesome street team which is getting too big to name everyone. I truly appreciate the input from each one of you ladies. You're so special to me. In writing this book, I seemed to need more from you—more questions that required answering, more words for beta reading. Thank you, from the bottom of my heart.

❧ Autumn Macarthur—your medical input to so many scenes was invaluable. Thank you to both you and Alexa Verde for reading through this manuscript prior to publication so that our Chapel Cove world remains constantly true.

❧ A very special thank you to my doctor, Dr. Melanie Kruger, for the great idea for Huntington's injuries. But not only for that, for being so eager to offer answers to all the questions I asked during my consultations. And then going the extra mile through phone calls and emails to give me the medical information I needed. Thank you for taking the time to check what I'd written too. You're simply the best!

❧ Thank you to my hubby and family for understanding when I needed to shut myself behind a closed door, especially when this book took so much longer to write (but then, it is almost double the length that I'd envisaged!).

❧ And my readers. Thank you not only for buying and reading my books, but for actively promoting my stories wherever and whenever you can. It is my prayer that my stories will never disappoint.

❧ Saving the most important for last, thank You, Jesus, for once again guiding my path through a story. It is only by Your grace that I make it to THE END with every book. Thank You that from the beginning of time, You chose me.

I hope you enjoyed reading *Choose Me*. If you did, please consider leaving a short review on Amazon, Goodreads, or Bookbub. Positive reviews and word-of-mouth recommendations count as they honor an author and help other readers to find quality Christian fiction to read.

Thank you so much!

Make sure you don't miss any new releases by following Chapel Cove Romances on Amazon:
https://www.amazon.com/Chapel-Cove-Romances/e/B07PZKWZMR

If you'd like to receive information on new releases, cover reveals, and writing news, please sign up for my newsletter.

http://www.marionueckermann.net/subscribe/

ABOUT MARION UECKERMANN

A Novel place to Fall in love

USA Today bestselling author MARION UECKERMANN's passion for writing was sparked when she moved to Ireland with her family. Her love of travel has influenced her contemporary inspirational romances set in novel places. Marion and her husband again live in South Africa and are setting their sights on retirement when they can join their family in the beautiful Cape.

Please visit Marion's website for more of her books:
www.marionueckermann.net

You can also find Marion on social media:

Facebook : Marion.C.Ueckermann
Amazon : Marion-Ueckermann/e/B00KBYLU7C
Bookbub : authors/marion-ueckermann
Goodreads : 5342167.Marion_Ueckermann
YouTube : UC_f4NDDO8p9YhwIMbdN9DNw
Instagram : marion.ueckermann
Twitter : ueckie
Pinterest : ueckie

TITLES BY MARION UECKERMANN

CONTEMPORARY CHRISTIAN ROMANCE

CHAPEL COVE ROMANCES
Remember Me *(Book 1)*
Choose Me *(Book 4)*
Accept Me *(Book 8)*
Trust Me *(Book 10 – Releasing 2020)*
Other books in this tri-author series are by Alexa Verde and Autumn Macarthur

THE POTTER'S HOUSE
SHAPED BY LOVE
Restoring Faith *(Book 1)*
Recovering Hope *(Book 2)*
Reclaiming Charity *(Book 3)*

A TUSCAN LEGACY
That's Amore *(Book 1)*
Ti Amo *(Book 4)*
Other books in this multi-author series are by Elizabeth Maddrey, Alexa Verde, Clare Revell, Heather Gray, Narelle Atkins, and Autumn Macarthur

UNDER THE SUN
SEASONS OF CHANGE
A Time to Laugh *(Book 1)*
A Time to Love *(Book 2)*
A Time to Push Daisies *(Book 3)*

HEART OF ENGLAND
SEVEN SUITORS FOR SEVEN SISTERS
A Match for Magnolia *(Book 1)*
A Romance for Rose *(Book 2)*
A Hero for Heather *(Book 3)*
A Husband for Holly *(Book 4)*
A Courtship for Clover *(Book 5)*
A Proposal for Poppy *(Book 6 – Releasing 2020)*
A Love for Lily *(Book 7 – Releasing 2021)*

HEART OF AFRICA
Orphaned Hearts
The Other You

HEART OF IRELAND
Spring's Promise

HEART OF AUSTRALIA
Melbourne Memories

HEART OF CHRISTMAS
Poles Apart
Ginger & Brad's House

PASSPORT TO ROMANCE
Helsinki Sunrise
Soloppgang i Helsinki (Norwegian translation of Helsinki Sunrise)
Oslo Overtures
Glasgow Grace

ACFW WRITERS ON THE STORM
SHORT STORY CONTEST WINNERS ANTHOLOGY
Dancing Up A Storm ~ *Dancing In The Rain*

NON-FICTION

Bush Tails
(Humorous & True Short Story Trophies of my Bushveld Escapades
as told by Percival Robert Morrison)

POETRY

Glimpses Through Poetry
[Bumper paperback of the four e-book poetry collections below]

GLIMPSES THROUGH POETRY
My Father's Hand
My Savior's Touch
My Colorful Life

WORDS RIPE FOR THE PICKING
Fruit of the Rhyme

What she most needed was right there in front of her all along.

At the age of thirteen, Clarise Aylward and her two best friends each pen a wish list of things they want to achieve. Deciding to bury a tin containing their life goals, the friends vow to unearth the metal box once they've all turned forty. But as the decades pass and each girl chases her dreams, the lists are forgotten.

Heath Brock has been in love with Clarise for over twenty-seven years and counting. As a young man, he'd plucked up the courage to ask her out on a Valentine's date, but the couple succumbed to pent-up passions, sending Clarise dashing for the other side of the country.

Years after Clarise's sudden departure, Heath serves as youth pastor. He'd held out hope of Clarise's return, but buries his feelings for his childhood sweetheart when he learns she's married.

Almost penniless, divorced, and with nowhere to go, Clarise returns home to Chapel Cove, her future uncertain. She's approaching forty with her dreams in tatters. When old feelings resurface, Clarise wonders whether she's ever really fallen out of love with Heath.

What's the man of God to do when his old flame returns, seemingly to stay?

With Clarise back in town, Heath is determined not to repeat past mistakes, but if he has anything to say about it, never again will he lose the only woman he's ever loved.

She came seeking her mother. She found so much more.

On her deathbed, Haddie Hayes's mother whispers a secret into Haddie's ear—one that she and Haddie's father had kept for twenty-eight years. The truth that Haddie wasn't born a Hayes sends this shy Kentucky girl far from the bluegrass of home to a small coastal town in Oregon in search of her birth mother. Hopefully in Chapel Cove she'll find the answers to all her questions.

EMT Riley Jordan can't help himself—he's a fixer, a helper, sometimes to his own detriment. A 911 call to Ivy's on Spruce has Riley attending to Haddie Hayes, the new girl in town. After Riley learns of Haddie's quest, he promises to help her find her birth family.

When Haddie makes the wrong assumptions, she vows to give up on her foolish crusade and go back to the only place she called home, a place she'd always felt safe and loved. But a freak accident hinders her plans of bolting from Chapel Cove.

And running from Riley…who has a secret of his own.

When love grows cold and vows forgotten, can faith be restored?

Charles and Faith Young are numbers people. While Charles spends his days in a fancy Fort Collins office number crunching, Faith teaches math to the students of Colorado High. Married for sixteen years, Charles and Faith both know unequivocally that one plus one should never equal three.

When blame becomes the order of the day in the Young household for their failing marriage—blaming each other, blaming themselves— Charles and Faith each search for answers why the flame of love no longer burns brightly. In their efforts, one takes comfort from another a step too far. One chooses not to get mad, but to get even.

Dying love is a slow burn. Is it too late for Charles and Faith to fan the embers and make love rise once again from the ashes of their broken marriage? Can they find their first love again—for each other, and for God?

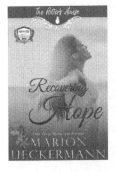

In a single moment, a dream dies, and hope is lost.

Lovers of the ocean, Hope and Tyler Peterson long for the day they can dip their little one's feet into its clear blue waters and pass on their passion for the sea.

Despite dedicating her life to the rescue and rehabilitation of God's sea creatures, when their dream dies, Hope can't muster the strength to do the same for herself. Give her a dark hole to hide away from the world and she'd be happy…if happiness were ever again within her reach.

While Tyler is able to design technology that probes the mysteries of the deep, he's at a loss to find a way to help Hope surface from the darkness that has dragged her into its abyss. He struggles to plan for their future when his wife can barely cope with the here and now.

If they can't recover hope, their marriage won't survive.

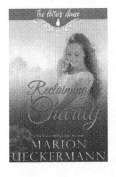

Some artworks appear chaotic, but it all depends on the eye of the beholder.

Brody and Madison Peterson have the picture-perfect marriage. Or so it seems. But their teenage daughter Charity knows only too well that that's not the case. Frequent emotive arguments—the bane of artistic temperaments—have Charity pouring out her heartache and fears in her prayer journal.

When Madison makes a career choice that doesn't fit in with her husband's plans for their lives or their art gallery, disaster looms. The end of their marriage and a bitter battle over Charity threatens.

What will it take for the Master Artist to heal old wounds and transform their broken marriage into a magnificent masterpiece? Could Charity's journal be enough to make Brody and Madison realize their folly and reclaim their love?

For thirty years, Brian and Elizabeth Dunham have served on the mission field. Unable to have children of their own, they've been a father and mother to countless orphans in six African countries. When an unexpected beach-house inheritance and a lung disease diagnosis coincide, they realize that perhaps God is telling them it's time to retire.

At sixty, Elizabeth is past child-bearing age. She'd long ago given up wondering whether this would be the month she would conceive. But when her best friend and neighbor jokes that Elizabeth's sudden fatigue and nausea are symptoms of pregnancy, Elizabeth finds herself walking that familiar and unwanted road again, wondering if God is pulling an Abraham and Sarah on her and Brian.

The mere notion has questions flooding Elizabeth's mind. If she were miraculously pregnant, would they have the stamina to raise a child in their golden years? Especially with Brian's health issues. And the child? Would it be healthy, or would it go through life struggling with some kind of disability? What of her own health? Could she survive giving birth?

Will what Brian and Elizabeth have dreamed of their entire married life be an old-age blessing or a curse?

Everyday life for Dr. Melanie Kerr had consisted of happy deliveries and bundles of joy…until her worst nightmare became reality. The first deaths in her OR during an emergency C-section. Both mother and child, one month before Christmas. About to perform her first Caesarean since the tragedy, Melanie loses her nerve and flees the OR. She packs her bags and catches a flight to Budapest. Perhaps time spent in the city her lost patient hailed from, can help her find the healing and peace she desperately needs to be a good doctor again.

Since the filming of Jordan's Journeys' hit TV serial "Life Begins at

Sixty" ended earlier in the year, journalist and TV host Jordan Stanson has gone from one assignment to the next. But before he can take a break, he has a final episode to film—"Zac's First Christmas". Not only is he looking forward to relaxing at his parents' seaside home, he can't wait to see his godchild, Zac, the baby born to the aging Dunhams. His boss, however, has squeezed in another documentary for him to complete before Christmas—uncovering the tragedy surrounding the doctor the country came to love on his show, the beautiful Dr. Kerr.

In order to chronicle her journey through grief and failure, Jordan has no choice but to get close to this woman. Something he has both tried and failed at in the past. He hopes through this assignment, he'll be able to help her realize the tragedy wasn't her fault. But even in a city so far away from home, work once again becomes the major catalyst to hinder romance between Jordan and Melanie.

That, and a thing called honesty.

Not every woman is fortunate enough to find her soulmate. Fewer find him twice.

JoAnn Stanson has loved and lost. Widowed a mere eighteen months ago, JoAnn is less than thrilled when her son arranges a luxury cruise around the British Isles as an early birthday gift. She's not ready to move on and "meet new people".

Caleb Blume has faced death and won. Had it not been for an unexpected Christmas present, he would surely have been pushing up daisies. Not that the silver-haired landscape architect was averse to those little flowers—he just wasn't ready to become fertilizer himself.

To celebrate his sixty-fourth birthday and the nearing two-year anniversary since he'd cheated death, Caleb books a cruise and flies to London. He is instantly drawn in a way that's never happened before to a woman he sees boarding the ship. But this woman who steals Caleb's heart is far more guarded with her own.

For JoAnn, so many little things about Caleb remind her of her late husband. It's like loving the same man twice. Yet different.

When Rafaele and Jayne meet again two years after dancing the night away together in Tuscany, is it a matter of fate or of faith?

After deciding to take a six-month sabbatical, Italian lawyer Rafaele Rossi moves from Florence back to Villa Rossi in the middle of Tuscany, resigned to managing the family farm for his aging nonna after his father's passing. Convinced a family get-together is what Nonna needs to lift her spirits, he plans an eightieth birthday party for her, making sure his siblings and cousins attend.

The Keswick jewelry store where Jayne Austin has worked for seven years closes its doors. Jayne takes her generous severance pay and heads off to Italy—Tuscany to be precise. Choosing to leave her fate in God's hands, she prays she'll miraculously bump into the handsome best man she'd danced the night away with at a friend's Tuscan wedding two years ago. She hasn't been able to forget those smoldering brown eyes and that rich Italian accent.

Jayne's prayers are answered swiftly and in the most unexpected way. Before she knows what's happening, she's a guest not only at Isabella Rossi's birthday party, but at Villa Rossi too.

When Rafaele receives what appears to be a valuable painting from an unknown benefactor, he's reminded that he doesn't want to lose Jayne again. After what he's done to drive her from the villa, though, what kind of a commitment will it take for her to stay?

She never wants to get married. He does. To her.

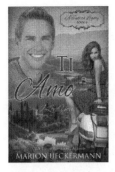

The day Alessandra Rossi was born, her mammà died, and a loveless life with the father who blamed the newborn for her mother's death followed. With the help of her oldest brother, Rafaele, Alessa moved away from home the moment she finished school— just like her other siblings had. Now sporting a degree in architectural history and archaeology, Alessa loves her job as a tour guide in the city of Rome—a place where she never fails to draw the attention of men. Not that Alessa cares. Fearing that the man she weds would be anything like her recently deceased father has Alessa vowing to remain single.

American missionary Michael Young has moved to Rome on a two-year mission trip. His temporary future in the country doesn't stop him from spontaneously joining Alessa's tour after spotting her outside the Colosseum. *And* being bold enough to tell her afterward that one day she'd be his wife. God had told him. And he believed Him. But Alessa shows no sign of interest in Michael.

Can anything sway the beautiful and headstrong Italian to fall in love? Can anyone convince her to put her faith and hope in the Heavenly Father, despite being raised by an earthly one who never loved her? Will her sister's prompting, or a mysterious painting, or Michael himself change Alessa's mind? About love. And about God.

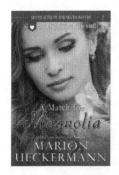

Womanizer. Adulterer. Divorced. That is Lord Davis Rathbone's history. His future? He vows to never marry or fall in love again—repeating his past mistakes, not worth the risk. Then he meets Magnolia Blume, and filling his days penning poetry no longer seems an alternative to channel his pent-up feelings. With God's help, surely he can keep this rare treasure and make it work this time?

Magnolia Blume's life is perfect, except for one thing—Davis Rathbone is everything she's not looking for in a man. He doesn't strike her as one prone to the sentiments of family, or religion, but her judgments could be premature.

Magnolia must look beyond the gossip, Davis's past, and their differences to find her perfect match, because, although flawed, Davis has one redeeming quality—he is a man after God's own heart.

Rose Blume has a secret, and she's kept it for six long years. It's the reason she's convinced herself she'll have to find her joy making wedding dresses, and not wearing one.

Fashion design icon Joseph Digiavoni crosses paths with Rose for the first time since their summer romance in Florence years before, and all the old feelings for her come rushing back. Not that they ever really left. He's lived with her image since she returned to England.

Joseph and Rose are plunged into working together on the wedding outfits for the upcoming Rathbone / Blume wedding. His top client is marrying Rose's sister. But will this task prove too difficult, especially when Joseph is anxious for Rose to admit why she broke up with him in Italy and what she'd done in the months that followed?

One person holds the key to happiness for them all, if only Rose and Joseph trusted that the truth would set them free. When they finally do bare their secrets, who has the most to forgive?

Paxton Rathbone is desperate to make his way home. His inheritance long spent, he stows away on a fishing trawler bound from Norway to England only to be discovered, beaten and discarded at Scarborough's port. On home soil at last, all it would take is one phone call. But even if his mother and father are forgiving, he doubts his older brother will be.

Needing a respite from child welfare social work, Heather Blume is excited about a short-term opportunity to work at a busy North Yorkshire day center for the homeless. When one of the men she's been helping saves her from a vicious attack, she's so grateful she violates one of the most important rules in her profession—she takes him home to tend his wounds. But there's more to her actions than merely being the Good Samaritan. The man's upper-crust speech has Heather intrigued. She has no doubt he's a gentleman fallen far from grace and is determined to reunite the enigmatic young man with his family, if only he would open up about his life.

Paxton has grown too accustomed to the disdain of mankind, which perhaps is why Heather's kindness penetrates his reserves and gives him reason to hope. Reason to love? Perhaps reason to stay. But there's a fine line between love and gratitude, for both Paxton and Heather.

Holly Blume loves decorating people's homes, but that doesn't mean she's ready to play house.

Believing a house is not a home without a woman's touch, there's nothing more Reverend Christopher Stewart would like than to find a wife. What woman would consider him marriage material, though, with an aging widowed father to look after, especially one who suffers from Alzheimer's?

When Christopher arrives at his new parish, he discovers the church ladies have arranged a welcome surprise—an office makeover by congregant and interior designer Holly Blume. Impressed with Miss Blume's work, Christopher decides to contract the talented lady to turn the rectory into a home. When they begin to clash more than their taste in color, will the revamp come to the same abrupt end as his only romantic relationship?

Despite their differences, Holly resolves to finish the job of redesigning the Stewart home, while Christopher determines to re-form Holly's heart.

Top London chef Clover Blume has one chance to become better acquainted with Jonathan Spalding away from the mayhem of her busy restaurant where he frequently dines—usually with a gorgeous woman at his side. When the groomsman who is supposed to escort her at her sister's New Year's Eve wedding is delayed because of business, Clover begins to wonder whether she really wants to waste time with a player whose main focus in life is making money rather than keeping promises.

Jonathan lives the good life. There's one thing, however, the London Investment Banker's money hasn't managed to buy: a woman to love—one worthy of his mother's approval. Is it possible though, that the auburn-haired beauty who is to partner with him at his best friend's wedding—a wedding he stands to miss thanks to a glitch in a deal worth millions—is finding a way into his heart?

But what will it cost Jonathan to realize it profits him nothing to gain the world, yet lose his soul?

And the girl.

Who am I? The question has Taylor Cassidy journeying from one side of America to the other seeking an answer. Almost five years brings her no closer to the truth. Now an award-winning photojournalist for Wines & Vines, Taylor is sent on assignment to South Africa to discover the inspiration behind Aimee Amour, the DeBois estate's flagship wine. Mystery has enshrouded the story of the woman for whom the wine is named.

South African winegrower Armand DeBois's world is shattered when a car accident leaves him in a coma for three weeks, and his young wife dead. The road of recovery and mourning is dark, and Armand teeters between falling away from God and falling into His comforting arms.

When Armand and Taylor meet, questions arise for them both. While the country and the winegrower hold a strange attraction for Taylor, Armand struggles with the uncertainty of whether he's falling in love with his past or his future.

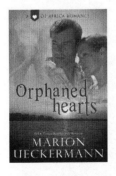

When his wife dies in childbirth, conservationist Simon Hartley pours his life into raising his daughter and his orphan elephants. He has no time, or desire, to fall in love again. Or so he thinks.

Wanting to escape English society and postpone an arranged marriage, Lady Abigail Chadwick heads to Africa for a year to teach the children of the Good Shepherd Orphanage. Upon her arrival she is left stranded at Livingstone airport…until a reluctant Simon comes to her rescue.

Now only fears born of his loss, and secrets of the life she's tried to leave behind, can stonewall their romance, budding in the heart of Africa.

Escaping his dangerous past, former British rock star Justin "The Phoenix" Taylor flees as far away from home as possible to Australia. A marked man with nothing left but his guitar and his talent, Justin is desperate to start over yet still live off the grid. Loneliness and the need to feel a connection to the London pastor who'd saved his life draw Justin to Ella's Barista Art Coffee Shop—the famous and trendy Melbourne establishment belonging to Pastor Jim Anderson's niece.

Intrigued by the bearded stranger who looks vaguely familiar, Ella Anderson wearies of serving him his regular flat white espresso every morning with no more than a greeting for conversation. Ella decides to discover his secrets, even if it requires coaxing him with her elaborate latte art creations. And muffins.

Justin gradually begins to open up to Ella but fears his past will collide with their future. When it does, Ella must decide whether they have a future at all.

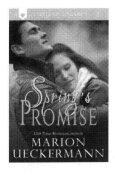

1972. Every day in Belfast, Northern Ireland, holds risk, especially for the mayor's daughter. But Dr. Olivia O'Hare has a heart for people and chooses to work on the wrong side of a city where colors constantly clash. The orange and green of the Republicans pitted against the red and blue of those loyal to Britain. While they might share the common hue of white, it brings no peace.

Caught between the Republicans and Loyalists' conflict, blue-collar worker Ryann Doyle has to wonder if there's life before death. The answer seems to be a resounding, 'No'. His mother is dead, his father's a drunk, and his younger brother, Declan, is steeped in the Provisional IRA. Then he crosses paths with Olivia O'Hare.

After working four days straight, mopping up PIRA's latest act of terror,

Olivia is exhausted. All she wants is to go home and rest. But when she drives away from Royal Victoria Hospital, rest is the last thing Olivia gets.

When Declan kidnaps the Lord Mayor of Belfast's daughter, Ryann has to find a way to rescue the dark-haired beauty, though it means he must turn his back on his own flesh and blood for someone he just met.

 While Ginger Murphy completes her music studies, childhood sweetheart and neighbor, Brad O'Sullivan betrays her with the new girl next door. Heartbroken, Ginger escapes as far away as she can go—to Australia—for five long years. During this time, Brad's shotgun marriage fails. Besides his little boy, Jamie, one other thing in his life has turned out sweet and successful—his pastry business.

When her mother's diagnosed with heart failure, Ginger has no choice but to return to the green grass of Ireland. As a sought-after wedding flautist, she quickly establishes herself on home soil. Although she loves her profession, she fears she'll never be more than the entertainment at these joyous occasions. And that she's doomed to bump into the wedding cake chef she tries to avoid. Brad broke her heart once. She won't give him a chance to do it again.

A gingerbread house contest at church to raise funds for the homeless has Ginger competing with Brad. Both are determined to win—Ginger the contest, Brad her heart. But when a dear old saint challenges that the Good Book says the first shall be last, and the last first, Ginger has to decide whether to back down from contending with Brad and embrace the true meaning of Christmas—peace on earth, good will to all men. Even the Irishman she'd love to hate.

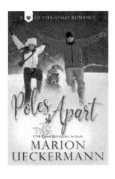

Writer's block and a looming Christmas novel deadline have romance novelist, Sarah Jones, heading for the other side of the world on a whim.

Niklas Toivonen offers cozy Lapland accommodation, but when his aging father falls ill, Niklas is called upon to step into his father's work clothes to make children happy. Red is quite his color.

Fresh off the airplane, a visit to Santa sets Sarah's muse into overdrive. The man in red is not only entertaining, he's young—with gorgeous blue eyes. Much like her new landlord's, she discovers. Santa and Niklas quickly become objects of research—for her novel, and her curiosity.

Though she's written countless happily-ever-afters, Sarah doubts she'll ever enjoy her own. Niklas must find a way to show her how to leave the pain of her past behind, so she can find love and faith once more.

Opera singer, Skye Hunter, returns to the land of her birth as leading lady in Phantom of the Opera. This is her first trip back to bonnie Scotland since her mother whisked her away to Australia after Skye's father died sixteen years ago.

When Skye decides to have dinner at McGuire's, she's not going there only for Mary McGuire's shepherd's pie. Her first and only love, Callum McGuire, still plays his guitar and sings at the family-owned tavern.

Callum has never stopped loving Skye. Desperate to know if she's changed under her mother's influence, he keeps his real profession hidden. Would she want him if he was still a singer in a pub? But when Skye's worst nightmare comes true, Callum reveals his secret to save the woman he loves.

Can Skye and Callum rekindle what they lost, or will her mother threaten their future together once again?

"If women were meant to fly, the skies would be pink."

Those were the first words Anjelica Joergensen heard from renowned wingsuiter, Kyle Sheppard, when they joined an international team in Oslo to break the formation flying Guinness World Record. This wouldn't be the last blunder Kyle would make around the beautiful Norwegian.

The more Anjelica tries to avoid Kyle, the more the universe pushes them together. Despite their awkward start, she finds herself reluctantly attracted to the handsome New Zealander. But beneath his saintly exterior, is Kyle just another daredevil looking for the next big thrill?

Falling for another wingsuiter would only be another love doomed.

When a childhood sweetheart comes between them, Kyle makes a foolish agreement which jeopardizes the event and endangers his life, forcing Anjelica to make a hard choice.

Is she the one who'll clip his wings?

Can he be the wind beneath hers?

Three weeks alone at a friend's summer cottage on a Finnish lake to fast and pray. That was Adam Carter's plan. But sometimes plans go awry.

On an impromptu trip to her family's secluded summer cottage, the last thing Eveliina Mikkola expected to find was a missionary from the other side of the world—in her sauna.

Determined to stay, Eveliina will do whatever it takes—from shortcrust pastry to shorts—to send the man of God packing. This island's too small for them both.

Adam Carter, however, is not about to leave.

Will he be able to resist her temptations?

Can she withstand his prayers?

 Their outdoor wedding planned for the middle of Africa's rainy summer, chances are it'll pour on Mirabelle Kelly's bridal parade—after all, she is marrying Noah Raines.

To make matters worse, the African Rain Queen, Modjadji, is invited to the wedding.

Mirabelle must shun her superstitions and place her faith in the One who really controls the weather.

Note: This short story is in the *Dancing up a Storm* anthology.

Made in the USA
Columbia, SC
11 June 2024

36973018R00169